THE SUN AND ALL THE OTHER STARS

THE SUN AND ALL THE OTHER STARS

A NOVEL

KARLA MONTALVÁN

This is a work of fiction. Names, characters, places, and incidents are either the product of the author's imagination or are used fictitiously. Any resemblance to actual persons, living or dead, events, or locales is entirely coincidental.

LCCN: 2026903206

ISBNs

Paperback: 978-1-7356469-1-6

E-Book: 978-1-7356469-3-0

Audiobook: 978-1-7356469-4-7

Published by Elizabeth & Minnie Publishing Los Angeles, California
www.elizabethminnie.com

Printed in the United States of America

Credits Cover design by Sol Cotti

For Mar, thank you for showing me the purest love I've ever felt.

Milo and Lucy, the sunshine in my days.

And Mami, Mima, and Pipo—the most important people in my life.

"But by now my desire and will were turned,
like a balanced wheel rotated evenly,
by the love that moves the sun and the other stars."

- Dante Alighieri, Paradise

1

WEDDING DAY

Mar

Madrid, Spain – 2023

The alarm rang promptly at 7:30 a.m. on my wedding day.

"Chapel of Love" by the Dixie Cups echoed through every Bluetooth speaker in my loft, flooding the apartment with the cheery chorus. From the bed, I could see the silhouette of my wedding dress hanging on the other side of the tinted glass closet door.

I had been awake since five, when the knot in my stomach couldn't sustain another melatonin-induced nightmare and proceeded to wake me. The alarm felt like an extension of those nightmares, an eerie reminder of the day ahead.

"Device, shut off." I groaned, turning over to find myself on the empty side of the bed. Maybe, just maybe, if I fell asleep again, by the time I woke up, it would be filled.

Lately, it wasn't just the bed that was empty.

There was no food in the refrigerator.

There was no money left in my bank account.

There was an empty closet where the groom's clothes should have been.

It was my wedding day, and I couldn't get myself out of bed.

Did I really have to get up? Would anyone actually give a shit if I didn't?

I searched my nightstand for some doxepin. That would do it. That would definitely get me back to sleep ASAP. Just as I was slipping the pill into my mouth, the doorbell rang.

"Maaaar!" Tania, my best friend, knocked loudly. "Maar, open the door."

I slid off the bed, straightening the wrinkles on the Britney Spears t-shirt I had been using as pajamas. I found a pair of dirty sweatpants clinging to the staircase and pulled them on as I rushed to open the door.

Tania looked like she'd been pulled out of an *El Corte Inglés* catalog. Auburn hair perfectly blow-dried by that vacuum air dryer she bought last week, big glasses perched on a nose covered in freckles, and a sweater dress that clung to her statuesque figure like a glove.

"You look like shit. What are you doing?" She waltzed into my loft.

I started pulling dirty clothes from the furniture and arranging cushions, feeling self-conscious that she had walked in on my mess.

"Eh...I'm just waking up." I escaped her gaze, moving into the kitchen, pretending to look for some coffee I could brew. "What are you doing here so early? It's not even 7:45."

She scoffed. "Trust me, I know what time it is. The only person I would get up for this early is you. But seeing as it's—"

"My wedding day." I paused my search for the coffee I knew didn't exist anywhere in this kitchen. I just couldn't get myself to look at her. The minute our eyes met, I knew I would have to face reality. And to be honest, I didn't want to.

"Your wedding day," Tania's tone edged on judgment.

She pulled a chair from my dining room table, pushing brushes still stained with paint to the side so she could set down her purse. Her tone softened. "I figured you would be needing a little more support than usual today, Mar..."

I finally turned to her. Smiling nervously, placing my hands on my hips, finally finding the courage to face her.

"Me? Nah, I'm fine." I almost choked on the words. I could feel the sobs rising in my chest. "Truly. I'm fine."

Tears blurred my otherwise perfect eyesight. "Why wouldn't I be?"

Tania walked over, placing her hands on my shoulders.

"Because even though it's your wedding day, you're not getting married today, *mi vida.*"

2

CLOUDS IN MY CAFÉ

Mar

Madrid, Spain – 2023

The morning of my wedding day, I sat in La Vaquería, my local coffee shop, hoping for answers I still didn't have.

It was true: I wouldn't be getting married today.

Or tomorrow.

Or maybe ever.

I watched steamed milk form clouds in my *café* while Tania, my best friend, cradled her tall Americano in one hand and swiped on eligible bachelors for me on a dating app with the other.

"It's time to move on, Mar. I know this shit sucks, but you have to put yourself back out there. It's not like he dumped you yesterday—it's been like three months."

Tania wasn't always like this. She was the friend who took the high road, pushing me toward forgiveness and sending wellness podcasts my way. But seeing as my zombie state had not changed since the breakup, she was opting for the tough love we grew up with as Latinas. A sort of, *una lloradita y seguimos* kind of vibe, that also wasn't working.

She sipped on her coffee while navigating the Yellow Pages of modern dating—AKA a dating app—to find me a "palate cleanser."

It was a term she liked to use to describe a man whose sole purpose was to have sex with me, and thus remove the imprint my ex-fiancé left on my body.

"No...nope...*ay Dios, no*. This is ridiculous..." Her face didn't give me much hope as she continued swiping for someone who might pull me out of my depression.

Opening an app gives the perception that there are millions of eligible bachelors out there who, like you, are looking for "*the one*." That perfect person that will come into your life and you'll just "know" they're right. That it's all a matter of numbers and time. The process seems simple, but when you're in the trenches of dating, it's like being awake during surgery.

You swipe on someone. Either you match or you don't.

If you do match, there's a possibility that you'll chat for a few days and actually meet. Or, more likely, never meet at all.

Instead, they'll just stalk your Instagram Stories like you're old pals. Perhaps, if you do go on a few dates, you will have passionate sex that you quickly realize is a one-night stand after getting ghosted.

This process goes on and on *and on* until you get tired of feeling like your love life is going nowhere and delete the app for the 500th time.

It was all the rage during the pandemic, but three years later, it has become a vicious cycle of judging before meeting, disappearing, and disconnecting before you even have a chance of knowing who that person was.

Sometimes, it's because you don't fit the unrealistic beauty standards and expectations of our time that reduce us to looking like avatars. Or, in most cases, you end up meeting people who think they want to connect, but in reality, they have no clue about what they want.

That's not to say it's better for couples. As a recently engaged woman, I can tell you *for a fact* that not all that glitters is gold. Even those of us who appear to have found the perfect person could be wrong. And everything you thought you wanted out of life, out of love, up until this point may have been an illusion.

The relationships, the kids, the career, the house, the vacations on credit—did we actually want those things, or did we think we wanted them simply because at some point in our lives someone told us we should? With this ache in my chest taking up all the space in my lungs, I didn't have much clarity on any of these questions. What I was *definitely* clear on was that the last thing I needed was to get under someone.

The coffee shop was nearly empty except for a few of its loyal daily customers, which included me. Joshua and his dog Thor were sitting at a corner table by the window. An elderly couple was sharing a slice of *pan tumaca* and churros. Lola, my downstairs neighbor, was on her laptop, a *cortadito* gone cold next to her. Mario, one of the baristas, was taking advantage of the slow morning to catch up on his reading for school. Every now and then, they would look in my direction with pity in their eyes.

What is the common denominator between all your relationships?

My therapist's words came to mind. I'd never found a common denominator. Instead, my mind always thought back to my thirteenth birthday, when *Abuela* Cristina, my paternal grandmother, passed on the Varela family curse to me. Until today, I hadn't given much thought to that humid afternoon at her house in Miami where she told me I was to carry on the fate of our ancestors and never love or be loved.

What had she said?

"You might meet someone, mijita. It may seem like you're in love and they love you back. But when you least expect it, POOF! That love will all disappear."

I gasped, turning to Tania, who was still scrolling through a dating profile on my phone. "Tania! Did I ever tell you about my family curse?"

She lifted her eyebrows. "Err...no. I would've *definitely* remembered that."

I leaned in to her just in case one of my neighbors overheard us and pinned me for crazy. They already knew me as the scorned bride. I didn't want to add to the *chisme*.

"I had written the curse off as bullshit, but I just thought about what my therapist told me the other day during our session, about identifying the patterns in my relationships and all that. My dad's mom passed the curse on to me when I was thirteen. This was years after he had died, and I never talked about it with anyone after that. We all thought *Abuela* Cristina was a little bit crazy..."

I bit on my fingernails anxiously. "But...with everything that's happened...I'm starting to think maybe everything she said was real."

Tania looked at me as if I had grown a third eye, but for the sake of humoring me, she went on.

"What's the curse?" She waved at the waiter for another coffee. "Does it say you're going to be single forever?"

"No, no, it's nothing like that. She said this was something her own grandma had passed down..." I closed my eyes, racking my brain for *Abuela* Cristina's exact words. "It was something along the lines of an *ancestra*, God knows when, back in Cuba, who cast a curse on everyone who came after her...that we would never fall in love, nor have anyone fall in love with us. Basically, when it looked like everything was going fine in our love lives, it would fail. It was meant to keep us from suffering for love."

Tania looked at me with concern, putting her hand over mine. "Mar, I know modern dating sucks. I know that your wedding *not* happening today sucks. This whole break-up and how it happened is a huge punch in the gut. But it won't suck forever....You're not cursed. *Everyone* is going through dating fatigue these days. *I* was going through this until I finally met Juan two years ago. And I'm thirty-five! You're not even thirty yet."

Frustration rose in me. "No! No! It's not like that."

The answers cascaded now.

"Now that I think about it, no woman in my family has had a successful relationship. The men have always either died, or gotten lost, or left with someone else." I panicked. "*Dios Tania*, what if the curse is real?!"

"Okay, okay, let's just calm down." Mario, the barista, brought her a second coffee. She took a sip, considering her words before relaying a new perspective. "Maybe you should take it as a blessing. If you can't fall in love, and no one can love you back, then there's no suffering, right? Maybe you just get over this hump. Go back to focusing on your art. Get on the apps..."

I pretended to gag at her last comment. "No, no, my dating life has always been a mess."

"Listen, for a woman with a curse, I think you've dated more than I have. That's not even counting your engagement. Other girls *would dream* of having your sex life. You know most of those people showcasing their 'perfect' relationships online are doing it for the curated Insta feed."

I thought again of my empty bank account.

The €1,000 wedding dress hanging in the closet.

The €5,000 deposit for a venue sitting empty today.

The extra €300 I paid the baker for the three-tiered cake in the flavors he loved.

I'd spent my savings on a wedding that never happened. On a guy who left me.

The wedding "save the dates" people had most likely tossed in their trash by now.

The people who had booked tickets to Spain and taken their precious vacation time to come to the wedding.

All of it, now gone. *POOF!*

Maybe the answers I'd been looking for had been here all along, in the decree of my family curse.

3

GUILLE

Mar

Madrid, Spain – 2023

Guillermo Bauer, also known as my ex-fiancé, walked into the coffee shop minutes later. He wasn't wearing his tux. Instead, he sported a fresh haircut and shave that made him look more handsome than he had the day he left me.

I took in my reflection in the mirror across from the table Tania and I sat at. My hair was wrapped into a messy bun. A random hair strand poking from the side. Hormonal acne on my chin and bags under my eyes screamed I hadn't slept properly in months.

Fuck. Why did he have to look so good?

Even with the way he'd broken my heart, my stomach would still churn each time I bumped into him. I turned my chair away from him to avoid his gaze, snatching my phone away from Tania.

We met at this exact coffee shop three years ago, straight out of the confinement of the pandemic. We were both there late as they closed. I was frantically sketching the final drafts of a mural proposal for a project at Torre de Espadas while downing a glass of red wine. He was wrapping up a meeting with a head of state, whom he was about to interview for an upcoming film. Just as he closed his laptop and turned toward the bar to pay, my drawings caught his eye.

"Are you an artist?" he asked in his Spanish accent. I looked up to find him staring back at me.

Caught off guard, I replied nervously. "*Sí*, I'm a muralist."

"Hmmm, *qué interesante*," he said. "Anything I would know?"

He was tall and serious, with infectious confidence. A gravitational pull that made you want to be a part of his solar system.

"Depends," I said. "Are you into good stuff or do you *pretend* to be?"

He chuckled.

I'd never noticed him around the neighborhood before, but he'd been living here for several years. Before me, for sure. Since I moved to Madrid smack in the middle of quarantine, it was difficult to make friends with other neighbors.

"You have two dogs, no?" he asked.

"Yes, Sirius and Romina," I said.

He frowned, looking down. "I used to have a dog, too. I lost him in my divorce."

Divorce.

"Oh, *lo siento*," I said, shuffling my papers together as the waiter called for closing.

"It's okay." He shrugged. "*La vida*, you know?"

I knew a thing or two about life, yes.

We walked out of the cafe together, making small talk until we realized we were headed home to the same place. "We live on the same block. I'm Guillermo," he said.

"Guillermo," I said. "I'm Mar. Do we? I've never seen you in all the time I've lived here." We walked home. I left him at his corner building before continuing to mine, wondering if I'd ever see him again.

4

THE VEIL

Mar

Madrid, Spain – 2023

The perception of intimacy can be a tricky thing. Especially when you look back at the moments you thought you were truly in love with someone. For me, that was believing Guille, my pet name for him, was *the one*.

Years before meeting him, I'd only been in one serious relationship that ended badly. The heartbreak had cut me so deep, I'd written off men as relationship potential, only keeping them around for the sake of sexual pleasure.

Tania was right in some ways. My issue wasn't meeting people. It was making my relationships work.

I met *plenty* of guys.

I dated them. I kissed them. I fucked them.

My list looked like a "30 before 30" lineup, but instead of entrepreneurs, it was emotionally unavailable men. They could be the perfect, cookie-cutter example of a man, and I wouldn't feel the connection. It all grew worse during the pandemic, when confinement led us to become even more disconnected than before. My body lusted for male attention, their bodies, but deep down I was afraid they would hurt me. I had all the sex I ever wanted, but none of the intimacy.

Until Guille came along.

We were friends first. Our proximity made it easy to bump into each other frequently. Three weeks after our initial encounter, we started ending the day with a shared glass of wine and laughter. Lots of laughter. He cooked me dinners at his apartment, telling me stories of his Sevillian grandmother and his upbringing in Andalusia. He loved records, especially Flamenco, which he would play while dramatically enacting a scene for me.

"Don't let these *Madrileños* fool you. Flamenco belongs to Andalusia," he said.

Aside from Tania, he'd become my confidant. The person whose door I could always ring or call for a walk in the park when I was having a bad day, or simply wanted to share a coffee. One day, a year after we met, he took our friendship a step further during a trip to Mallorca.

We were on a sailboat owned by one of his close friends from work. He approached me with his wide smile, covering the sun for just a moment as I lay tanning on the deck.

"Mar," he said. "I don't think we can continue being friends."

Startled, I removed my sunglasses to look up at him. "*¿Qué*? Why?" I sat up.

Holding a glass of white wine in one hand, he reached for a loose curl covering my face and moved it to one side. "Hmmm...maybe because in the last year since I have known you, I've fallen deeply in love with you."

He said deeply *in love*. As in, *LOVE, LOVE*. With my own "I'm in love with you too," Guille and I unraveled a perfect plan for our future. Within the next six months, we moved in together into my loft, renting out his place. My dogs, Sirius and Romina, had accepted him as part of the pack. I met his family in Sevilla. He flew to Miami for the Cuban interrogation process every new boyfriend must go through. And to my surprise, at the end of that trip, with the help of my mom, Tania, and my cousins, he proposed.

He was the kind of guy you thought could be *the one*.

Until he wasn't.

5

THE BETRAYAL

Mar

Madrid, Spain – 2023

Guille left me for Silvi. Nine months into our engagement, just three before our wedding, he showed up at our apartment, covered in rain from head to toe, breaking things off between us. During the nearly three years we'd been together, he'd failed to mention Silvia—or as he called her, *Silvi*. His *ex-girlfriend*. The one who had left him for another man during the pandemic, who had now returned after "realizing" he was the one for her.

The tight, gnawing knot I felt in the pit of my stomach when he sat me down, his face stoic, to tell me he was leaving, still hadn't relaxed.

"She's the love of my life, Mar. I have to see it through." He didn't even flinch.

I drowned in my breath as he rambled on, trying to explain his reasoning. Things had ended with Silvi months before he met me. He had been her lover while she struggled to make her marriage work. She had chosen another man, blocking Guille out of her life entirely. Now, as if by magic, she'd reappeared.

"What am I supposed to do?" he said.

His words, and my loss for answers, echoed in my head.

"Not leave" is what I should have said back then. Instead, I let pain vibrate through every cell of my being.

Her resurgence threw our seemingly stable, happy relationship into the dumpster, hurling me into the depths of depression I'd kept at bay for so long. It was as if he'd removed a veil, and suddenly, I could see that he, too, had been carrying fears he never spoke about. He had been showing me just one facet of who he was, finding in our relationship a refuge from the pain someone else had caused him. Pain he had never told me about or shared, even though I thought I knew every piece of him. And now, he was inflicting on me the same kind of pain she had forced on him years before.

He slept somewhere else that night. I didn't sleep at all.

Instead, I lay awake, focusing on my breathing. On how hard it was. My lungs felt suppressed by the stabbing pain of my shrinking heart. The tears came days later.

Within a week, he'd moved in with Silvi, leaving everything we had built behind.

6

AN UNEXPECTED REQUEST

Mar

Madrid, Spain – 2023

Despite avoiding his gaze, I felt Guille's eyes on me. *Everyone* in the coffee shop seemed to feel his eyes on me. His look said I was the real reason he was here.

We hadn't run into each other in months, but the coffee shop awarded him an opening my blocked contacts list hadn't. Guille walked over with his espresso in hand, nonchalantly.

"Mar. Tania."

Tania scoffed at him. "*No me lo creo, chaval.*"

Ignoring her, he directed himself at me. "Do you think I could come by the loft tomorrow and grab the rest of my stuff?"

I could smell cigarettes on his breath. He'd quit when we were together.

Guess Silvi is just as poisonous to the body as to the soul.

My face felt hot, irritated by the saltiness of the tears that hadn't stopped for months. Or was it because he looked like our separation hadn't affected him at all? Did he even know what day it was today? Had he realized that if he hadn't abandoned our relationship, we would be two hours away from becoming husband and wife?

Yet here he was, looking better than ever and asking for his stuff back. I wish I could be as oblivious as he was, pretending everything was fine and back to normal. As if we'd never existed.

"Sure, whatever," I said. "I think Tania will be there in the morning."

Tania snapped up to look at me. Mouthing "hell, no!"

"If you don't mind," Guille looked down at his hands, "I'd like it if we could speak."

His request came as a shock. He'd had three months to speak, keys to our apartment, hands to write a letter...

"About?" I asked, feigning amnesia. "I have nothing left to say to you."

Guille knew me too well. He knew I was bluffing.

"Mar," he said. "*Por favor*. Just a few minutes as I gather my things."

"Tomorrow at seven. Don't be late, or I'll leave everything at the door."

7

SECOND CHANCES

Mar

Madrid, Spain – 2023

The next day, I walked up to Lucas Brown, standing in the archway of the Torre de Espadas building. It was the project I'd been working on over the last three years that was nearly ready to be revealed to the public at one of Madrid's newly restored buildings.

The historic location, once home to diplomats, was sold to investors who turned the space into what they hoped would be the newest "it" spot for locals and tourists alike. Although the building still radiated with the splendor and architecture left behind by the previous owners, three selected artists, including myself, were called on to give it a "modern-yet-antique" look.

Finally, the reformation of the building was coming together, transforming into something even Lucas couldn't grasp. The Madrid sunset seeped through the stained-glass entrance, forming rainbows across the foyer that danced up the staircase to the first floor.

I watched him close his eyes, taking in his breath as the warmth from the sun hugged his body and the butterflies painted on the entrance mural that were previously fluttering around him returned to their place on the wall. It was exactly as he had imagined. No. It was better. Now all that was left was for the last two murals to be finished, and he would be able to open the doors to the public. The only problem was that the artist hadn't been around to finish it, and he was on the verge of firing her for good.

But I couldn't allow him to do that.

Because that artist was me.

Tiptoeing through the front entrance, I tried not to disturb his concentration, but whatever spell was cast on him by the sunlight, the door closing behind me broke it.

His eyes widened in shock at seeing me appear. "Marisol Varela! Is it truly you, or am I seeing a ghost?"

Lucas was one of the most respected—and peculiar—people in European art work. At thirty-six, he had already won several architecture and design awards in London, Berlin, Copenhagen, and now in Spain. It was every person's dream to work with him. A rare privilege I'd discarded alongside most things in my life three months ago when my world had fallen apart.

"I'm sorry I've been a little bit *desaparecida,"* I said. "A lot has been going on lately...and—"

"And you ghosted me," he said in his posh London accent. "Darling, one hardly imagines the woman who fought so fearlessly to get this commission would give it up so easily. I'm guessing you're here for your next round of payments?"

I wasn't. But it *would* be great if I could afford to live again. Most of my savings and income had gone to paying cancellation fees for the wedding, refunding orders that couldn't be returned, and losing security deposits.

Lucas had known me through pivotal life changes. Before

moving to Spain, I'd gotten a law degree from the University of Miami. Got a corporate job at one of the largest firms in the world, handling Latin American accounts. Bought an apartment. Rescued two dogs. But underneath the façade of the perfect Cuban daughter, and a closet full of long-sleeved blouses and blazers to hide my tattoos, I was miserable.

After a few years suppressing who I was, I decided I'd had enough and shed all my possessions like old skin. I quit my job with all its benefits, vacations, and burnt coffee, and instead, applied to this project at the hands of Lucas. I sent him dozens of samples of the work I'd done while I painted as a hobby. What truly did it for him was the mural of the Orisha Oshun I did at the Wynwood Walls. It had gone viral on social media, and he wanted the same type of virality for his project.

"Actually, I was hoping you would forgive my totally unprofessional, zero notice, leave-you-with-the inauguration-in-your-hands move and perhaps let me come back to finishing what I started," I said, all in one quick breath.

"Hmm..." He crossed his arms, thinking about it for a moment. I knew he was prideful. *Everyone* knew. He didn't like making mistakes, and I had told him he wouldn't regret hiring me. Of course, I hadn't foreseen that I'd be clinically depressed just as I was on the verge of wrapping up my dream project.

"Please, Lucas?" I remembered I had brought him croissants from a Hungarian bakery he loved in Chamberí. I took them out of my tote bag, handing them over as a peace offering. "I'm working on myself. I even brought my paints, brushes, and cans today. If you let me, I can finish this for you right now."

He took a croissant halfway out of the paper bag, pausing before taking a bite. "Mar, do you know why I picked *you* out of the hundreds of applicants that came my way for this project?"

"Because you like taking risks?" I asked nervously.

"No. Because your art was different. Your murals had soul, they spoke, they transmitted something. Here was someone with little to no experience in the art world, a law graduate from the University of Miami, who one day decided to give it all up to paint *murals*."

He took another bite out of the croissant and looked up at the ceiling mural I'd completed just three days before Guillermo left me. "I thought back then, 'Wow, this woman has bollocks.' Typically, I get sent some trust-fund snobby kid whose father thinks they are the next Picasso or Renoir. Rarely do I get a Cuban woman whose primary paintings focus on shedding light on her cultural history, depicting the power of Yoruba goddesses, and showcasing women as anything *except* sexual objects. Even more, that person is rarely a muralist who hoists herself up to the highest point in a structure to decorate it with art. The question is not whether you can do this today or tomorrow, Mar. The question is, do you *truly* believe that you can? Because anyone else can finish this and do it well enough. I trusted you to be able to, yet you didn't trust *me* to ask me for what you needed."

His words hit me like a sucker punch. He was right. I could have picked up the phone and called. I could have asked for more time, and I didn't. Not for lack of wanting, but for fear of losing yet another important aspect of my life. Or worse, fucking it up.

The first few days post break-up, I stopped myself at the door before heading to the building. I barely got out of bed to go to the bathroom. I scarcely ate. At some point, I misplaced my phone charger and didn't even bother to look for it. By the time I found it and charged my phone, I was so overwhelmed with hundreds of messages that I could barely get myself to text anyone back.

I had lost who I was in my relationship, feeling as if a piece of my identity had gone, and in that loss, I had also forgotten the woman Lucas was talking about.

"Just let me stay today. I promise I won't disappoint you."

8

PIECES OF HIM

Mar

Madrid, Spain – 2023

The doorbell startled me, even though I expected Guille. I'd arrived home about a half-hour earlier, covered in paint, after Lucas agreed to let me finish the mural at the entrance of the building. It felt like a balm to pick up my brushes again, to feel the paint glide on the canvas of an enormous wall of plaster and create something new. The entrance piece was meant to immerse guests in the world of water, similar to my mural of Oshun that first drew Lucas to me. Oshun is a Yoruba river goddess, whom I brought to life with intricacy not often found in murals.

I'd always felt connected to the water, a deep fascination, even though I was terrified of it. Each time I got close to the ocean, or a river, or even a harmless pool, a primal fear would overcome me. I would avoid the water at all costs.

Maybe it was my father's drowning when I was a child that had instilled a fear of it.

Still, the water and I had a unique relationship, which I transmitted through my current mural. The rage was a tempest, pulling a darkness from previously still waters that could prove deadly. The misunderstood depths of lakes, whose darkness scared people away. The clarity that came from stillness in shallow waters. The calmness that allowed light to seep in and create life beneath the surface. I mixed in different tones of blue for the cosmic depth of an ocean that hadn't yet revealed all its secrets.

Returning home was a reminder that while my art was still my refuge, my depths still held feelings unresolved. I had a quick sob session in the shower, the warm water running down my face, as tears of anger and sadness rose and fell swiftly.

I watched the hues of blue paint tint the shower floor as they ran down my arms. My hands were tight fists, gripping the loofah as I remembered his words, his detachment. How easy it had been to leave me and our life behind. I let go when I realized I had torn through it. The hollow pain that comes with disappointment is never given enough credit. The hole it leaves in the middle of your chest, the way it strips you of any hunger, be it for life or even just food.

I turned the shower off, placing my curls in a turban and stepping out into the steamy bathroom. I wiped the moisture off the mirror, revealing a puffy face I still didn't recognize, but I knew was me. Or a version of me. My round eyes, one green, one brown, stared back, and I felt the tears returning. I felt the unavoidable grief I'd been living with wrap around me, showing me the wounds that still lay open, the ones I had to face. Perhaps the healing of that grief began with accepting that Guille had moved on, and maybe I should too.

I threw on some clothes before heading to the living room to gather his things. Two trash bags held everything: his motorcycle helmets, Polaroids of us on a road trip, a hoodie he'd given me one day as we walked home and I got cold, the wine cork from the bottle we drank on our first trip together, when we got so drunk we had to nap in a field of red poppies before driving back to the hotel. And, of course, my engagement ring.

As I collected the material remnants of his presence in my home, I wondered if my love would have ever been enough for him. If, at any point in our relationship, he would have reached the point of thinking, "Thank God things didn't work out with Silvi so I could meet Mar." This thought alone reignited the stabbing pain from the beginning of our breakup.

But now he was here. I was closing this chapter of my life for good. I knew I would never count the freckles on his back or sing him to sleep again.

I opened the door to my apartment. His freshly shaved face from yesterday had grown into a shadow of stubble, exactly the way I always loved it. Pursing his lips, he tried stepping into my apartment, but I stopped him at the door.

"*Hola.*" I grabbed the trash bags, laying them at his feet. "*Tus cosas.*"

"*Vale,*" he said. "My helmet, the sweater...?"

I nodded. "*Sí*, everything."

He looked down at the bags, avoiding eye contact with me.

We stood in suffocating silence, opening a space that neither one of us knew how to bridge. He dropped one bag, then faced me. Tears formed in his eyes, and he bit his bottom lip. I wanted to run to him and hug him, and I had to catch myself.

"I'm sorry, Mar." He picked up the trash bag he had dropped and called the elevator back. "*Lo siento mucho.*"

He paused.

Then he pierced through me with one last sentence.

"I want you to hear it from me, not the rest of the neighborhood"—he sighed, not meeting my eyes—"I've asked Silvi to marry me."

I suddenly forgot how to breathe.

For so many years, I'd clung to the idea that what we had was the real thing, the kind of love and intimacy people spent their entire life searching for, not realizing I'd overlooked all his red flags. How had I been so stupid not to see the lies, the distance? I told myself that modern love required a level of detachment I never felt comfortable with but accepted. That deep down, Guille had chosen me, and I had chosen him in a forever type of love. A part of me secretly hoped this was all a phase, that it would pass. That he was still that person for me. But he killed it all with that sentence. The man in front of me was not the man I fell in love with.

And seeing Guille now without the filter of hope, seeing him move on so quickly from everything we built, I realized I wanted nothing more than to see him disappear. To never run into him again. That maybe I didn't actually *want* this man who stood before me.

"*Adios*, Guille."

As I closed my front door, I let go of him.

9

THE CHAIN

Mar

Madrid, Spain – 2023

An hour later, Tania came over with a bottle of wine and a proposition.

"Okay, Varela, I've brought the goods, my shoulder is ready, and I'm down for whatever you want to watch. But first, I need to talk to you about something."

She walked into the kitchen, rummaging for a wine opener. I didn't have the heart to tell her about Guille's news yet.

"So, do you remember in the summer when we went to El Prado to see that exhibition on women painters from the Renaissance?"

That summer, we had been invited to see "The Secret Women of the Renaissance." It was there that I learned of remarkable women artists who were part of secret societies, forced to disguise their identities, and reliant on the help of other artists to get their work out. Some of them even helped famous painters with their art.

"Yeah, it was amazing."

I leaned on the kitchen counter, crossing my arms as she popped open the wine bottle.

"Remember how I told you I'd run into a doctor who specializes in past life regression when I went to the bathroom? I'd recognized her from a TED talk that randomly popped on my YouTube feed, and *una cosa llevó a la otra,* and she gave me her card so we could stay in contact."

"*Vaale*...so what are you suggesting?" I asked.

"Well, I know this is going to sound wild to you, but she's the one who helped me fix my relationship issues with Juan, and I think you should go see her." She handed me a glass. "It came to me yesterday when you told me about that family curse and all your troubles."

"Wait till I tell you about my latest trouble..."

"Oh my God." She drank from her glass. "What happened now?"

"Guille is going to marry Silvi."

She spat out her wine. "WHAT!?"

"Yep." I was so numb from crying that I barely flinched at her reaction. At this point, nothing surprised me. "You see what I meant yesterday about maybe the curse being real?"

"Well! Even more reason for you to go visit this doctor, then. You've been going to therapy and doing all this work on yourself and crying it out. And now you're remembering this curse from your *abuela*. All the unresolved shit you have with your family and your dad. Maybe this is it. Maybe you just need to go back into your past lives and see where it all started."

I arched an eyebrow. "You're telling me you think I need to go back into my past lives to see how I can change my future?"

"I think you should go see her. Everything that has happened to you in the past three years, everything with Guillermo, how you've been a total mess. Last week, you had yellow paint on your forehead for three days and had your electricity cut off because you forgot to pay the bill. It just feels..."

"Like I'm desperate?"

"It feels like you are being led somewhere. I think there are things you aren't seeing and that you're going to continue repeating until you break through," she said. "And I think this could help. I wouldn't suggest it if I didn't think this was something that could make a difference. You know I'm on your side every single time, but I think we have to call in reinforcements here, *hermana*. From. The. *Other*. Side. Whatever it is that is tripping you up goes beyond our understanding of this."

"Fine, send me the TED Talk." I sighed. "I won't promise you that I'll go see her, but I'll listen to what she has to say."

10

PAST LIVES

Mar

Madrid, Spain – 2023

I queued up the TED Talk Tania sent me of Dr. Adriana Almaguer, Ph.D., while I worked on one of the ceiling murals at Torre de Espadas. The exhibit would be opening in about three months, which meant I spent most of the day hoisted onto scaffolding while I wrapped up the final pieces.

One of the best parts about being a muralist was the quiet. The pockets of time I had to immerse myself in the world of color and form. On rare occasions, I shared spaces with the architects or sculptors who came to work on the other installations, but for the majority of the time, it was me, my cans, my paintbrushes, and my headphones.

Dr. Almaguer's clear voice ruptured through the roar of applause that opened the TED Talk. Her tone was steady and measured, with an ease in her cadence that let you *know* she wasn't here to play, but to heal. I found my shoulders relaxing, my breath easing for the first time in months, as she posed a question to the audience.

"Have you ever felt like you've been here before? Perhaps you walk down a street and get a sense of *déjà vu*, or you meet someone and it feels like you've known them forever. Over the last few decades, past life regression therapy has become more and more popular. First, with the rise of the Theosophical Society led by Helena Blavatsky. Then, psychiatrist and hypnotherapist Brian Weiss brought his findings into the famed book *Many Lives, Many Masters*, and Dr. Ian Stevenson, who documented thousands of children's accounts of past-life memories."

I'd heard of Weiss before; his book had been such an international success even outside the realm of psychotherapy or if, like me, you had no idea what past life regression was about, you'd at least heard his name mentioned in passing.

"The concept of reincarnation surpasses Weiss, dating back as far as the 8th century before Christ. We can find information about reincarnation in the Upanishads, foundational Hindu texts. The Egyptians saw death as a portal into a new world. Buddhists and Jains believe our souls reincarnate, coming back after every visit on Earth. Even if one day our bodies leave us, our souls continue, and they don't continue alone. They always travel with soul families, to which they are loyal. It is not uncommon for us to return as our parents' parents, or even as siblings of people from our families, as we're here to fulfill our soul contracts."

I put down my paintbrush, sitting up to replay what she had said.

They always travel with soul families, to which they are loyal.

"In past life regression, we work with the foundation that some of the patterns we live out, especially the ones that feel 'bigger than us,' may be rooted beyond our consciousness. Beyond even our own personal history. Perhaps you may have noticed the same patterns repeating across generations. Abandonment, scarcity, betrayal. It feels inexplicable in this lifetime, but through regression, we can find its origin."

She went on to explain how past life regression therapy was a window into understanding not just the past, but helping us integrate lessons into the present that could keep us from repeating patterns in the future. I thought back to the curse.

The women of my family had swallowed and lived it as truth for centuries. I wondered where the deep-rooted belief that we could never fall in love came from? Was there a way to remove this curse if it was real? Would I, one day, have to pass this down to my own granddaughter?

Until now, I blamed my stern upbringing by strong women who had only lived glimpses of happiness amidst suffering, loss, and adaptation as the root of my emotional stuntedness. For centuries, our mothers and grandmothers were forced to choose strength as their driving force, not joy or love. As if the only way to be strong was to be stoic.

My great-grandmother didn't have time to nurture her daughter through love and affection. Living in a dictatorship, she had to survive. Survival is not tender—it's sharp-edged, unsmiling. *Abuela* Cristina wasn't raised on kind words, but commands. Her mother's hands didn't offer gentle caresses as they were always calloused with work. Affection wasn't a luxury she could afford, so she taught her children to be vigilant, not vulnerable.

My other *abuela*, Mariana, had raised my mother and aunt alone while my *abuelo* served time as a political prisoner. She never showed her anguish in front of her daughters. Who has time for tears when they have two daughters to clothe and feed and a roof to keep from leaking? She gave them everything they required for survival, but never softness. That was how you kept daughters safe.

And so, the cycle was passed on like an heirloom. *Abuela*

Cristina's decree of the curse, my own mother's sternness. When *Papi* drowned in the Florida Strait, I only saw her break down once. She never spoke of him again or even attempted to rebuild her life after his passing. She had to raise me in a new country, with or without him. I knew her inflexibility before her warmth, nearly having to beg her for it. She taught me that to survive, sometimes you had to lock love away.

I needed answers. If, as Dr. Almaguer said, soul families travel together, could past life regression therapy lead me back to where it all began?

11

DR. ADRIANA ALMAGUER

Mar

Madrid, Spain – 2023

A month after listening to the TED Talk, I journeyed through the cavernous depths of Madrid's metro to my first past-life regression therapy session. I observed people on the train's platform, wondering where they were headed. Were any of them interested in finding out what had happened to them in a previous existence? As if dealing with our current one wasn't challenging enough.

It's an interesting place, the metro. Everyone in the city braved their way through the labyrinth to get to their final destination. You never knew who you'd stumble upon when entering a *coche*. On occasion, you'd be lucky and find yourself nearly alone, just a few other souls around. You'd grab a seat, ride a few quiet stops, and be at your exit before you knew it. Other times, especially when heading beyond the city's central core, whether for some tedious bureaucratic task or to your friend's house in the suburbs, you'd see it all.

A group of friends on their way to a party. A couple who couldn't wait to get their hands on each other the moment the train slowed to a stop. Immigrant musicians from all over the world busking for a few euros to make ends meet. I always carried a few loose coins for them.

I'm not even sure why I chose the metro today. Typically, when I'm in a rush to get somewhere, especially an appointment, I take an Uber or a cab. Today, it felt like a necessary part of my journey. I traveled five stops to the San Bernardo station, just a short walk to Almaguer's office in Olavide Plaza in Chamberí.

"It's right above the wine shop on the corner. Not the one with the wine tastings, the other one," she had noted on our call.

I exited the station to a clear blue sky. After two weeks of non-stop rain, Madrid had returned to its usual sunny-all-the-damn-time weather. It's everyone's dream scenario unless it's summer and you're suffocating from the heat. Fall, however, had a way of making everything more beautiful. The leaves were now a full kaleidoscope of reds, oranges, and yellows. An occasional pine snuck through, as a memento of what once was eternal heat and sunshine.

At the plaza, I followed Almaguer's instructions, spotting her office right above the wine shop. The entrance to the building was on the side, nearly hidden in plain sight. A white door blended into the concrete walls of the colonial building. I pressed the button to her office, A1.

"*¿Sí?*"

"*Hola*, it's Mar," I said.

The door buzzed, and the intercom beeped, granting me access. From the regal, manicured white walls of the outside, you'd never expect the eclectic interior that awaited. A long, arched stone-lined wall led the way to a giant indoor patio where ferns hung wildly. At the center was a marble fountain decorated with traditional arabesque designs, brought by the Moors who lived in Spain for 800 years. Wild ivy covered an entire section of the indoor patio, shaped like a perfect square. The tenants had set up a garden, smack in the middle of urban Madrid, their own piece of heaven.

Still in awe, I walked toward the staircase to the first floor, where Almaguer waited for me. She was tall, statuesque almost, with milky skin. Her eyes were a bright blue that reminded me of Caribbean waters behind red-rimmed half-moon spectacles. They transmitted a kindness that made me feel like I'd known her for several years.

Her relaxed elegance mirrored my own love of fashionable comfort. She wore loose tailored pants with a blue silk blouse that was lazily folded halfway up her forearms, revealing constellations of freckles. On her neck, a single silver moon necklace, and a sheer scarf decorated with gardenias hung on her shoulders. In the video, she'd seemed like a no-nonsense figure of authority, yet up close, she was whimsical.

I followed her into a small room in her office with a sage green couch, a chair, and a bookcase. Philodendron hung abundantly from the ceiling, creating a rainforest-like ambiance my artistic senses were in awe of. A small salt lamp dimly lit the room, although plenty of sunlight came in through a window on the right corner that led to the plaza.

"Sit down on the couch, *hablemos*," she started, making herself comfortable on the chair.

I placed my bag down on the bookshelf and promptly plopped onto the sofa. Its soft surface was inviting, almost therapeutic. Was it possible for me to already feel relaxed even if we hadn't started? I couldn't help a small, nervous smile as she watched me take it all in.

"So, a curse." She raised her eyebrows, leaning back on her chair and inviting me to share. "That's what you mentioned on the phone."

I could feel resistance building up. I didn't like admitting that romance or the possibility of the curse was something that caused me to lose sleep. I'd been raised to believe romance was a second-hand desire, that it was weak to cry over a guy, let alone come to a consultation to find out if this was something I'd struggled with for several lives. It also opened a can of worms I wasn't sure if I was ready to face.

"I mean, not just a curse. Not just love. I've been thinking about all these other areas where my life just feels...stunted. It's as if just when things are going well for me, it suddenly gets destroyed." I rolled my eyes, diminishing the impact it supposedly had on me.

"It's never just a curse. Most of the time, we think our life is going fine until something happens that shakes us and makes us see things from another perspective. Isn't that what is happening now?" She could see right through my bluff.

I took a deep breath, sighing. "You could say that. Honestly, I'm tired of being that woman who feels like she's never going to know what it's like to be chosen, or have a partner, or fall in love. When I listened to you talk about soul families, something about it just..."

"...made sense?"

I nodded, frowning. "It made me realize that this is not just something related to me. It may be connected to my entire family, and if it is, then I want to know. I don't want to carry that burden for the rest of my life, or worse, pass it on to the next generation."

"Interesting. And why is it so important for you to be chosen by someone else?" she asked. "What does love mean to you, Mar?"

"*No sé*," I continued, looking down at my hands, finding bits of yellow paint still stuck underneath my fingernails. "Maybe it's the fact that none of my relationships have ever worked out, just as this curse said they wouldn't. Or that I don't think I've ever *truly* fallen in love with someone, just the idea of false intimacy. And now it goes beyond that, because I'm questioning things I wasn't even thinking about before."

"Like what?"

I bit my lip. "Like maybe I've been carrying the weight of something much bigger. After I moved to Spain and left my life behind, I had considered myself to be this person that rebelled against all the things she was supposed to want. That she was taught to want."

"And those were?"

"The 'perfect life,'" I said.

She raised an eyebrow. "The perfect life...interesting. What happened in your last relationship that made you want to come see me?"

"He broke our engagement and got back with his ex-girlfriend. He's going to marry her now," I said.

"I'm sorry to hear that. Has this exacerbated your feelings of not being chosen?"

"Yes, of course. But I'm over him now." I downplayed the breakup.

I also didn't tell her that since the day things fell apart with Guille, I had been avoiding my neighborhood altogether. I would take a different route to walk the dogs, visit a different park, do all my sketching at home rather than at the coffee shop. I had abandoned Alberto, the centenarian I had breakfast with three times a week. Even when his daughter called to ask if I was all right or needed anything, I lied, telling her to tell him I had a horrible cold and didn't want to get him sick. It wasn't until Tania forced me to return to La Vaquería that I took up my old routines.

A subtle pout formed on Almaguer's bottom lip before she turned her face down toward her notebook to write.

"Is there anything else I should know before we start your first session? Any traumas, or anything you're scared of that you want to mention? This would be a good time to do so," she said.

"No. No personal trauma. I'm afraid of bodies of water. Rivers, oceans..."

She jotted this down in her journal.

"Do you know how past life regression works?"

"I don't," I said. "I've read a little bit about it, seen some videos, but I'd be lying if I said I understand how it works. I'm honestly a little nervous. I have no idea what to expect. Is something going to happen to me? Can I get stuck in one of them?"

"It's normal to be nervous." Almaguer closed her notebook, establishing eye contact with me. "However, there's nothing to worry about. We'll be together for about two hours. I always like to chat briefly before and after the session to make sure you're as comfortable as possible or to hash out details from the session."

Almaguer shifted in her chair, leaning in my direction as if we were signing a pact. "This is a form of gentle healing. During each session, you'll journey safely to your past lives through hypnosis. I'll ask you questions as we go along, never suggesting anything. This is your journey, not mine."

"How is it possible for us to even explore this?"

"Our bodies spend a very limited time on Earth, but our souls are eternal—they remember. When you are born here on Earth, your body takes on a new physical form, but it carries memories from previous lives."

My heartbeat accelerated as Almaguer got up and pulled the blinds closed, dimming the lighting in the room. I closed my eyes, clutching my hand to my gut.

"Mar, I know you're nervous, and we don't know each other that well yet, but you're going to have to trust me through this process if you want it to be effective," she said. "I'll be your guide the entire time."

I thought about all the times I cried myself to sleep, felt

lonely, and was disappointed by the choices I made in my relationships. In my life. Perhaps this was the start of healing. I took a deep breath. "All right, let's do this."

"*Bien*. Go ahead and lean back on the sofa. Get as comfortable as possible," she instructed. "Take off your shoes. You can grab the blanket behind you and cover yourself if you tend to get cold."

I relaxed onto the soft couch. It smelled of lavender and some other herb I couldn't distinguish. Looking up at the ceiling, I released as much fear as I could at that moment.

"I'm ready," I said.

"One more thing before we start. Is it all right with you if we record our sessions? It will help us document your process."

I agreed.

Sitting back, she began. "Mar, start by taking three deep breaths and softening your gaze..." Her voice trailed off as I focused solely on her words. "At the count of ten, you will allow your subconscious mind to guide you into any past life memories relevant to us today..." she continued, her voice steady and low.

I took several deep breaths, relaxing deeply as Almaguer instructed me to walk down a staircase.

"Now, slowly, each step taking you deeper into relaxation as I count down. *Ten.*"

Her voice grew distant as my body became lighter, almost as if I were falling asleep.

"Nine. You are safe, taking another deep breath as your body releases all tension, your eyes feeling heavy."

Eight.

Seven.

Six.

"Five. You are almost at the bottom of the steps. You see a door in the distance. Walk toward it."

I could see it clearly, a door and a light. My body led me to it as if by inertia.

Four.

Three.

Two.

"One. Open the door, Mar. Behind it is a memory, a life you've lived before. Tell me what you see."

12

BEATRIZ VELÁZQUEZ DE CONCEPCIÓN

Beatriz

Florence, Italy – 1484

"Stand still, *cara*!" Sandro said as I shifted from my right leg to the left while posing in his *bottega*. "The lighting has to hit your body perfectly to match Simonetta's mannerisms."

The smell of egg yolks, lead, and red iron oxide burned through my nostrils. My stomach churned, my eyes blurring as I felt the remains of my breakfast rise and fall in my stomach. He was working on a painting in honor of the goddess Venus emerging from the ocean in a shell with sea foam caressing her feet. She was divine, ethereal, and perfect in every way—just as Simonetta Vespucci lived in Sandro's imagination.

He mixed yellow ochre and white lead to form different tones for the goddess's skin, the scent of exuding minerals adding to my discomfort. Despite the open windows framing Sandro's *bottega*, not a single breeze passed through, forcing this particular lesson to feel like a slow, deliberate form of torture. "I will be buried at her feet one day. I have requested it, and her husband has agreed."

"He has?" I took a moment to sit on a stool and breathe while he searched for something around the *bottega*.

Simonetta's husband, Marco, was well known within Florentine society for his close association with the Medici family.

"He has. Oh, Beatrice, while she lived, Marco permitted her to model for me—secretly, of course. How could a woman of her stature pose for a young painter such as me? It enthralled her. *Mia musa.* It is now the duty of my love to immortalize her as the subject of my art."

Simonetta had passed years before from tuberculosis that took her in the spring of 1476. Sandro's secret love for her turned into an obsession, a forbidden melancholy he exuded through his paintings. The *bottega* was covered with drawings and memories of her face. The subject did not matter—somewhere in his paintings, she appeared. It was evident that the love he never lived would be perpetuated in his art.

Simonetta and I did not have a likeness. My eyes, for one, were not blue, and my locks were not copper. We were similar in stature and manner, and that was enough for me to pose as her for Sandro in exchange for painting lessons. All in secrecy, of course.

Unlike Simonetta, I did not come from a wealthy Genovese family, or a Florentine family, for that matter. My father, Luis Arturo Velázquez de Concepción, was invited by the Pope on behalf of the Castilian monarchy to spread the word of the Catholics' conquest of Spain from the Moors. I was ten upon our arrival in Florence. My younger twin sisters, Margarita and Isabel, were three, and my brother, Luís Lorenzo—who we called Enzo—was ten and three. We were greeted by families close to the Medici, not for our riches but my father's proximity to the arts. It made me proud to be his daughter.

In Spain, Isabel la Católica chose him as her royal servant in the court. He was charged with traveling throughout Europe, collecting the most exquisite pieces of art for her. The Moors ruled widely in the Iberian Peninsula for nearly 800 years. Whether the Catholic monarchy wanted to or not, Christians, Jews, and Muslims had blended throughout the centuries, creating a cultural tapestry that ran through my very own blood—and was evident in my image. My skin bore a golden brown hue. This was one of the reasons my father was enthralled by his new post. Having a daughter of darker skin was a target he did not want for his family.

At *Papá's* gatherings, I crept through the darkness of our home to catch glimpses of the brightest minds of Florence who graced our halls. I hoped to one day be fluttering amongst them, not as a girl in hiding, but as someone they considered a contemporary. It was at one such gathering, two years past, that I became acquainted with Sandro.

It was nearly dawn, yet the musicians still played in the courtyard of our home. The notes floated up to my room, where I lay restless, keeping sleep at bay. I knew the kitchen was a haven for spying on our guests as it sat just above the courtyard. I tiptoed down the stone staircase the servants used to reach the bedrooms, which descended directly into the cellar. Quietly, I made my way up a wooden stool that sat just beneath a secret window to the festivities. Suddenly, I was startled by a man's voice.

"Sneaking around is unladylike. Or so I have heard, *signorina*."

"¡*Madre mía*!" I cursed as I fell off the stool, stubbing my toe. I steadied myself quickly, wrapping my robes tighter around me.

"*Sei la figlia di Luís?*" He asked in a playful tone. I could tell he was not scandalized by my presence.

"*Sí*. I'm his eldest daughter, Beatriz....or Beatrice, they call me here."

He snickered. "You are lucky it is me running into you, Beatrice. I'm not sure my contemporaries would react kindly to a young woman of—"

"Fifteen years," I stuttered. My body tensed from his presence.

"*Quindici*...wandering around in her robes at this hour of the evening." He put the apple down, wiping away its juices on a cloth.

"Alessandro Botticelli," he extended his hand. "*Ma,* you may call me Sandro."

My eyes widened. SANDRO BOTTICELLI?! *The* Sandro Botticelli himself. "Oh! Your work commands my deepest admiration, *Signore* Botticelli," I blabbered. It was one thing to meet my father's contemporaries, another to meet my idol.

"*Veramente*? Interesting, for a young woman."

I sprouted on, speaking of my deep admiration for his technique, of my own modest attempts at painting, and of how life, for me, was like a canvas waiting for someone to illuminate it with color and form.

I had been enthralled by Sandro's work since childhood, longing to one day be a painter myself. I was not interested in learning a new craft to please a husband. I wanted my work to hang in the halls of palaces and homes. I wanted my signature imprinted at the bottom of the sigil "Velázquez de Concepción y Higuero."

"I know society grants little space for women to delve into such pursuits, but in the depths of my heart, I am certain this is what I am meant to become. I wish to immortalize Florence and Spain. Paint the reflections of the sun in the Arno...the people."

He leaned against the wall of the kitchen. "It provides

women *no* space in the arts, darling. The only time I have seen a woman pursue any sort of discipline it is for the entertainment of her husband and his guests. Have you any experience?"

"A little! I mean—yes! I've painted a bit with charcoals with lessons *Papá* allowed for me to partake in. Not much else, but I would love to learn more."

He listened intently to my words in a way few men had in the past. With care.

"Hmmm...." He put his hand up to his chin. "Well, I shall return to the festivities, but do hope to see you around, *signorina*."

"Maestro Botticelli," I whispered loudly. "Not a word of this to my father, *per favore*."

He chuckled. "Do not fret, *cara*. This will be our little secret."

A few weeks passed before I stumbled upon him again, this time at a market.

"*Signorina Velázquez*," he whispered, pretending to stare at leather samples. "Do not fret, I have not told anyone of our meeting in the kitchen."

I looked around before responding politely, "It's quite all right, *signore*. *Il nostro segreto*."

"Your father would mark me if he found out about this, but I think I may have a solution for you, *Signorina* Velázquez. Should you be brave enough to snatch it."

I hesitated to ask him what it was. He drew a piece of parchment from his robes, ensuring no one was watching.

Cordial invitation to Madonna Clarice's knitting group.

"Do not be afraid. You must learn to keep secrets. If you are interested, send your maid to the district of Santa Maria Novella, along Via Nuova. Have her visit the window beside my workshop and tell *Signora* Clarice: *Firenze è viva*."

Before I could answer, he left.

"Beatrice," Sandro called, returning me from my thoughts.

"*Scusa, scusa*! How much longer must I stand? At this rate, I shall resemble Simonetta in the last days of her life."

He gasped. "Do not ever speak in that manner of my *amore* again."

I stepped away from the window, searching for my robes. Daria, my *nana*, would be coming by shortly to escort me home. For the past two years, we had fooled *Papá* into thinking that I was receiving knitting lessons at the home of *Signora* Clarice. The elderly woman was Florentine through and through and loved Sandro as her own son. After her husband's untimely death, she dedicated herself to two things: her children and collecting art pieces. A stunted sculptor herself, she always wished she could pursue her artistry or pose for another, facing the consequences of what society would gossip about her. Unless you were posing for a portrait, it was considered indecent. It was a job for slave girls or those who needed a florin or two for living.

"When do you think you'll be finished with the painting?" I asked him as I stepped closer to the large canvas. The absolute perfection of the blue hues of the sky and the ocean, the details of Venus's hair.

"Very soon. After today, I believe I have advanced in the most important pieces, her body and hands. *Grazie.*" He winked. "You are very brave, you know? Not everyone is as willing as you are to pose or even sit alone with a man in a workshop."

"I am aware, but I also know you have other preferences." I winked back.

We both laughed. "Well, aren't you clever? And what might those preferences be, *signorina*?"

"Let's just say it's another one of our little secrets."

Secrets bonded Sandro and I together, and I knew Simonetta was perhaps the only *woman* Sandro had ever loved.

We could hear Clarice's steps approaching the workshop. For the sake of caution, I hid in a secret corridor behind a bookcase covered in plaster figures. She knocked.

"Alessandro...eh, *Signore* Botticelli," she said softly. "There's someone here to see you—*un uomo*."

I could hear Sandro covering his work. He detested the idea of someone entering his workshop and seeing it unfinished, unless it was me or another one of his students at the *bottega*.

"*Uomo*?"

"Yes, he is quite, er...statuesque—" she was interrupted by a deep voice. "*Sono io*."

Sandro opened the door abruptly, letting out a loud "EYYY!!!!"

Light steps and the scent of Bergamot flooded the workshop. The aroma was captivating. Deep, musky, soft.

"Sandro, may I come out now?" I asked.

"*Cara*! *Sì, sì,* come out*!* I would like to introduce you to someone," he said, his tone filled with glee.

I readjusted my robes and my bodice, covering what had just minutes before been exposed to the sunlight, and stepped out from the corridor.

The figure before me towered with the grace of a recently polished marble statue. He glanced up at pieces of parchment drying from the workshop's ceiling, his gaze falling upon me as it descended.

Deep, dark eyes embraced me, and momentarily, I was breathless. He tucked one hand in his pocket, reaching for mine with the other.

"Beatrice, meet my marvelous friend who has just arrived from Roma," Sandro said. "One of our empire's most promising writers. He is a poet."

I wiped my sweaty hand on my skirt, stepped forward, and lifted my right hand, "*Piacere*, *sono* Beatriz."

"Beatriz." He paused to kiss my hand. Then murmured, "*Sono* Dante."

13

DANTE LUPO

Beatriz

Florence, Italy – 1484

Dante.

His name was so simple, yet it played like a melody in my mind for weeks after our initial encounter. Although we had only exchanged a few words, those moments left me wanting to know more. Somewhere deep within me, I felt as if I already knew him.

I left the *bottega* flustered, eager to know when I would cross him again. Aside from my brother and Sandro, I had rarely spent time in the company of other men. Dante's presence felt different. I thought about his black eyes, his lips brushing my knuckles, and his raven hair catching the light in Sandro's sunlit workshop. I burned to ask Sandro about him, but he was away in Siena, pausing our lessons at the workshop, and with them, my only hope of seeing him again. Not being able to bear it any longer, I enlisted Daria for help.

"I need you to do something for me," I said.

"Surely, *signorina*, what is it? Are you well? You have seemed troubled lately."

"Yes, I am all right. It is just heat. Summer does not sit well with me." Daria was clever, but easy to deflect. "I need you to go to *Signora* Clarice's house. Pretend you are getting something for me, say I forgot a handkerchief or something of the like. Then, ask her when *Maestro* Botticelli is returning. That I must see him at once."

I trusted Daria with my life. She was the only person who knew what the lessons at Sandro's *bottega* were really about. Without asking for too many details, she agreed, telling the other servants she was stepping out to fetch something for my knitting practice and would return shortly.

Hours later, she walked into my bedchamber, silently holding a platter with a glass of water. The whispers of her footsteps woke me. I'd fallen asleep contemplating a sketch I'd done in Sandro's *bottega* in the early days of our secret meetings.

"Bea..." Daria sat at the edge of my bed, removing hair strands that stuck to my forehead. "I went to the home of *Signora* Clarice, as you requested."

I was suddenly wide awake. "What did she say? When can I return?"

"*Signore* Botticelli shall return by next week. It appears his sojourn in Siena was extended."

"Praise the heavens." I sighed—at last, good tidings.

"There is more." She edged closer, lowering her voice to a whisper. "There was a young man there. He inquired after you."

Could it be... "Did he say his name?"

My heart rushed in anticipation.

"Yes, eh...Dani—*eh*—DANTE!"

I squealed, grabbing her hands and kissing them, which made her slightly uncomfortable. Regardless, she allowed it.

"He said that if you wished to go to the *bottega* before *Signore* Botticelli's return, he would open it for you."

"Daria! This is splendid!"

Daria's casual way of speaking about this encounter calmed me. Perhaps she was in fact my accomplice. After all, she knew I was going to Sandro's *bottega*, not to *Signora* Clarice's to knit. She knew all the socks, scarves, and blankets I brought back were items *Signora* Clarice knitted herself and gave me as a way of disguising my true actions.

I rose from my bed, devising a plan for our next meeting.

"This is what we shall do," I said. "Tomorrow, we will tell *Mamá* that we are going to the market and perhaps the modiste. Then we shall make our presence known."

Daria and I headed to the market the next day with my twin sisters in tow under the guise of seeking wool for knitting. *Mamá* knew we were up to something and thought sending an army of maids would keep me in tow. Little did she know of the daughter she raised.

I intertwined arms with Daria.

"Are your nerves all right, *signorina*?" she asked, low enough for the rest of the party to miss.

"Have you ever fancied anyone before, Daria?"

She blushed. "In truth, I have."

"What did it feel like?"

Her eyes brought sunshine to the otherwise cloudy day as she looked at me. "It felt like recognizing myself in the other. I know not how to explain it, but it felt as if I urgently needed to be close to them. Is that how you are feeling?"

"How did you—?"

"My job is to anticipate your every need and wish before it happens. I know you."

The market buzzed around us. Conflicting smells of jasmine, meat, and leather became more prominent as we approached the dozens of stands surrounding Santa Maria del Fiore. Immediately, the twins were engulfed by the fuss, driving their *nanas* from one stand to the next. They sampled from every vendor—a raisin, almonds, a dab of oil on the wrist.

We reached a stand with wide fabrics and ribbons. It was my chance to escape. Daria unlatched herself from my arm. I swiftly hid behind a large violet fabric, covered my head with my shawl, and headed toward *Signora* Clarice's home. The cobblestone felt heavy beneath my slippers. The noise of the market was distant in comparison to my heart beating in my ears. I turned onto the street, seeing the heavy wooden door to the place where I could always be myself.

I knocked three times in our secret code to be allowed in. *Signora* Clarice's hands opened the door carefully, a wide grin adorning her face when she saw me. "*Allora, ragazza!* You have returned at last."

Embracing me, she said, "He has been waiting for you many weeks; let me take you to him."

She led me along the usual path to Sandro's *bottega*; without knocking, she opened the door, revealing Dante in the dim lighting. Droplets fell on the glass windowpane, providing us with a minor curtain of privacy in the otherwise empty room.

"Ah, I've forgotten the stove," *Signora* Clarice said. "I shall return."

Several pieces of parchment sat in front of him, covered in the most eloquent calligraphy. His forearms were stained with blotches of ink.

"Beatrice." He stood, heading toward me. "I did not believe I would see you, *ciao*. Sandro has not returned, but I am looking after the *bottega* for him."

I removed my shawl, revealing unruly strands of my cascading hair. The smell of rain and musk filled the room. The wind blew through the open windows, sending flowers in from the almond tree outside.

"I do thank you for telling Daria I might come. I am fond of the *bottega*. You should know, I do not only pose for Sandro; I am a painter myself."

He leaned against a wooden stool, crossing his arms. "I know. He told me, and I surmised as much from the day we met, that you were not the kind of lady who would be visiting Sandro Botticelli's *bottega* to aid him in painting the goddess Venus more clearly. Albeit, I must say—"

"You must say what, sir?"

"Nothing, nothing." He paced around the room, running his fingers through his long black hair, creating messy waves around his face. His beard had grown since I last saw him. He was unlike the men who frequented society. He seemed free.

Moving closer to me, he stopped at an arm's length, standing over where I sat. My hands perspired at his proximity.

"Beatrice, there's one more thing I must say if we are to share this space. It would not be polite of me to deny you the knowledge of this."

A tingling sensation overtook me. The only thing I could focus on was the shape of his lips as he spoke.

"From the moment I beheld you, all I could think of was the moment I would see you again. When you are here, know that I hold your beauty as high as that of Venus. One whose presence is what a mere human like me longs to be around."

His brown eyes embraced me. His words still traveled through me, my hand reaching for his. Did he truly compare me with Venus? Gathering myself, I spoke first in a whisper. "If you are here, I will come."

My hand rested in his, feeling like it belonged there. Our fingertips gracing each other softly. We looked at each other without speaking, just recognizing our faces.

Remembering my sisters and Daria at the market, I pulled away gently.

"I shall return."

14

THE VOYAGE OF NO RETURN

Beatriz

Florence, Italy – 1485

In the year since our first meeting, Dante and I had grown together like intertwined vines. His deep sincerity and passion drew me to him like a force I could not detach myself from. In all this time, he had been more than the person I shared my deepest secrets with. He was also the only place where I felt like I could truly be myself. Our love unshackled me from the constraints of society.

My eighteenth birthday loomed over us. We knew our time together would end shortly as the threat of my *mamá* arranging a marriage was imminent. But I trusted *Papá* would hold up his promise to wait until I was nine and ten before discussing it. It still did not keep us from finding every opportunity possible to be together.

With the city recovering from the plague, my parents left Florence with the twins after I announced I felt ill and required Daria's mother, Apollonia, to assist me in recovery. My feigned illness had in fact been a hidden desire to spend the night with him.

We met at a cottage with a vermilion door hidden entirely by trees. One could have missed it had it not been for the man sitting on its front steps awaiting me. Daria accompanied me just beneath the hill where the cottage lies, saying she would meet me in the morning so that we might return to the house together without others perceiving my absence.

I sprinted toward Dante like a child, jumping into his arms, and he lifted me to the canopy above. This would be our first night together. At his lodgings in Florence, we had only met for a few hours before I could return, and as much as Sandro pretended to ignore our connection, he would never allow us to stay there together longer than my lessons.

"*Amore. Amore mio.*"

My skin radiated with bumps. The branches swaying vigorously with the essence of our love seeping from us.

"I have missed you." I nibbled on the lower part of his lip. He carried me through the threshold of the cottage into a warm, stone-lined room. A chimney stood in the middle of the house with firewood already burning to keep the still chilly air of spring at bay.

The cottage was quaint, with dried herbs hanging from the wooden structure holding up a circular rooftop. Lavender and rose perfumed the air, intoxicating me with awe and desire.

In a corner behind the fire, hidden by a curtain, was a large tub. Gazing at Dante, I concluded this was no coincidence, and perhaps, today, we would bathe in each other.

"That is an interesting tub. Is the water currently boiling by the fire for that purpose, or are you fixing a meal for us?"

His deep voice suppressed a coy "Uh." Then, he cleared his throat. "Well, it could be for both. Although I traded a few translations I have been working on for a while for delightful cheese and other fruits. My *nonna* also prepared something for us. Not knowing I was bringing a lady to our family cottage, *certo*."

"You are rather sneaky, are you not?" I pushed back against him. "Asking a *signorina* to this cottage under the pretenses of exchanging ideas and conversation, only to prepare her a bath with dry flowers."

Leaning into my neck, he pressed his lips lightly on the space underneath my ear. "Was that always the plan? To exchange...ideas?"

I closed my eyes to his gentle touch, his hands now pressing my hips against him as we stood at the center of the room. "That is...what...I thought..." a quiet moan escaped me. "I am also quite all right with whatever else you have planned."

His lips trailed up my neck, but eventually, our lips found each other. I may not have been able to travel to a new world yet, nor become the famed artist I longed to be, but not a soul could take this voyage away from me. As night fell, Dante lit candles like stars and filled up the tub with the same dry flowers that decorated the ceiling above us. I was meant to remain chaste until marriage, but I refused to give my future husband the privilege of my virtue. It was mine to do as I wished. I wanted to love on my own terms, and there was no one else I wanted to love more than Dante.

We neared the tub with our garments still weighing heavily on us. Our heartbeats rhythmically bounced off the walls, forcing the boiling water to vibrate with each beat. Dante edged closer, his hands nearing the crown braid Daria had worked on earlier in the day to keep my hair from knotting during our walk. He removed each pin delicately, placing them on a log-turned table near the bathtub. I watched him, tugging at the lace, keeping it all together, allowing my locks to drape down my back. At this, his breath deepened, his hands now fumbling with the buttons of my bodice. One by one, he peeled away each layer of garments until only my chemise remained between us.

Then, unbuttoning his shirt, he revealed his warm ivory skin speckled by freckles, his abdomen a combination of canyons and valleys where a trail of dark hair led to the rest of him, hidden in his trousers. Bewitched by each other, I removed my chemise, my breasts bouncing back like fresh-picked oranges from a basket. My mother's words rang momentarily through my mind: "A man should never see a woman bare. It is sin." How could this be sin, when it felt like the most natural act in the world?

"*Dio*. May I touch you, Beatrice?"

"You may."

With that, our bodies collided, becoming one. Forgetting the boiling water for an instant, our skins melded. "Are you sure you are poised to do this? We do not have —"

"I want to. *Voglio te.*" I reached for his face, pulling it closer to my mouth.

He breathed into me. "*Non ci ritorna da questo.*"

"*Non voglio tornare.*"

15

A BARGAIN FOR A MAIDENHEAD

Beatriz

Florence, Italy – 1485

Torrential rains flooded Florence over the coming days, forcing us inside. The rain had taken over the entire Tuscan region, leaving *Papá* around more, which I loved.

Papá joked that if the weather kept up, he would not know how to differentiate our city from Venice. But no one, except for a few servants who had traveled with us, understood the jest. After all, many of the servants had never left the city walls, even to nearby towns, let alone another kingdom.

He was not a typical father, or at least not like the ones I saw in the families we acquainted ourselves with. *Papá* was joyful and caring; he was openly affectionate with all of his children. While many fathers often neglected their daughters' company to spend time only with their sons, he devoted himself to us all equally. He was interested in our hobbies, would ask about our days, and would listen to what we had to say—even if it was his daughters saying it. My mother blamed him for my rebellious character, often implying he had spoiled me into thinking that women could have an opinion or govern their own lives. While she continually tried to marry me off or send me away, he pushed for my liberation—within the realm of possibility, of course—saying, "We'll find her a suitor soon."

Ever since *Mamá* and I quarreled on the subject months prior, I had avoided marriage discussions entirely. I would run off into the garden and pretend to cut flowers for a bouquet. I was at the *bottega* twice a week. I would even pretend to be asleep when she approached my chamber. I knew I could not keep her away forever. After three days of nonstop rain, she called a family meeting in the sitting room with *Papá*. They had an important announcement for all of us.

One by one, the six of us marched into the sitting room, finding our usual spots in the large, rectangular space. My favorite corner was by the giant windows that overlooked the Magnolia tree. Raindrops weighed heavily on its branches, collecting leaves and flowers around its trunk. Enthralled by the scenery, I barely noticed that *Mamá* had started the family meeting until she called for me.

"Beatriz, would you like to join the tree outside?" she said.

I wished to roll my eyes, but opted for ignoring her instead.

"As you all know, your father and I have been meeting with potential families regarding your marital status. After all, Enzo and Beatriz, you have been presented in society for some time now, with no matches made. Part of it was because your father insisted you both studied—particularly you, Enzo. We have been dwelling away from Spain so long that I wish we could have married you there, but your father has found it more prudent that we join a Florentine family instead. He wishes we become a more serious component of this society. Enzo, you will meet your betrothed tomorrow. "

Until hearing Enzo's name and not mine called out, I held my breath, anticipating she would stab me with the news of upcoming nuptials. I looked over at my brother, who only stared down at his hands, quietly nodding his head in acceptance of *Mamá*'s words.

"Her name is Giovanna Baldovinetti, daughter of Constantino and Simona Baldovinetti. They will dine with us tomorrow for your meeting, then we will arrange the marriage as soon as possible."

The room fell silent except for our breathing and spatters of rain as she observed all of us, contemplating whether the news brought joy to any of us. *Papá* leaned against the large wooden piano at the center of the room, scratching his beard, his lips pursed. He gazed over at Enzo, who looked up at him with worried eyes. He winked back and mouthed, "*We will discuss later.*"

Without saying much else, we stood in unison with little interest in staying around for tea. Not even Margarita, who loved pretending to be a hostess, was up for the task. I walked to *Papá,* leaning my forehead on his chest to receive a scratchy kiss or a pat on the back. While my heart ached for Enzo, the immense relief of my own safety comforted me, filling me with an immeasurable peace. But it was short-lived.

Breaking away from *Papá,* I started walking toward the door of the sitting room to join my siblings, but *Mamá* called my name, stopping me. Her tone forced me to trip over my dress. I turned to face her.

"Beatriz, I know you've probably been thinking a lot about your own nuptials, but don't worry, *hija*, we have already arranged it."

I could sense the pleasure in her tone. She enjoyed forcing her will upon others, particularly her daughters. It fed her controlling nature. My eyes darted to *Papá,* who still leaned against the large wooden piano, his gaze fixed on the raindrops sticking to the large window.

"The last time we attempted discussing your engagement,

you were unwell, but what better time to do so than right after sharing the news of your brother's betrothed?"

"Papá," I whispered, but he pretended not to hear me. He didn't look up at me. He had never ignored me in the past, and the only moments he remained silent were when he was in agreement with a decision *Mamá* had convinced him of taking.

Mama's nose flared. "Beatriz, you will marry Niccolo de Rossi. This is not a silly hobby your father can support or be manipulated into thinking you should do. This is what is best for you and for the entire family. End of discussion."

"No, not end of discussion! I will not marry. I would rather you take me to the convent, but I will not marry a man I do not even know." I turned to *Papá*. "How can you allow this?"

Disregarding my calls for *Papá's* help, *Mamá* continued.

Niccolo de Rossi. My future husband's name spewed off her tongue like a curse cast upon me by the fates. Followed by other similarly-sounding phrases like: *son of Filippa and Quintino de Rossi, a prominent family in the Kingdom of Bologna. She is quite lucky* and *such opportunities do not come about often.*

An invisible glass dome descended around me, reducing her voice to incomprehensible blabber. I could only stare at *Papá*, looking down at the floor. Behind him, a storm raged outside, the Magnolia tree's branches swaying harshly against the wind as it rained sideways. Thunderstroke punctured my shield, forcing a single plea from my lips.

"*Papá.*" He looked up at last. "Speak, *te suplico*."

He straightened himself away from the piano, running his hands through his beard.

"Bea, as you may know, I desired that you marry whence you felt ready—"

Mamá attempted interrupting, but he lifted a finger to hush her.

"*Pero*, the de Rossi family took interest in your betrothal to their son Niccolo, who your mother has made a strong case for.

They are a family of great wealth. Niccolo shall be count shortly. At the moment, he is the viscount of his family's estate. That, *mi amada hija*, shall provide a steadfast safeguard for you. Herein, I am not disposed to bargain with you in accordance with this."

"I do not wish for safety. I do not wish to be married," I said firmly. "You gave your word to wait until I was at least nine and ten for us to speak of it. That year is yet before me, *Papá.*"

"Say what you may about me, but know this: I am a man of my word. Most of all where matters of my daughter are concerned. You will be nine and ten by the time of the nuptials, Beatriz. Our accord with the de Rossi family stands firm that you shall not marry until after Niccolo returns from the war in France."

My heart beamed with a small droplet of hope as he uttered his last words, relief pouring over me.

"If it were up to me, you would be married *before* he comes back from war. However, your father believes it best to await confirmation of Niccolo's survival. We must ensure your virtue not be tarnished," *Mamá* huffed.

"My *virtue*? This is all a bargain for my maidenhead?" I scoffed. "Of course, you would trade your eldest daughter for station and favor."

"It's no more than reassurance of your future, *mal agradecida*. What do you expect would occur to you if war arrives and your *papá* isn't here to protect you? Did you truly believe our position to be unassailable? You are but a foolish child, Beatriz. You always have been. Do you not see how many maidens younger than you would give anything to be in your position? Praying their parents might secure matches for them that they might start a household of their own." She stood up from the edge of the *sedia*. "¡*Dios mío, esta cruz que me ha sido dada*! I do pray one day you shall awaken to see the truth. Give thanks upon your knees for all that we have wrought on your behalf.

Know this, you insolent child: marriage is not born of love. It is a contract. A matter of alliance and estate. You are a woman, and you must do as women are born to do: wed, bear an heir, and bring honor to your husband's household. The sooner you accept this, the lighter your burden shall be. Now, if you will excuse me, I shall attend the preparations for your brother's betrothal feast on the morrow."

I looked over at *Papá* one last time, realizing my hero had betrayed me and would not save me.

16

THE RETURN

Mar

Madrid, Spain – 2023

I gasped, returning to the familiar smell of lavender in Dr. Almaguer's office. I lay quietly for a moment, taking in what I had witnessed. My heart beating fast.

"Welcome back," Almaguer said as my eyes flickered open. "How do you feel?"

"Not well, my heart is racing. That...who was that? Who was that woman? Who were those people?" My tone edged on hysterics.

"Who, Mar? Here, let me pour you some water."

I began gathering my things. "I thought you said this was gentle healing. This was *not* gentle. I felt everything she was feeling...."

"Everything Beatriz was feeling?"

I turned to her, shocked she knew her name, "How did you?"

"I ask you questions during our sessions. You mentioned her name. It's normal to feel a little distraught; this is a journey that requires much of your energy."

"I don't think this is for me. I'm really sorry, truly, but I thought this was meant to be a way of healing me, not furthering my feelings of grief and sadness....and now *anger*."

"Perhaps it's not so much about placing expectations on how you're 'supposed to feel' and just feeling it. You're going on a journey that takes you to places unknown to your consciousness but known to your subconscious. Sometimes those events from the past are not what we hoped. But tell me, what do you remember?"

"I was a young woman during the Renaissance. I was posing for someone... I-I myself was an artist as I am now. I—She was a painter. And she met this man that I—she—fell in love with, but they couldn't be together because her parents arranged a marriage to someone else. She was terrified. How can it be possible for it to be so similar to my current life? Did they even end up together?"

"Anything is possible, Mar. What's important is not to judge the experiences. Just as in your normative life, we are here to live, not to question the way we do it at every turn, otherwise we will live our life regretting our existence rather than enjoying it...."

"That's bullshit, Almaguer. That's not what I came for. What about learning why these things are happening to me and why things just don't seem to work out for me, and if the curse is real?"

"Things *are* working out for you, Mar. Just not in the way your rational mind thinks they are, and that is not only terrifying, but often difficult to understand. In the coming sessions, we might get the answers, or they might surface outside this office. Take some time to step away from what happened here today, and before we meet again, we'll see what happens."

"No." I turned toward the door. "I'm not coming back. Keep the deposit for the other sessions. I'm already broke. Thanks, but this esoteric shit is definitely not for me."

17

MUSEO DEL PRADO

Mar

Madrid, Spain – 2023

I woke up in the middle of the night feeling like I was drowning. It's common for me. Sometimes it feels like I'm at the bottom of the ocean, scrambling for air, trying to reach the surface and failing. Staring up at the ceiling, I took several deep breaths, closing my eyes, and tried to conjure calming thoughts.

It's okay. You're in your bed. You're safe. Everything is all right.

After the fourth deep breath, I felt tension ease from the pit of my stomach, releasing like a flower in bloom. I opened my eyes slowly, taking in the emptiness of the vaulted ceilings in my loft. I placed one hand over my heart and the other over my stomach, where the sadness of my world pooled.

I couldn't stop thinking about the past life session and what I had just experienced. I stormed out of there so quickly, so rudely. I even texted Tania, telling her it was a waste of time. I still had questions.

I picked up my phone to check the time. *Fuck*, it's 5 a.m. *Again*.

I got up, peeled the sheets off my body, went to the kitchen, and made myself a *cafecito*. With my return to work, I had managed to get a single payment of my commission and afford coffee again. One small step for mankind, a giant leap for Mar. Or something like that.

There were still many areas of my life in which I felt like a failure, but making coffee was one of those things I could do with my eyes closed. I moved through the routine without thinking. Grab the container where the finely ground Colombian coffee I loved was stored, open it to release the familiar aroma that instantly made me feel at home. Then came the Italian moka pot—pack the coffee into the filter, close it, and set it on the hot stove.

I waited for that first concentrated drop to emerge. Placing two spoonfuls of sugar into a jug, staining them with droplets of coffee and stirring quickly to form the Cuban coffee token of victory—a perfect *espumita*. On the frother, streams of milk turned into soft clouds, gathering before they met the coffee. I let it all touch my lips, and I felt the warmth of home—even if home wasn't always that warm. It's the hug I wished I had right now, the words of comfort that I often knew how to give to others but not to myself. The kind of words others didn't seem to understand that I also needed from time to time.

That was the problem with being strong all the time. With seeming like you have everything under control. Like you've "got it." Because even when you do got it, you're rarely awarded space to melt. For me, that space was this coffee and the rising streams of its comfort pouring into me.

I took my *cafecito* and walked over to the couch in my living room. The dogs followed, all of us plopping down on the puffy mustard-colored sectional. I rested the mug on the coffee table in front of the couch and pulled out my phone, searching for more information on past-life regression. Thousands of videos came up, many of people who had gone through it, and it helped them tremendously. But the ones that interested me the most were the TikToks of children who claimed to remember their past lives, choosing their parents, and all that stuff Almaguer had told me about before I went into hypnosis. These kids had never been through a regression, but claimed they remembered things from their past lives.

A three-year-old boy from Argentina insisted he was a sailor in a past life. He had an obsession with boats and ships, even drawing sequences of numbers his parents later figured were coordinates. At first, the mom laughed it off, but then he recounted details of his life as a sailor, the routes he took during the First World War, and what he had lived through that were so intricate that the child could not have known about them unless he had lived that life. I was still skeptical. He could have watched documentaries about ships or seen movies at some point. I kept looking.

I came across one about a seven-year-old girl with an irrational fear of airplanes. She had never been on one, but she would tell her parents they were dangerous. She would often awake in the middle of the night yelling, "We're going to crash, we're going to crash!" When prodded about it, she told them she had been in an airplane crash in 1998 near a field in Virginia, detailing the exact route of the plane. I felt shivers crawl up my spine when her parents looked into the information and found it was factual. A plane had crashed exactly where she said it had.

"Okay, let's look at one more," I said out loud to the dogs.

The final one completely floored me. A little girl from Brazil told her family she remembered the moment she left her former life and came to this one. She told her family detailed stories of how she had been her grandmother, her mother's mother, in her previous life. "I came back to be with you, ma," she said. "I didn't want to leave you the first time, when you were just a little girl. So, I came back as *your* little girl." Her grandmother had died when her mother was just an infant from a rare disease. Her mother had never known her, raised by a stepmother instead. The little girl's recounting of her disease and watching her mother from another plane had me in tears. Everything Almaguer had said about soul families and their loyalties suddenly felt real.

I sat on the couch with my legs crossed and looked out into my quiet neighborhood, thinking through everything. I steeped in the silence that held my pain, now even more intense after my session, and let it wash over me.

What if what I experienced was real? What if all of this wasn't bullshit, as I had told Almaguer? I had felt it, after all.

I still couldn't wrap my head around how the hell a woman from the 1400s could have anything to do with what I was going through now? I was struggling with relationships in the 21st century in a post-pandemic world. It didn't even make sense that the root of my issues could go back that far. Perhaps it had worked for other people, but it wouldn't work for me.

Either way, I had things to do today, and I already had enough with my personal shit to be dwelling on something that may or may not have happened in the past.

Alberto was a ninety-four-year-old widower I met at the coffee shop. If there was one thing I missed about living far away from Miami was my grandparents, so when the coffee shop started an "*hora de abuelos*," I was the first to sign up. He was a retired military guy with a great sense of fashion and a lot of philosophizing on life. From the moment we were paired together, I knew he was far beyond just my friend, but the newest part of my Spanish family.

We had breakfast together every morning—or at least most mornings. I'd missed the last few months of them. He always ordered the same thing: a *porra*, one brown sugar, and a *café con leche* to dip it in. Some days he waited for me, others I waited for him. He still had a flip phone that didn't receive text messages, so our meetings were left to trust, routine, and hoping for the best. On this particular winter morning, we changed our usual lodging for a different plan, a visit to the Prado Museum.

"*Lo siento*, I know I've been absent for a few months and hadn't found a moment to catch up with you," I said on the phone two days ago when we planned it. "I've been going through a lot, but I'm working on moving past it now. I can come pick you up on Thursday morning if that works for you," I said.

"I heard what happened, Mar, no need to explain it to me. I understand this kind of situation is terrible," he said. "The ebbs and flows of life. And the answer is yes, yes, come for me. We don't know how long I have. Better make the best of it."

You see, when you're ninety-four and have lived as much as Alberto had, every day was the hope and the peril that it could be your last. I walked over to his building, just a block away from mine, where he was already waiting for me, leaning on his cane.

"Alberto, I told you I'd ring the bell. It's freezing," I bickered.

"*Ba*"—he waved his cane—"at my age, I don't have time to be waiting around for the bell to ring. Plus, I have to be back early for my doctor's appointment. I don't know why they keep doing all these crazy check-ups. I already know my time is up soon."

This kind of talk made me nervous. I knew death was imminent at his age, but the reminder of it left a bitter taste in my mouth. And he knew it. We got into a cab to the museum, both of us hoping the line wouldn't be too long.

"Mar," he looked up at me. "*Ya sé que no te gusta hablar de la muerte*, but you should know, I'm not afraid of dying."

I chuckled, "I know, but you don't have to jabber on about it, *señor*. I like the fact that you're here. You're like my family. "

"*Ay* Mar, when you've lived as long as I have, you'll realize that this whole thing about the wonders of getting old is a bunch of *tonterías*. Yeah, you get to be alive. But you barely have control of your life anymore. You have to enjoy it and do everything you want to do *now*, while you still have time to steer it in the direction you want it to go. Hopefully, it won't take you that long to realize it, because by then, you won't be able to do anything, and you'll need someone to escort you to the museum."

I thought back to all the unanswered questions I still had.

"*Vale, vale*, that's the end of all that talk." I paid for the taxi and helped him out.

There was something so majestic about the Prado Museum. You could come for days and still not see it all. Sometimes, I'd come just to sit in the cafe and experience the energy of the art around it. Goya's dark period was my favorite installation. As a muralist, how could I not fall in love with pieces taken from the walls of his home as he went mad with the horrors of war?

There was no need for perfect lines or form. Color was only used when it was strictly necessary. In war and grief, the only swatches available are shades of white, black, and red—in no particular order. When fear and death rule life, it's all a blur.

We walked through the galleries at Alberto's pace. He would stop now and then with commentary. He had his favorites. Among them, El Bosco's *El Jardín de las Delicias*, *Las Meninas* by Velázquez, and Goya's *La Maja Vestida*.

He also had his views on how art could be improved, something he never failed to let me in on.

"One thing I still don't understand about humanity is that all this art is great and all, but so much of it still doesn't represent the majority of the people found in history. I mean, look at this painting of Philip IV on horseback. Who cares about his horse? Very few works show the trials of people outside of the monarchy. Same with books, every other literary piece—at least the ones I read—have been about these people in high society. What about all the other classes? Do they not deserve their own applause as well?"

"Well, that's what modern artists are here to do, no? People like me? Maybe I won't be in a museum like this, Alberto, but perhaps it doesn't need to be preserved to have a long-lasting effect," I said.

By this point, we moved on toward the back of the museum, beyond the sculptures, to a space so secluded you could almost miss it. Taking the opportunity to rest in the dimly lit space, Alberto sat at a bench while I continued walking around the room.

That's when I saw her.

I felt a pull, almost like gravity, that called me to a corner where a small painting sat almost imperceptible between two large canvases. Anyone could have passed by it without noticing it. But once you got close to it, it was impossible to miss.

The canvas's golden frame looked ancient, without much restoration done to preserve its original form. Perhaps this was done on purpose, or perhaps it was beyond repair by the time someone found it. The wood was carved with lilies and vines, and on the inside of the frame, a blurry scripture in Latin that I couldn't quite make out. "Vincit omnia," *conquers all,* were the last words, but the first one was still blurry to me.

But what caught me most was the woman. Staring back at me were a pair of eyes exactly like mine. One green, one brown. Slightly parted lips, and a dimpled chin. I recognized the painting straight away, having a flashback to my session at

Almaguer's office, where the woman I was in a previous life was painting a very similar piece.

"No fucking way," I muttered. The room closed in on me.

Looking at the description, my suspicion was confirmed, "BVR 1493."

Beatriz Velázquez. That was her name!

I was so enthralled by the portrait that I barely noticed Alberto approaching me. The tick-tock of his cane beat against the surface of the Prado's marble floors. He stood next to me, leaning on the wooden support system, and stared at the portrait. He let out his usual tired sigh as he stood next to me, but then, he gasped.

"*Ave María*, Marisol." He turned to look at me with wide eyes. "Who painted this portrait of you?"

18

THE SEARCH

Mar

Madrid, Spain – 2023

I paced back and forth in my apartment while the dogs stared at me from their beds. In all my studies in art history and the Renaissance, I had never come across a painter with the name BVR. And if this portrait was hanging in the Prado, then it must be important. Whoever BVR was, she certainly wasn't *ninguna pelagatos.*

I ransacked my brain for any and all traces of these initials in my studies, pulling out every book I had on the Renaissance at home. Botticelli, Leonardo da Vinci, Michelangelo, Donatello, Caravaggio. Hundreds of images emerged. Frescoes, portraits of noble Florentines, muses, images from ancient history and literature. But nowhere, BVR.

Since we weren't allowed to take photographs at the Prado, I looked through their online archive to see if I could find the piece and do some extra research on it. Unfortunately, the page was currently under construction, sending me into an even deeper fervor of frustration. *How could I not know who she is!?*

As the evening passed, I couldn't shake my thoughts away from the painting that—as Alberto said—resembled me. How much of a coincidence could it have been that I go through past lives therapy, find out I was this Renaissance painter, and then I bump into her painting at the Prado? Seriously, just take me to the psychiatric ward now. I shut down my laptop, staring at the ceiling. There was another thing from the session I couldn't stop asking myself about: Beatriz's relationship with Dante. Part of me wished to know more. Did she have to marry the person her parents wanted her to marry, or did they find a way of escaping?

She even had a romance that I felt oddly jealous of. If she, in fact, was my soul, she had lived that experience at a time when I couldn't remember. Hundreds of years ago, I may have had something special, a love that risked it all, that felt destined. And now, in this lifetime, all I'd had were could-have-beens. Looking back, there wasn't a single one of my exes I could say resembled Dante. No one had devoted themselves to me in the way he had her. The way he had looked at her and longed for her, their friendship. Even with Guille, whom I had felt deeply connected to, I hadn't found that devotion.

Now, on the couch, my world was not what I imagined it would be. Instead, it was a puddle of confusion, sorrow, a deep longing to move past what was holding me back and embrace a different kind of future. A life where dreams come true, a different way of having it unfold. Celebrating my murals at the world's greatest art galleries, taking a year off to perfect the art of bread making, or perhaps even joining a theater group. Meet someone who wanted to get to know me, the real me. Who wasn't scared of peeling back the many layers that encompassed the person I am. Just as Dante had done for Beatriz.

"You're the only person I know that hasn't clicked with Dr. Almaguer," Tania said. "I can't believe you stormed out of her office on your first session. That's a bit unhinged, *tía*."

We were meeting for lunch at an Asturian restaurant in Goya before heading to an art show Lucas was throwing at the Fundación Juan March.

"It's not unhinged. I just don't think this kind of therapy is for me after all. When you went, did you end up feeling like it was worse for you? Because I just feel angry all the time, like if this is really what my life used to be like and I had this amazing romance, then honestly, I feel robbed."

Tania sighed. "Robbed of what? You've already *lived* that life. Now you have to live *this* one. I think you're looking at this all wrong. The point of going for multiple sessions is that you see the patterns you have to change in yourself. To heal."

"What about the painting of BVR I saw in the Prado? The one that looks like me," I said. "Do I just ignore that?"

"No. Just go back and talk to Dr. Almaguer. Keep figuring it out. You can't run away from your problems and your traumas, Mar. You'll have to face them eventually, and what better time to do so than now?"

We walked over to the gallery exhibit a few blocks away in Lista. The show served as a teaser for the opening of Torre de Espadas, the exhibition I was working on. First, we would hear a few words from the curator and then get a chance to look around at the pieces of contemporary Spanish art that were part of the collection. There would be an after-party in the same building.

Everyone from Madrid's art world was there. Lucas looked fierce as he moved through the crowd, proud of yet another accomplishment. He had helped curate this collection, too. Tania's boyfriend, Juan, had joined us, taking her away for a bit of prosecco, and I went my own way, looking around the room at the pieces hanging from the walls.

I came toward the end of the room, where a tall man stood with a glass of prosecco. From the back, all I could see was a head of unruly hair poking out in all directions. He was wearing a lapis lazuli blue jacket over jeans. I stood next to him as we both watched the same piece by a Spanish sculptor, Marianela Ortega.

"She's quite good, *no*?" The man said. It took me a moment to realize he was talking to me. I was enthralled by the sculpture.

"Marianela? Ye—yes! She's very good."

Jesus, my conversational skills were really lacking these days.

"I love her use of different media for sculpture. The clay, the pieces of stone. You don't see much of this kind of artistry these days," he went on.

I turned to face him. He had a kind face made even kinder by his smirk. He had been looking in my direction the entire time.

He stretched out his hand. "Dario Messina. Nice to meet you."

I caught a hint of an accent that wasn't Spanish at all.

"Marisol Varela," I said. "But, everyone calls me Mar."

"And what do you like to be called?"

Shit. No one had asked me before what name I liked going by. It was surprisingly sweet.

"Mar is fine. Marisol is a bit strong...plus it has a weird meaning."

He cocked his head. "What would that be?"

"Woman of sol—solitude."

Why the hell was I relaying this information to a total stranger?

He chuckled. "I have to say, that is a very smooth way of telling someone you are single."

I felt heat rushing through my cheeks as they turned red with embarrassment.

"Oh, no, no, no, that wasn't—I was just—"

Use your words, Mar.

"Don't worry, I'm just teasing. But now I will find out what Dario means. Maybe something like 'handsome Italian man who cooks very well.'"

I laughed, noticing the pain I'd been carrying with me as a constant companion had disappeared for an instant in Dario's brief company. There was something familiar about him.

"Have we met before?" I asked. "I recognize your face from somewhere."

He thought for a moment. "No, we haven't. I don't come to Madrid often. I'm only here for a few weeks, and then I return home."

Bummer.

"Where is home?"

"*Firenze.* I am a professor there. I teach poetry and art history."

Seriously? Florence?

"Wow, I've always wanted to go to Florence. It was one of my dreams when I was in high school."

"Ah, well, if you ever come to my city for a visit sometime, let me know."

"Mar!" I heard Tania's voice calling me from across the room. "Lucas is looking for you." She gestured for me to follow her. I looked up at Dario, a bit bummed that our conversation had to be cut short.

"It was great meeting you, Dario. Have a great time here in Madrid. It's a pretty amazing city."

"*Grazie, grazie.*"

I turned and started walking away when I heard his voice again.

"Ey, Mar!"

I looked back.

"I would have definitely remembered meeting you."

19

ANOTHER TRY

Mar

Madrid, Spain – 2024

I dreamt of BVR's painting. My own eyes staring back at me, soft copper curls cascading down her neck and shoulders, the green and blue gown that draped down her body, the black choker adorned with embroidered hearts on her neck. This wasn't a portrait of a joyful lady in waiting; this subject was angry, and the woman behind the brush was too.

I didn't know what her other work was like, but as an artist myself, I knew that when you felt that kind of anger, the only way of finding catharsis was to transform that emotion into something tangible, visceral, beautiful. Art had a way of helping you get back to who you were—or become who you were supposed to be—by giving you a place to channel everything you felt without having to make it about you. I could relate to that resentment toward the world; it had done me wrong more than once.

I couldn't stop thinking about how the girl in this painting might be *me*. Five hundred years ago, a painter in the Renaissance knew exactly what I would look like. How? How did she even know?

But the Beatriz I saw was happy, full of life. Vivacious. Where had that anger come from?

I knew what I had to do, and as much as it sucked to admit it, I pulled out my phone and booked my next appointment with Almaguer.

"I'm surprised to see you here, Mar. Happy New Year." Almaguer cradled her teacup while I played with the tassels of a blanket draped on the sofa. I wasn't always the best at admitting I was wrong, and she could tell. Even in our short time together, I could see how perceptive she was.

The entire trip to her office I debated on whether to tell her about BVR or not. Would she understand my wishes to know more about the painting? Could she know who BVR was? After all, Almaguer had appeared in my life after my own friend met her during the "Women Painters of the Renaissance" exhibition.

"Maybe the last time I left was a bit impulsive," I said. "I got spooked, honestly, I'm not going to lie to you. I guess I had this idea that I would come here and suddenly everything would make sense, all would fall into place, and I would heal everything I felt."

"Hmmm," she said. "That happens. That's why I was adamant about telling you to release expectations. When you are on a healing path, it's important to ask yourself if you're on that path because you truly want to heal or if you just want to feel better."

Shit, she was good.

"Feeling better is not always healing. There are many ways

to trick the mind and the body into thinking you're better. Distracting yourself from your own issues, drinking, partying, having sex with strangers, jumping into a new relationship right away. All of those things we engage in when we're tired of being sad or angry or dealing with difficult emotions come with a price. Often, they come with a price to our soul."

"*No entiendo*."

"Mar, every lesson, every hardship that you go through in this life, your soul has already chosen. Your soul, and probably your exes, chose this path. You chose your parents. You chose this life experience so you could learn *something* and your soul could transcend."

"Wait, but doesn't that eliminate the concept of free will?"

"No, not at all. When we come to the earth to experience this, our conscious mind doesn't retain these memories. We come in as a blank slate. Otherwise, imagine how easy life would be. We'd just come into the world, know our mission, stay away from all those things we know will slow us down, and move on. Being here gives us *choice*. Despite what your soul has selected, you can *choose* a new destiny. Like how you chose to be here today. Now, please tell me why you've returned for today's session because I'm very curious."

I decided to fess up about the painting. I would leave the YouTube videos and everything else for another time.

"I saw something three weeks ago that startled me a bit," I said. "It was a portrait, by this artist BVR. She was the woman whose life I had gone back to. She had this crazy portrait at the Prado that looked just like me. It was such a coincidence."

She looked up at me from her half-moon spectacles, inquisitively. "Hmm, really?"

"I know, I know it sounds crazy. But I felt insanely connected to the painting; it was like looking at myself in the mirror. Even Alberto, a neighbor of mine I went with, thought the same thing. It has been driving me mad since I saw it."

"Understandably. I'm sure it must have had an impression on you." She sipped on her tea. "How do you feel about all this?"

"Confused? Is there any way that I can go back to that life specifically? Like, can we choose to go back there?"

"Theoretically, we can guide the mind to go toward a specific life, but in the end, it's your subconscious that chooses what you see."

"I want us to try to go back to that life. I want to know what happened to Beatriz...and to Dante."

I could tell she was searching for the right words, measuring their impact on my already fragile mood.

"*Está bien*. I will try leading you there. Perhaps we can find the answers you're looking for regarding your relationships. How this experience with Guillermo is helping you evolve."

I scoffed. "Evolve? I have to fear seeing my ex doting on his girlfriend around our neighborhood. If anything, I've regressed."

"*A ver*, Mar." She leaned forward, her silver hair cascading over her arms. "Sometimes, even though it can feel like we're not moving in any particular direction, that is the moment when we're moving the most. It's like winter, the season we're in now. In our physical plane, it seems like everything is dead, like nothing is happening. But deep in the ground, the trees, in nature itself, everything is preparing for the year ahead."

She put her teacup down. "Are you ready to go back so you can prepare for the future?"

"Yes," I said. "This time I'm ready."

20

THE THIN WALLS OF SOCIETY

Beatriz

Florence, Italy – 1485

I stormed through my bedchamber, tearing the garments off my body. I ripped the minuscule flowers off my hair, undoing my braid, staying only in the freedom of my sheath robe. My skin burned as heat waves of anger coursed through me.

Niccolo de Rossi. *It couldn't be.*

After all the years I spent crafting my future with *Papá*. Ensuring I would not be wed to a man whom I did not know from one day to the next, that I would not be bartered like a beast at the market. And yet, here I stood, no better for all my striving, sold. He granted me the gifts of letters, of education, when most women—my mother among them—could scarcely tell one word from another. All to what end? That I might set my own soul and hand to a marriage contract?

Niccolo de Rossi. *It wouldn't be.*

Sitting cross-legged at the foot of my bed, questions raced

through my mind. I ransacked memories of the gatherings and feasts *Mamá* held here. Had I seen him before? Could we have been introduced, and I was too distracted to remember? This was *Mamá's* design all along. To marry me off. To send me forth from this household. This imperfect daughter of hers would rather be covered in charcoal than shuffling cards and sipping on fancy teas with her acquaintances. Surely, there must be some path by which I may be delivered from this. It *must not* be.

Soft knocks came from the hall. My hands still clenched into fists, I pulled the sheet on the bed over myself, leaving only my face uncovered, pretending to be asleep. Daria's head peeked through the door.

"Daria! *Grazie Dio*, come in, come in." I threw off the sheets. "Did you hear what transpired in the sitting room?"

"Who *did not* hear what happened in the sitting room, *signorina*? The household is so quiet, you can hear the floorboards."

Closing the door, she sat with me at the foot of the bed. I had known Daria long enough to know when she had news to share. She bit her bottom lip nervously, drawing circles on her apron with her index finger. Servants were the secret keepers of every household, the unsung historians documenting the story from every viewpoint. Not even priests were as informed.

"What news do you have?" I urged. "Do you know of this Niccolo? Have we met previously?"

She straightened the apron atop her skirt. "We have hosted his parents on several occasions, *signorina*. The Count de Rossi and his wife. Filomena, the cook, says that they have been here quite often, the *mamma* taking tea with yours every other fortnight or so. We attempted to draw information from Diana; however, she is strictly loyal to your mother. But other servants say his mother is highly unpleasant, spitting orders at them."

"Surely Diana would not utter a word against my mother. Although I recall *Mamá* saying something about Bologna." I raised myself from the bed, pacing across the room. "But *if* they are from Bologna...how is it possible for *Mamá* to take tea with her so frequently? Is it not almost a fortnight away?"

I groaned, flopping onto the bed once more. Even if the servants didn't know who Niccolo was or his family's dealings in Florence, then I would have to take on the investigation myself. The real question now was how. While my *Papá* awarded me certain liberties within the walls of our home, to the rest of society, I was still just a woman of seven and ten.

Oh yes—*society*.

The following morning, preparations for Enzo's engagement luncheon were taking place. From my chamber, I could hear *Mamá* howling at the servants. She would not allow a single piece to be out of place on the engagement of her only son. Oh no. If there was anything my mother cared about, it was how she was perceived by society.

The implications were of little consequence to her. People were peons in a game of chess where she was the queen in disguise. Every other piece, including my father, was one she moved around to her benefit. Since we were not close, I could not bring myself to understand her or the reason she acted the way she did. The only moments that shed light on her strategy reminded me that women were subjected to the rules of society.

Before descending for the luncheon, I sent Daria on a mission to gather information about Niccolo de Rossi. She would go to *Signora* Clarice's home. I recalled *Signora* Clarice had spoken previously of a secret society and how they often met with prominent city members. Many *mammas* took their daughters to Clarice's "official" courses, where she taught women how to be "good wives." She was often in rooms where

Niccolo's name could've been spoken. Perhaps his family tried to marry him off previously, to someone else. In any case, it was worth a try.

The guests arrived promptly at midday. Ladies, sires, members of the chamber, patrons of the arts. For the most part, none of them knew my brother, still attendance at these ceremonious events was pivotal to being a member of society.

Mamá established specific protocols for receiving the guests. We would stand in the salon, by birth order, greeting each one until the last of them arrived. She and *Papá* would remain just beyond the doorway, seeing all was done with due order. The twins gleefully accepted this task, while I dreaded it. I was still not speaking to either of my parents. Enzo, as usual, was indifferent.

Enzo's betrothed, Giovanna, arrived last to the feast, as was tradition.

The luncheon began promptly after a toast from both families. Perched in my corner of the hall, I observed how my brother quietly accepted the fate laid out for him by our parents. Men, in contrast to women, had a choice. Had he protested as I had, there was a possibility he would have been released from this? But he had not. I was beginning to realize that our family, in more ways than I had grasped, conformed more to what society thought and expected of them than to their own true nature.

While I mused, a familiar voice approached me. "No greetings for your arts master, then." I turned to find Sandro smiling wryly. He pretended to find something to eat at the table beside mine as we spoke, under the pretense that we knew each other only through my father.

"I had not seen you. Otherwise, I may have asked you to help me plot an escape plan."

He sipped wine from his goblet. "As enticing as that sounds, *signorina*, I would not lay such turmoil upon your father. Now, tell me, what are you escaping from? Have they plotted your wedding as well?"

"Yes." I sighed. Then it dawned on me, perhaps Sandro knew of Niccolo, or at least heard of him. "Sandro...er—*Maestro Botticelli*—have you heard of a Niccolo de Rossi?"

His face paled. "Oh, *cara*, is that who you are to wed?"

I felt the reeds of my bodice encircle my ribcage. "Wh-what have you heard?"

He pulled me behind one of my mother's ornate flower arrangements, feathers covering our conversation.

"I urge you not to panic, *Bea*, for it will make it worse and there is not much you can do about this sort of thing. I have met with his mother more often than with him; she is a ghastly old hag. I was sent to meet them once while they were visiting. They wanted a painting of Niccolo to be done for his title as count."

"Wh-what does he look like? Was he awful?"

"He has hair the color of wheat fields, with piercing blue eyes. They are as beautiful as they are uncomfortable to gaze upon. He does not say much, so I would not be able to judge his character. It is as if he is...how should I put it—*contained*?"

"Contained?"

"Like there is much within that has not yet risen to the surface," he said. "But when it does, *cara*...it is likely best not to be near him."

"What?!"

Sandro edged closer, his voice a whisper. "I have heard rumors that he once beat a servant nearly to death in the courtyard of his home for soiling his boots. He was also previously engaged to Cecilia Garibaldi. The poor girl never spoke of it, but it is said he was verbally forceful with her on occasion. Her family sent her away for several months before Niccolo went off to the war."

My stomach churned further upon this description. The room started spinning.

His eyebrows had not separated throughout our conversation. “His reputation as a general is of concern as well,” he said. “I do not mean to scare you, but you *must* be careful not to bring attention to yourself. He could have anyone he liked killed under the pretense it was for the protection of the kingdom."

I closed my eyes, finding a wall to lean against to catch my breath. “Oh, Sandro. What can I do to free myself from this? My parents are keen on having me marry him. Particularly *Mamá.*”

“What of your father?”

“I can no longer count on him. He sides with my mother on this. I am on my own now.”

Sandro sighed, then took another sip from his goblet. “When is your wedding, dove?”

21

MUSES

Beatriz

Florence, Italy – 1485

Winter turned into spring and spring into summer, as I edged closer to ten and eight. Florence also turned turbulent, with religious groups threatening the soul of the city. Too concerned with my dwindling time with Dante, my artistic pursuits, and the looming doom of my future husband's temper, I did not concern myself with the turmoil.

The weight of my engagement had lessened as my mother focused on Enzo's wedding and ensuring she perfected her hosting skills while our societal ranking increased. I found solace once more in my first true portrait. I had yet to identify the woman I was painting. She was, in many ways, a mirror image of me.

We had the same eye shape, except I saw her with one eye a different color. They were glossy with loss and confusion. Occasionally, I caught her staring back at me, seeming more determined. Today, I dwelled on her locks. They were a blend of copper and honey in all its forms. I had mixed the colors earlier, adding a bit of golden powder my father gifted me in an attempt to assuage my fear of my arranged marriage. Well, *Papá*, here I am, alchemizing it.

I still had not deciphered what to do with the expression on her mouth, as she was ever changing like the sea.

"You are getting quite good at this,." Sandro snuck up behind me. "Do we know this young woman?"

"No, we do not." I frowned. "She came to me by chance during my first lessons here. Yet I still cannot riddle her out."

He dragged a stool next to mine, grabbing the smallest brush he found. I noticed gray hairs on his copper beard.

"Beatrice, have you read *La Divina Commedia?*" he asked, fiddling with the tip of the brush.

"I have not," I said. "*Mamá* moderates the books we are allowed to read at home."

"Ah, of course." His eyebrows came together. "The reason I am asking is that when it comes to muses, they happen to appear in very strange ways and accompany us in our journeys quite differently."

"Like Simonetta—"

He interjected, "Yes, like Simonetta for me. *Ma*, Dante Alighieri, the author of *La Divina Commedia,* also had a muse, a love unlived. She was also named Beatrice, like you."

"And his name was Dante..." I murmured.

"Yes—exactly as my beloved poetic friend, for whom I know you have a fondness. " He winked, having noticed my nervousness at his observation. "Do not fret, *Bea*. As you are aware, I believe taking a wife is a horrible task. You are safe."

"You believe the lady in this portrait is my muse?"

"I believe you should continue allowing her to speak to you." He took the brush, pointing it at the canvas. "There are a few ways in which you can work around her while you figure out her expression. One such way is using this gold powder in her eyes to bring out that flame. I have to say this is quite excellent work, for an amateur such as yourself."

My face heated with flattery. He pressed his hand against mine before pushing himself off the stool.

"Uh—Sandro, does a muse ever abandon you?"

He sighed. "Sometimes I wish they would."

22

AN INVITATION

Beatriz

Florence, Italy – 1485

An invitation arrived at my doorstep.

To the admirable Lady Beatriz Velázquez de Concepción.

It is with great esteem that I request your presence during our next lesson, not at my home as is customary, but at Via de Sant' Antonino 11, at the secret garden known only to its members as Casa dei Fiori. We would be delighted to receive your joyful company. Seek Daria for further instructions.

-S

23

CASA DEI FIORI

Beatriz

Florence, Italy – 1485

In the coming days, my lesson was not at the *bottega*, but in a home two doors down, where an indoor garden revealed itself to me. Towering walls covered in murals made of mosaics and tempera told the stories of the women who painted them. Women, who like me, hid behind sacred walls to be themselves and express their art.

My mouth gaped open as *Signora* Clarice led me through a garden. In the back, ladies huddled, embracing each other. Among them, a familiar face emerged, red locks in a braid that reached her hips—Daria.

"Daria!?"

Shock rippled through her expression, as if she had done something wrong.

"No, no, I am so happy to see you!" I ran toward her, embracing her like a sister.

The women circled us in an invisible embrace. *Signora*

Clarice took the lead. "I would now, with good grace, present Beatriz to the company. Welcome to *La Casa dei Fiori, Amapola*."

I sat in the middle of a circle of fifteen women draped in white dresses. The courtyard, alchemizing sunlight into rainbows that bounced off stained glass, smelled of copal incense. Water cascaded from the small fountain on the side of the room, drowning the tumult outside the walls.

Each woman wore a different flower in their lapel, a sign of her affiliation with "*La Casa dei Fiori*." The flowers were far beyond a simple nod to the name. Each one symbolized a specific trait of the member named after it, and how they represented the properties of that particular bloom.

I knew a few of the ladies at the gathering, though I had spoken but little with them in the past. I had known Daria best, or so I believed. I could have never imagined my *nana* was part of a secret society. All along, I thought I had been the only one keeping secrets, while she had kept silent on an entirely different life. Her flower was the Daffodil, representing uniqueness and sunshine. Francesca, one of the society's founders, wore White Heather for protection and wishes come true. There were Hibiscus, Holly, Tulip, Myrtle, and Magnolias.

The rite was singularly strange; anyone could have deemed it as witchcraft. We would all be cast into the fire or drowned for setting ourselves against the will of God and the Church. And yet I had found that neither religious affiliation nor status were the pillars of purity of soul. There was perhaps more kindness in this indoor garden than in all of Florence. For God lived within the love we emanated and fought to preserve in kinship, partnership, sisterhood. *Signora* Clarice, or Orchidea, approached me holding two poppies. I was given the name *Amapola*. It was Spanish for the crimson herb that journeyed from Mesopotamia to Europe, casting a dreamlike spell over the continent with its properties.

"Beatriz Velázquez de Concepción, from this moment forth, in the confines of this secret society, you shall be known by your blossom: Amapola," she decreed. "You are our bright, dreamlike, and perilous poppy. In our darkest and deepest melancholy, we look to you to relieve us of our troubles, reminding us that peace is forthcoming. Your petals may be gentle, but within them lies a substance strong enough to topple empires." She leaned in closer to me. Almost whispering, "It is often those no one believes in that have the power to change the world. We shall do the oath now. No one joins this society without being sworn in."

She extended her hand to reveal a pin made of red Murano glass. Perforating the left breast of my white robe, she settled the glass poppy above my heart.

"Beatriz, repeat after me, right hand above your heart, *per favore*." *Signora* Clarice smiled.

"I, Beatriz Velázquez de Concepción, swear my loyalty, service, and artistry to the secret society of *Casa dei Fiori*. I vow to uphold the virtues of the women within it, honoring the grand risks of our work. Knowing my thoughts are pivotal for the betterment of society, accepting the responsibility that art is beyond form and color—but protest—and from now on, my new voice."

The thrill of being a part of something as special as this was muted by a simple notion: *this would not last*. If *Mamá* ever knew, she would find a way of severing me from this new identity.

Each woman in the circle drew closer, embracing me and each other like a bouquet. Somehow, with the promise of my engagement looming like a dark cloud over me, I knew this was the sunshine that would help me blossom in the darkest winters of my life. Daria held on to me the longest.

All these years we had shared, I realized we had never embraced. She had gifted me her youth, a life of devotion. Her hair was decorated with ribbons and braids. On her, I could smell the light scent of the lavender oil her mother so lovingly concocted so she would always smell wonderful.

"I shall never leave you, Amapola. You may rely on me for this. I shall follow you to the horizon and fall off the edge of the world if I must. But you shall never endure alone."

Tears flowed from my eyes as her words pierced my heart with loyalty. I pulled away from our embrace to look upon her. "I apologize for overlooking you, Daria. My mind fills with questions. Forgive me for being a foolish child all these years and not seeing your brilliance."

"Mistre—"

I placed a finger upon her lips. "Bea."

I attempted to feel joyful as the evening continued with endless dancing. Women from all circles were equals within these safe walls. Laughter and song carried us through, helping me forget that outside, other fates awaited. I had found purpose in community, and as much as I wanted not to fear what was to come and believe in the light, a feeling of strange melancholy permeated the joy of belonging.

A petal from the dried poppy I received earlier flew from my skirt pocket, bursting into shimmering red dust that filled the courtyard. The room froze, the crimson substance enveloping us in its powerful enchantment. Under its spell, everything seemed possible. As my steps left footprints on the dirt floor below them, I saw him.

Dante.

Cloaked, his face hidden by his disguise, he stood at the closed door of the courtyard, watching me. In the haze of the poppy, I performed for him. The rich silk of my white dress swayed like a whisper around my hips as I moved rhythmically to the lute, my eyes locked on his. My heart thumped against my chest, sweat trickling down my spine as I spun gleefully, gliding, my fingertips brushing the air as they would soon be brushing against his wide chest. The music paused. Firelight caught a glimpse of his face, painted with desire. I stepped toward him, intoxicated by the effect of Dante and the poppy. He was another thing I loved and stood to lose.

"Are you real?" I reached for his face.

He grinned. "I am."

"Are you also a part of this?"

"Of this, and of you."

24

MYRTLES AND ROSES

Beatriz

Florence, Italy – 1485

My first work for *Casa dei Fiori* came from the hand of Sandro himself. He left a few pieces for me to work on during his absence. His assignment was very specific: to work on the Birth of Venus, the painting I had posed for the year before. It was so large, it engulfed nearly an entire wall of the studio.

Sandro left a note by my paintbrush, detailing my task.

Amapola,

Now that you are in bloom, it is time you painted the roses and myrtle belonging to the birth of Venus. Botanical sketches on your table. Worship this goddess with all your talent.

See you soon, cara.

-S

He had left materials for me. Rosa Rubiginosa, Rosa Canina, Rosa Gallica. I gathered them, forming the colors of each flower the goddess and the scenery around her required. The bright morning light seeped through the frosted windows of the *bottega*, illuminating every corner.

First, I crushed cochineals, their vibrant red hue bursting as I ground them in the mortar. The smell of musk and dirt rising against my nostrils. Then, I added lead white and linseed oil, forming a smooth substance ready to honor the canvas Sandro worked on so lovingly, his homage to Simonetta.

Is the love that lasts forever the one we never have the opportunity to live? I pondered, observing Simonetta's face representing Venus.

Will I love Dante forever because I will not have him? Will I love him even after I am forced to give myself away to another man? Carry another man's children? Endure another marriage?

My hands moved with precision, barely touching the canvas with the delicate brush stained with pale pink. The scent of linseed oil and fresh pigment hung in the air, mingling with the faint hint of dust and fresh-cut wood used to build the easels.

I dipped the tip of the brush in the pigment, capturing the curled edges of each rose as it flew in the ocean breeze. I could almost hear the waves crashing on the shore, the strong winds rustling everything around it. With each stroke, I added layers of petals, each flower diverse and equal to the others.

I had not noticed time fleeting until *Signora* Clarice knocked three times, signaling my exit. The *bottega* had fallen under the spell of my silent brush whispering against the canvas. I stepped back to admire my work. I stood still, taking it in, feeling the pulse of creation rush through me.

25

EIGHT AND TEN

Beatriz

Florence, Italy – 1485

My eighteenth birthday arrived with the Florentine autumn and unexpected joy. I awoke before dawn to crisp, chilly air and the hint of nostalgia that arrived with the changing of leaves. Even when the most beautiful days of the season came along, with their bright blue skies and their changing leaves, I could feel her creeping in my stomach, making her way up my throat and through my eyes, often resulting in a few tears.

Still in my night robe, I tiptoed through the empty halls of the house. Not even the servants were awake, the sun giving the moon a final glance before peeking up from the horizon. I grazed the textured walls of the house while the cold kissed my bare feet. One and eight was a big number. The last one before the weight of expectations that came with marriage descended upon me. Rumors of Niccolo's rage had reached me once more, this time through Daria. Women of the *Fiori* who knew his mother had told her of their conservative nature and Niccolo's temper. Which he had been sent away to the war to quell.

I stepped into my father's study, curtains draped on the big windows like virgins at church. *Let's unveil you*, I whispered, tucking the pieces of long fabric behind ornate holders at each side. The Magnolia tree stood tall in the courtyard, and I watched how it swayed as the morning breeze awoke. The sky started turning a lighter shade of blue as the sun's rays penetrated it with its golden perfection and warmth. There were still some Magnolias left from this year's bloom falling. *This would be the perfect gift for myself*, I thought, heading to the courtyard door to feel the leaves covered in morning dew under my feet.

Even though they were cold and wet, I felt relieved as they held me. With each step, the leaves formed a bed for me, calling me to sit next to them, witnessing the spectacle the sun was forming in the sky. I rested my body against the soft leaves, letting the leaves lull me into a daydream. The clouds moved in tandem as birds flew through them. Deep down, I envied their freedom. If I could grow wings, I would join them too, seeing this city from above, freeing myself from my future husband's rumored temper.

"*Feliz cumpleaños, hija.*" *Papá's* deep voice startled me.

"*¡Papá!*" I gasped, realizing my father had not seen me in my night robe since I was a child. "Pardon me, I was just—"

He raised a hand, stopping me. Aside from a few pleasantries and polite interactions, we had not spoken since the announcement of my engagement. A smile creased under his grand beard.

"No need to explain yourself—I am leaving and will be back for an afternoon meal with the family." He turned. "Perhaps you should return to your chamber before the rest of the household finds you like this."

I laughed nervously. "Yes, of course. I figured I had more time."

"We all believe we have more time, *hija*. Imagine my surprise at realizing the child I once held in one hand is now a woman of eight and ten."

I wanted to tell him my fears, how I longed for him to be my hero again.

"I'm sorry, I am not the daughter you expected, *Papá*. It would please me if we could start speaking again."

I looked down at my hands. To my surprise, he walked up to me, raising my head to look at his confused expression.

"*Escúchame,* Beatriz. You are far more than I ever expected. I never imagined such a brilliant daughter could be born of my loins. I am the one who is sorry that I cannot provide you with a world that views you as I do. But to me, you are a most impressive young woman. I do hope you never lose that fire within yourself. Even if I have to face the damages later, with your mother and such—" He laughed. "Now, go on with your day."

His words still lingered in the air, forcing tears from my eyes as I watched him disappear into the house.

26

A QUESTION OF VIRTUE

Beatriz

Florence, Italy – 1485

The rest of the day was spent in family formalities. *Mamá* had arranged a birthday breakfast with the twins, then I would accompany her to the priest for confession and counsel before my wedding, and finally we would have a meal with Lorenzo and *Papá* in the afternoon.

The day was intoxicatingly perfect and slightly warm for autumn. Daria and Diana, my mother's maid, accompanied us to church, waiting outside as we entered. *Mamá* led me to the priest's chamber, where he questioned me about my devotion to God, my understanding of the marriage sacrament, and my willingness to enter this union.

"Do you go into this marriage willingly, my child?" the priest asked. He examined me closely, his weathered hands holding a cross tightly to his swollen belly.

Mamá shot a piercing look toward me.

"Yes, *padre*." I said.

He rambled on about the importance of wifely obedience, my daily chores, and Catholic duties. I allowed his words to wash over me, nodding in agreement to expedite his sermon.

We emerged from the church to find a woman near our carriage. Dressed in all black, her face pinched with disapproval upon our presence. I soon realized she belonged to the de Rossi household.

"*Signora*," *Mamá* said, her voice tight. "What a surprise."

"The family has sent me forth," she interrupted. "There is a pressing matter that must be tended to before the wedding." She fixed her gaze on me with cold appraisal. "The *signorina* must prove her virtue."

Virtue? Her words hung in the air like a slap.

"But of course I am virtuous..." I interjected. "I am a woman of eight and ten that has never lain with another man. That is a disgraceful thought."

"Quiet, Beatriz," my mother snapped. "We will discuss this further with Niccolo's parents if this is a condition they have requested. Remember, he is to be your husband and you shall do as he says."

"Will Niccolo's virtue also be attended to before our wedding day?" I retorted, ignoring her warning.

My mother's hand struck me before I could utter another word. Droplets of blood dripped on my robes, red as the poppy I had been given on my initiation day at *Casa dei Fiori*. I touched my face, and my fingers came away bloody. Her ring had split my cheek and lip.

I rushed away from the carriage, past Daria and Diana.

"Mistress!" Daria ran after me, but I did not stop. The blood kept coming. I did not notice where I was running to until I arrived at *Signora* Clarice's door. When she flung it open, shock filled her face. I burst into tears.

"Beatrice." She rushed me in, ensuring no one else saw us. "What has transpired, *cara?*"

I cried into her bosom, staining her dress with my blood and tears.

"I cannot do it, Clarice. I cannot marry Niccolo. I cannot do what my mother and my family expect of me. I will not make it through another year of life if this is the case—" I sobbed.

"*Calma*, *cara mia*. Hush now." She stroked my back. "All will be well. Pardon me a moment, while I boil water for some tea. It will help."

Dante, disturbed by the commotion, appeared at the *bottega* door. His eyes widened at the sight of me.

"Bea." He ran toward me. "What has happened?" His hands lifted my face to inspect me more clearly.

"Someone from Niccolo's household accosted my mother and me outside the church where I was receiving marital counsel. She demanded assurance of my virtue, to which I replied by asking if Niccolo would face the same scrutiny. My mother then struck me."

He pinched his nose between his fingers as he shook his face.

Signora Clarice returned with tea, and a cloth to clean my face before excusing herself once more. "I shall leave you both to speak."

Dante looked over at me. "I cannot watch you be hurt like this. I do not want this to be your life. And each time you mention your wedding, it is as if a spear is pushed through my guts and ripped out repeatedly. I am, as Prometheus, doomed to having my liver eaten each night by an eagle. Except that liver is my heart, and my eagle is reality."

He came to me and pulled me into his chest. In the silence of our cries, Clarice reappeared with a bowl of fresh warm water.

Dante took it from her, whispering he would tend to me. He seated me on the bench and knelt, placing the basin beside him on the floor. He dipped the rag into it, gently stroking my face. I winced at his touch, the sting of the gash my mother left burning my face.

"*Mi dispiace*," he whispered.

"No," I cleared my throat. "I do not need your apology. Sitting with the pain of this is enough. Do you think it will leave a mark?"

"I believe with a dab of rose oil, it shall heal." He smiled.

"How do you—" I started.

"My *mamma* and *nonna.* The poor have a way of knowing how to heal with herbs and

such. I was a troublesome child. Now, *cara*, I shall ask you.What do you want to do?"

Resigned, lost, hurt, all I wanted was sleep. Perhaps never wake up. I would not be

surprised if my mother sent everyone searching for me. I knew I could not stay hidden for long.

"If it were my will we would flee far away from here today, Dante. But we cannot." I thought back to what Sandro said about Niccolo's temper. He was a general, a man with a title and resources who could have us both killed if he felt disgraced. Our safety came before all else.

"*Amore*," I said. "I am afraid this is a fight we are not poised for. I must return home."

He breathed angrily. "No, I will not—"

"Please," I begged. "If my father finds out about our acquaintance, I will surely never see you again. We must wait. Please, do this for me. Let me go for now, for both of our safety."

"This is not the end. I refuse. What kind of man would I be if I let the woman I love marry another? I cannot lose you like this, Beatriz. We must escape. We must devise a plan now. An uprising is coming to Florence. It may not be today, or tomorrow, but one is coming. That will be our escape."

Florence had been buzzing with talk of another revolt against the Medici. Talk of a preacher from Ferrara who condemned the arts was heard around the city, yet no one believed this would cause any real trouble.

"Let us run away. No one will find us." Dante insisted.

As he edged closer to me, I realized he was crying. His desperation nearly broke me. "We can ask Sandro to help us. No one will come looking for you."

I had to turn to stone to protect him and myself. Cut it off like a wounded limb. There were some things one must sacrifice in life, and I realized mine would be this love.

"We cannot," I said almost in a whisper. Wishing I could say *sí*. "I promise I do not wish to marry Niccolo, Dante. *Credimi*. You are the only person I will ever love. We simply cannot at this moment. There is too much at stake if we run away. His family is dangerous. *He* is dangerous, Sandro told me himself. It could get you killed—and—"

He peeled my palm away from his cheek, stepping back from me. He breathed in and closed his eyes. When he opened them again, his dark gaze held mine.

"Have it as you will, *Beatriz*. If you are willing to sacrifice *us* for this marriage, so be it. It is absurd, all this while I believed you would come with me. That we would find a way to escape together."

"Dan—" I edged forward, he lifted his hand to stop me.

"No. Do not come closer. I will respect your wishes. I will not ask you to run away with me. I will not ask you to leave him or your family or your life. *Dai*. If you will not come with me, then I will leave. I have no desire to witness your new life. To see you as someone else's wife. To see you carry someone else's child. It may seem selfish, perhaps it is. But that for me is an *inferno* I will not survive."

He snatched his satchel and stormed out.

My gown weighed heavily on me. The sumptuous deep blue silk brocade shimmered with gold embroidery. Each thread woven into delicate floral patterns. I had ensured the modiste included this subtle nod to the *Fiori*. The bodice, adorned at the neckline with tiny pearls, flowed seamlessly into billowing sleeves, matching a cascading skirt. As part of my wedding gift, Niccolo's family sent a sheer veil and delicate gilded crown with miniscule irises, carnations, lilies, and orange blossoms pulled together by an olive branch. All flowers representative of Tuscany and Spain.

It was the last fitting before the wedding took place. By this point, my face had healed significantly with minimal swelling.

The modiste pulled back on the bodice, constraining my breath.

Outside, *Papá* waited for me. We would rehearse our arrival to the church before the wedding. I stepped down from the fitting stool, stepping forward to where he sat looking in the other direction, I tapped his shoulder. He turned, his eyes sprinkled with a mixture of joy and worry. "*Hija*." He held my hand up to his lips. "You look *hermosa*. Radiant. How I would have loved to commission a wedding portrait of you in this gown. Although, I am certain this image of you will live in me for all eternity."

I found his hand, gripping it in mine, and he led me around the modiste's fitting area. "Beatriz." *Papá* broke through the silence. "*Hija mía*. I have been waiting to say this since your birthday. We may not have another opportunity to speak before you wed. *Siento mucho* that this choice has brought you such sorrow. I hope in time, you will comprehend us."

I thought of my choice, of choosing to marry for the sake of our survival, of our family. Beyond my personal interests, the only way forward was here. Niccolo was not Dante, but he was what my family had chosen. From now on, I would have to carry on astutely; I needed to embrace the new woman I would be. Niccolo would be a count. I would soon be a countess. There was much I could do with that title to further my cause.

"*Te perdono, Papá.*" I held his hand. "Let us move forward with this."

27

SOUL MATES

Beatriz

Florence, Italy – 1486

I snuck out through the back entrance of the palazzo in the middle of the night on the eve before my wedding. I had not seen Dante since telling him Niccolo had returned from war early, our families forcing our wedding to happen hastily. I was not sure if I would find him in his lodgings, but I needed to see him before I married. Those could not be the last moments we spent together or the last words we uttered to each other.

I knocked on his door, my heart pounding, praying he would be there. Praying he was not enjoying someone else's company. He pried the door open, half asleep. The candle he held cast shadows across his pained face. Inside, candlelight illuminated pieces of scaffolding in a corner where I had painted two sparrows months earlier.

I did not utter a single word. Nothing I could say would change the course of our destinies. For that moment, all I wanted was to be held by him. As if reading my thoughts, he pulled me into his room, our wet faces crashing into each other. Then, our lips met for soft kisses that soon turned into a passionate embrace. He groaned, pulling me closer, grasping at my hips, lifting me and carrying me over to his bed. He stripped off the laces of my bodice one by one. I became exasperated until finally, he released the cast of my confines.

My skirts ballooned over him while I straddled him, holding his face while I kissed him deeper, desperately. He roared, pinning me to the bed, stripping off my skirts, leaving me fully exposed to him. I dove into ripples of pleasure that overpowered me as we continued. He draped my legs over his neck, licking me. His tongue traveled above the opening of my womanhood, moaning with pleasure as he did it.

I grew desperate from the distance between our bodies. I wanted him inside me. I pulled his hands toward my chest, cupping my breasts. "Have me*, ti scongiuro*."

I begged further, feeling his smile as he reached down to remove his trousers. Then, he pulled away, his hot breath lingering between us. His bare chest hidden behind the curtain of his black hair. Pulling me toward him, our lips found each other again. I ran my fingers through his hair as he found his way inside me.

He buried himself deeper into me, breathing with pleasure into my neck as I moaned loudly. He hushed me with a kiss to keep the others from waking. I begged him to thrust into me with greater force.

"*Amore*"—he kissed me–"*Amore mio*."

"I am afraid I shall never be able to sleep on this bed again, not after knowing you shall never lay upon it," he said. "*Ti amo*."

"I love you too, Dante. You are the love of my life. I will never love anyone again as I love you."

"Perhaps our souls have met in the wrong lifetime, where

we could not choose to be joined. That does not mean you do not deserve a chance at being your happiest, Beatriz. My heart will always be yours, from now until eternity, and until I see you again, in this life or the next."

It was the last words he would utter to me.

28

THE WEDDING

Beatriz

Florence, Italy – 1486

P*apá* and I walked in through the doors of Santa Maria Novella, where Niccolo, his family, and our guests rose to welcome us. Unlike Enzo's festivities, due to Niccolo's absence in the war, we did not have a traditional courtship. This was the first time I would see him.

He was not at all what I expected. His body was a muscular husk towering over the altar steps. Golden locks blended into a reddish beard he caressed whilst awaiting my arrival. As I edged closer, his piercing blue eyes set on me like a predator. With poise, he walked over to me, extending a hand to take me from *Papá*'s arm.

I curtsied, extending my gloved right hand toward him. He smiled as he lifted it to his lips.

"*Piacere,* Beatriz," he whispered. "I was hoping we would meet last night, but in the morrow, you are more impressive than what had been described."

His gentleness took me by surprise. This was not the man Sandro could have described to me before.

After the ceremony, we had a few moments to ourselves before heading to the wedding banquet. We stood at the garden in front of the church, awaiting our carriage. His blue eyes were nearly white. They reminded me of paintings I had seen of wolves once at the market.

"That went on without a hitch, did it not?" he flashed a wide smile toward me, raising one of his eyebrows.

"Y-Yes, yes it did," I said. I was unsure what to expect of Niccolo, but part of me hoped he would continue being this pleasant.

"You will be delighted by the palazzo. I am sure you know, but I will inherit the title of count soon, which means you will have to attend many social events. The fact our wedding went smoothly soothes my worries of your social abilities."

"What do you mean, *sir*?"

"I need you to understand this city and the people in it. I heard you were not very social. Do you indulge in any pastimes?" he asked.

I hesitated for a moment, wondering if it was safe to mention my love of art and painting, yet I figured it would be helpful to know now.

"I like to paint," I said.

He snorted. "Paint? How quaint. Are you any good?"

"I *am* quite good," I scoffed. "Did you think I was a woman who spent all day practicing her needlework?"

"You are surely spirited, *mi piace,*" he smiled. "Wild beasts heed me."

"I am not a wild beast, *signore*."

"Oh, *Madonna*. My mother does know me well to have selected you as my bride," he said, stroking his beard. "Do not worry yourself, *dolcezza*. There will be plenty of time for you to work on your drawings and pastimes. Florence is a city of artists. We will entertain some in our home. Surely, it will give them a giggle to know that my wife finds herself inclined to the arts."

The carriage came around. "Let us go now. Our guests await."

29

ALL THAT GLIMMERS

Beatriz

Florence, Italy – 1486

The wedding festivities began promptly after we arrived at the palazzo. Every so often, someone would mention the bedding ceremony. My stomach rotted at the thought of Niccolo touching me. As everyone around us became drunk with dance and spirits, I took in the spectacle of my new home. Statues and figures of the Greek myths, Murano glass sculptures, opulent furniture. The wealth overwhelmed me.

Niccolo held a smoldering smile, showing off his family's power. "This is your home now, *bella. Mamma* took over decorations for us while we were engaged."

The reception took place in the hall. The extravagant banquet with courses of roasted venison, peacock, and even suckling pig. An overflow of exotic fruits and cheeses from the region, pastries dripping in honey and rose water.

Entertainment abounded, with musicians performing madrigals, while dancers whirled in lively courtly dances. The wine flowed as did the gifts, something Niccolo didn't mind. He gulped down the wine while guests approached us with fine textiles, chests overflowing with dowry gifts, jewelry brought from other kingdoms. Needing some air from the frivolities, I walked around the hall, gazing at the paintings. Atop the fireplace, a fresco caught my eye, I edged closer to it.

The delicate strokes of the brush were incredibly familiar.

'Twas impossible. No, when would he have done this?

In front of me was the myth of Pygmalion and Galatea. The sculptor Pygmalion had forged a statue of his perfect woman, then prayed to Aphrodite to bring her to life. The goddess agreed, breathing life to Galatea.

"I hope you are not upset by it." Sandro's voice felt like a warm embrace behind me. I turned to face him.

"When did you find the time to do this? I have not seen you in months at the *bottega*," I said.

He snickered. "Your betrothed's family is quite powerful, my dear. They sent word to me, offering a handsome sum to create a fresco in this grand hall to welcome you. Niccolo had taken note that you admired my work, somebody must have told him, and he wanted you to be impressed by *this* detail."

I thought of the moments outside the church, how I snapped at him for mocking my artistic skills.

"I am not the greatest supporter of your husband or his family, but you, my dearest Amapola, are worth it all. Take it as a wedding gift. I thought of a myth that could encapsulate the realities you rebel against. Any time you need to remember, you may look at this."

"*Grazie*, Sandro."

Niccolo walked over to us, interrupting our conversation.

"Are you surprised at your wedding gift from *Maestro Botticelli, bella?*" I could smell the wine on his breath even from a distance. I smiled politely.

"Yes, *husband*. I was just telling the maestro how impressed I am by your thoughtfulness. *Grazie*."

He placed a hand on Sandro's shoulder. "If you will s'cuse us, *maestro*. The time of the evening has come for my wife and I to retire to our chamber. Our witnesses await."

Witnesses?

Sandro's eyes flicked to me, his gaze dropping to the ground in horror. Daria appeared, alongside a group of others who would bear witness to the consummation of our marriage.

"Niccolo." I reached for his arm. "May we speak for a moment, *per favore*?"

"Surely, what is the matter?"

I lowered my voice, avoiding the ears of others, "I was unaware there would be witnesses to our wedding night."

His eyebrows furrowed. "My mother insists upon a more traditional approach to the consummation of our marriage, given your family's objection to the examination of your virtue. All who matter in Florence will know of your purity and my virility. We shall be covered by the sheets, *belleza*, do not fret."

I hesitated. "Niccolo, I am not in agreement with this. *Per favore*. They can wait out—"

His hand buried into my elbow. I recoiled in sharp pain.

"This is how it will be done. I will not hear any further complaints," he said angrily. "You will obey what has been established. *Capisce*?"

I shook as he released my arm, his face returning to a pleasant smile. Underneath my skirts, I felt fear creep up my spine.

Each step toward the bedding ceremony treading a groove in the marble floors beneath, I flushed, breathing heavily as Daria took off my wedding dress, and I hesitated, pushing forth. Beads of sweat formed in my brow. I breathed deeply. *Calma, Beatriz. Calma.*

"Bea." Daria held my face between her hands. Other maids

appointed by Niccolo's mother circled us. "Think of something beautiful. Remove your body from your mind."

She held my cold hand, leading me toward his bedchamber. The room hummed with the presence of Niccolo's parents, de Rossi family advisors, the priest who married us, and two men I knew nothing of. After my escape at the church, the families agreed that a blood stained sheet would suffice as proof of virtue.

The lingering scent of incense in the chamber pierced my nostrils, and the taste of iron invaded my mouth as it became increasingly dry. Daria prepared to leave, but I pulled her back in, begging her to stay. "I need someone on my side, Daria, please."

What came next was a silent blur of motions. I could only hear my heart thumping in my ears, the maids circling around me, their warm hands removing my shawl, then removing the sheets off the bed and inviting me to climb in. Niccolo sneering at me, as if I were an animal poised for slaughter. Ready to be dominated by a force greater than itself. He climbed onto the bed, then onto me. The heat of his breath and the smell of wine on my neck. The bedsheets covered us like corpses with the distant sound of chattering around us. His hands, cold and wet like a frog, pulled my arms over my head. I could feel the tip of his hard member gracing my belly. His giant body enveloping mine. How was it possible he could be aroused by this?

Without a single caress, he spread my limp legs, forcing himself inside with a single heavy thrust, a groan escaped me as the sharp sting shocked my body, leaving me breathless.

Applause followed from the gallery. Pain rushed through me in an unrecognizable way, as it had not with Dante the night we made love in the cottage. I closed my eyes, trying to return to the moments of passion where my body was worshiped.

There was no passion here. No love or altar where my body

would be cared for. No lips lightly pressing against mine. I could forget that it even existed, that it ever happened to me. With one final moan, Niccolo's seed emptied inside me, as my soul escaped me. The sheets bore witness to his brutality. He and our audience took the blood as proof of my innocence, never suspecting the truth that my heart and body belonged to another. In some perverse way, I should thank him, a gentler man might have discovered my secret.

30

THE PHANTOM

Beatriz

Bologna, Italy – 1491

In the five years since my wedding, my entire world shifted. First came the beatings at the hands of my husband. Then, my father's death. The pain of losing him remained untouched. He was everywhere and in everything, yet in nothing. I could still hear his voice in my mind, but I drowned in the silence of his absence. He was in the paintings that arrived at our palazzo in Bologna, in my brother Enzo's aging face, in the smell of old books and the Gregorian chants of the monks at church.

No matter how much I tried to distract myself, I relived the day of his death repeatedly. The wake of his loss left me in a swirling anger that lived permanently within me and this dark world I had come to live in.

Despite his absence, I still spoke to *Papá.* Since relocating to Bologna with Niccolo, I promenaded with Daria every morning through Piazza Maggiore and San Petronio, strolling through the arches of the porticoes, the sun quietly slanting through them. I would tell him about the artisans and the students striding past in their robes, discussing politics and philosophy, engaging in heated debates over one thing or another. Other days, I told him about my role as a noblewoman in the city, and how I could no longer let my sharp tongue loose. My job now was maintaining decorum, making sure Niccolo was well respected, and the wives of other noblemen in the city admired me. I was no longer the daughter my father knew.

I'd tell him I quit the herbs that stopped conception. That I wanted a child, and would he grant me one from heaven, or wherever he was. The problem was not conceiving, but remaining with the child. Keeping them alive. I had birthed a beautiful *bambino* with his father's golden hair and translucent skin, but he'd only lived for a few minutes before leaving me.

We buried him at the church in hallowed ground, Papá. Search for him in heaven. He was baptized as soon as he was born; the birth was so difficult that they called for the priest.

At this point, I had lost so many children, I hid the conceptions from Niccolo. He had no patience for my difficulty conceiving either way. His mother tortured me with a morning diet of six raw eggs mixed with cumin and fennel. She even found a mandrake root for me to sleep with. No matter what they brought on, the babes would find a way not to come into this world. Today, I buried the most recent one of them. Even though *Padre* Clementino told me that until they reached a certain age in the womb, it was unnecessary, I could not simply let the maids remove sheets stained with blood. I had created a special place for them in our palazzo, where no one bothered to observe me or follow. Where they would rest in peace, and where I knew I'd have them close to me.

"Bea." Daria held me up, dusting wet dirt off my green velvet dress. "I know it is not my place, but I think you need to take a break…from conceiving."

I wiped my hands on a towel she brought with her, choking

back tears. "I want a child, Daria. It is my duty to my home and to the world." I started walking back toward the house. "I need a purpose. *Un bambino*. It will give me purpose."

"I understand you feel that way," she trailed behind me. "*Ma*, you already have a purpose, Bea. You always have."

I kept walking rapidly, ignoring her words.

"*Guardami,* Bea," Daria's voice suddenly became stern, leaving no choice but to turn to her. "I need Beatriz Velázquez de Concepción to return. That woman who was not afraid of the world, or men, or anyone who stood in her way. *La artista* who only cared about painting the world she saw through her eyes. You have become so intent on being the woman everyone wants you to become that you have lost sense of who you are."

"*Non posso,* Daria. *Non è così semplice.* It's not that simple."

"*É così, certo che lo è,* but you are afraid and you have conformed. You forgot about who you were. I have cleaned your wounds and watched you weep and buried every single one of your children with you as your maid....But as your friend, as your fellow *fiore*, I cannot watch you do this anymore. *Non posso.*"

"And what do you suggest I do? *Dai, dimmi,*" I crossed my arms. "*Se è così semplice.*"

Looking around to ensure no one was watching, she reached into her apron, handing me two things: a piece of charcoal and a sealed letter with my name written on the outside. Then, she pressed into my hand, uttering a single word in Spanish: "*Pinta.*"

Cara Amapola,

Sei tu o è un fantasma che vive adesso? Since your departure from Florence, now grown distant with the passing of the seasons, this humble bottega has been bereft of the wonder and ardor once kindled by the hand that, like the poppy from

SEED, DID BLOOM HERE INTO TRUE ARTISTRY. THE ABSENCE OF YOUR SPIRIT LINGERS HEAVY IN THE AIR, A SILENCE WHERE ONCE PASSION AND DEVOTION DANCED UPON CANVAS. I GRIEVE WITH YOU FOR THE LOSS OF YOUR DEAR FATHER—A GRIEVOUS STROKE, INDEED, THE SORROW OF WHICH CAST LONG SHADOWS UPON MANY HEARTS. YET, I BEG YOU: LET NOT MOURNING BE YOUR ONLY COMPANION. THE WINDS IN THIS CITY DO SHIFT, AND THE TIDES OF GOVERNANCE GROW HOSTILE TOWARD THE ARTISTS' SOULS. MORE THAN EVER, THE FIORI NEED YOU, YOUR BLOOM OF HOPE. RECALL YOUR VOW, SPOKEN NOT IN HASTE BUT IN FIRE AND TRUTH. RETURN TO IT, AS TO A SACRED CHANGE. ENCLOSED IN THIS LETTER, YOU SHALL FIND THE FRAGMENT OF CHARCOAL LEFT UPON YOUR WORKTABLE—UNTOUCHED SINCE YOUR LAST PASSING THROUGH THESE DOORS. MAY IT SERVE AS A SPARK, YOUR FIRST STEP BACK INTO THE LIGHT. FOR WE SHALL REQUIRE YOUR FLAME, AND SOON.

WITH A STEADFAST HEART,
-S

31

SOL

Beatriz

Bologna, Italy — 1491

The Fiori had found me.

A parcel arrived on a rainy spring day on the doorstep of our palazzo in Bologna. It was wrapped in heavy wooden panels and muslin cloth that carried the smell of the Apennines and the Tuscan countryside. Figaro, one of my trusted guards, notified Daria of a large container that had been delivered conspicuously in the night. No one had seen the carriage that brought it, and it was too big and there were too many for it to have simply appeared out of nothing.

Keeping it hidden from other servants not as loyal to me, they brought a grand total of six crates into a small art *bottega* I built out in the back of the palazzo, facing the garden. It was not nearly as grand as Sandro's, but it had abundant lighting, smelled of lavender flowers from the garden, and was far enough to be kept hidden from servants, visitors, and my husband, alike. We stacked the crates against the wall, Daria and I staring at each other in pure confusion over the delivery.

Since Daria handed me the letter from Sandro, I knew things in Florence were becoming increasingly worse with the rise of Girolamo Savonarola, and soon after the death of Lorenzo de' Medici, Florentines were captivated by the friar's sermons on corruption and vanity. Sandro's paintings were being scrutinized for being too mythological, and through his letters, I could feel how the changing tides in religious beliefs were affecting him.

Nonetheless, his words had sparked a fire in me I considered extinguished. I still remember peeling the red "B" with his insignia open as soft cold rain washed the years of sorrow away from me. Now, his calling had arrived at my door, and I was prepared to live up to the vow I made all those years before.

We cracked open the crates, unveiling canvas upon canvas of works I'd never seen before.

"*Madonna mia*," Daria exclaimed, holding open a sketch that had been rolled and tied with string. "Beatriz, this... this is..."

"*Resistenza*," I affirmed. "Whatever is brewing in Florence, we must protect these pieces of art at all cost—who knows what shall come of it or when we shall need to return it to its rightful home."

We continued well into the afternoon undisturbed, as servants were given strict instructions to refuse guests or come fetch us. Slowly, we created a system of separation and storage, realizing the best way to keep them safe was to return them to their original wrappings and hide them behind a bookshelf I'd installed to keep my painting supplies. Although Niccolo had been away for nearly a year supporting Ludovico Sforza in Milan, if he returned unexpectedly and found the paintings, I would have no way of explaining what it all meant. He was not tolerant of bringing things into the home he had not approved of first.

"What about this one, Bea?" Daria held up a small canvas wrapped tightly with a red ribbon tied around it. It was attached to the back of a larger canvas, most likely to preserve space. In the turmoil of the larger canvases, we overlooked it completely.

She pulled on the tight red string, giving in to her touch like a sigh. As the cloth unraveled, a stamped note fell out. I reached over to grab it, recognizing *Signora* Clarice's calligraphy and my name across the front of it.

Bologna, Italia
Anno Domini 1491

Amapola,

I believe she is most deserving of a proper ending, none other than at the hands of her creator. Perchance, you can have a happy one as well. Go forth to this address on Mercoledì alle undici del mattino.

Via dei Librai, No. 7
Quartiere di San Donato

-Orchidea

"Hand it over to me, Daria." I reached for it, placing the letter on the shelf behind me. Like being handed a newborn babe, I removed the cloth to find *her* there, her eyes staring back at me like a feline, her expression still unfinished. I felt my heart radiate with inspiration, as I held her up to the light. *Benvenuta a casa, Sol.*

I walked over to the corner where my first painting stood, unfinished. I held it up, resting it on the easel.

You're the answer to everything, aren't you? Something in my heart told me she was. As if the day I finished her would be the moment the pieces of the puzzle would fit and this life would all make sense. As if she knew what I needed to do all along, and that's why she had been born.

Later that week, I returned to the *bottega*, reaching for my sketchbook, untying its soft leather cord. The cover was worn from years of being stowed away in a trunk. The mixture of linen pages and parchment rekindled memories of the twins, who by now were married women. Their sweet little faces mid-laugh.

I began working on Sol. Her wide almond eyes. She has a lot to say about what she has seen, a secret she's not ready to reveal. I shade lightly, avoiding sharp definition, to give her the elusive quality that evaded my imagination for so long. Just like her name, she shines through the pages of my sketchbook as if she had never been eclipsed by time. I pull the sketch up next to her in the easel, closing my eyes, imagining the final painting. She will be clad in a gown of deep green velvet and sapphire-blue brocade. A black ribbon choker embroidered with small crimson hearts, as if plucked from a whispered vow, decorates her neck. And of course, flowers sustain her. Wild roses, violets, poppies, and narcissus. Just like the sun, they all turn to her.

You are and always will be my fate, and that of all who come after us. For unlike me, you will be immortal.

32

"L'AMOR CHE MOVE IL SOLE E L'ALTRE STELLE"

Beatriz

Bologna, Italy – 1491

I prepared for my morning walk to the Quartiere di San Donato, where *Signora* Clarice had sent me. I chose a discreet blue frock with a cloak to go along with it.

"This is a scholar's address, *no*?" Daria asked. "That *quartiere* is typically where literature scholars teach."

Bologna was home to one of the world's oldest universities, founded back in 1088. It was the epicenter of law, philosophy, and literature, with streets woven in a tapestry of the old and new world. The city itself was the campus where scholars taught in private homes or even churches.

"I figure we'll find out," I placed the letter with the address in the pocket of my cloak. "Although I am intrigued that the *Fiori* have such connections here. Of course, there's the matter of the uprising in Florence, but do you imagine it has become so dark that they would need to establish systems outside to protect it so?"

The distant chiming bells of San Petronio announced our arrival at Quartiere di San Donato. The address *Signora* Clarice had given me led to a narrow, ivy-clad home with brick walls, just off Via dei Librai, nestled between a printer's shop and a spice merchant. I approached the wooden door with caution, instantly noticing the brass wolf head knocker decorated with a single poppy above a carved plaque that read:

D.Lupo, Magistri
Studiorum in Litteris Recentioribus et Poetica Vulgari
Diebus Lunae, Mercurii, Veneris
Hora secunda
"L'amor che move il sole e l'altre stelle"

My eyes skimmed over the quote at the end of the plaque that might have meant a scholarly admiration for *La Divina Commedia* to others, but represented a love long lost, yet never forgotten, to me. My heart paused for a moment before bursting into life with a thousand fluttering beats as it realized who was behind that door. Daria gasped behind me as she reached the same conclusion. Finding my sweaty palm, she pressed against it, whispering in my ear, "I will be at the apothecary fetching herbs, *madonna*. This is something you must do on your own."

She walked away, my hands reaching for the knocker as if it were a lifeline.

"*Un momento, per favore.*" His deep voice echoed far into the lodgings. "If you are a student, tutoring hours do not commence until one."

I took a deep breath, finding my voice, petrified of how he might react or if he would even recognize it after all these years.

"I am not a student. *Anche se ho imparato così tanto di te,*" the rustling stopped. After seconds that felt like centuries, the door opened wide, and he stepped forward. His long raven hair, tied neatly with a ribbon, allowed the sun to illuminate the lines on his slightly aged face. His hazelnut eyes scanned me, his mouth barely agape as his hand still gripped the edge of the door.

Still silent, he motioned me to enter. We stood in the threshold of the small courtyard where I imagine he held lectures by the arrangement of chairs, bookcases, and scattered pieces of paper on a desk in the corner. The five years that had passed since we last saw each other stood between us.

"I—" we said simultaneously.

"Go ahead," he motioned, crossing his arms across his chest in the same familiar way he used to when he watched me paint.

"Dante. What are you doing here? In Bologna, I mean. How long have you..."

"For three years," he interjected. "I've been teaching contemporary literature and poetry at the university."

I felt slightly nauseated at the thought that we'd been in the same city for years. My face started to feel hot with anger. "But, but I thought you were in *Roma*—"

"*Certo.* I *was* in Roma for some time after you wed your *marito*. Then, a few years ago I received an invitation to teach here at the university, and I could not reject it. Things are not well—politically—in Roma, and I was not going to return to Florence..."

"Of course, the political situation is not well there either." I looked down at the tiny pearls embroidered in my bodice.

He scrunched his eyebrows, pulling his hand up to his beard, now peppered with tiny white hairs, "*Eh*...and you were also there. Or so I thought."

"Did you know I was here for the last three years?" The question escaped me, and as much as an affirmative answer would hurt, I needed to know.

He edged closer to me, his hand reaching over to the end of my braid, intertwining it in his fingers. "No, not the entire time. But long enough."

I snapped my braid away from his hand. "You knew I was here, and you did not reach out to me? You were not curious as to what was happening with me?"

"That is unfair, *Beatriz.* I was clear that I required to be away from you, to take space from your life or—"

"—Or what?" I yelled. Unable to restrain myself.

"Or I would have snatched you from your home and done what I should have done all those years ago. I considered it a few times. I saw you promenading in San Petronio one afternoon with Daria. You wore a yellow dress with a green cape and flowers in your hair. All I could see was your golden silhouette, like the veil on a statue of a virgin. When you turned...I realized you were with child. The air was knocked out of me again. It struck me that your life must be full and beautiful, and like many things left in the past, better not be touched for the chance of ruining it."

I knew the exact day he was referring to. We had left an offering at the altar of the *Madonna* for my child, with just a few weeks until his eventual birth. I stopped feeling him move in my belly, his kicks gone.

"You should have reached for me," I whimpered. "Taken me out of the *inferno* I've been living in all this time. The last time I felt anything was our last night together. That was my first death. My second, the day my father died. The third, when I birthed and buried the only child I have carried to term."

Tears flowed from him as he embraced me, the warmth of his body reviving me with its tenderness. The years had passed and *still,* I loved him. I never stopped. Now, the question was whether he still loved *me.*

This home was too large for a man to live in alone, and I did not expect Dante to have a solitary life simply because we could not be together. The thought alone destroyed me. The idea of his touch on another woman, his children running around the piazzas in Bologna, someone else feeling his touch.

I pulled away, finding composure within the shock of our reunification. For so long, I wondered about him. In my darkest moments, I cursed him for leaving me to live that reality, cursing myself for dissuading him from it. I watched his parting letter on my wedding day burn at the fireplace through angry tears. Now, standing in front of him, I could not fathom the thought of losing him again, but I needed to know. Before anything else, I needed to know.

"Dante." I hesitated, feeling a mixture of nervousness and curiosity. "Are you...? Have you? Are you wed?"

He looked down at his hands, my voice shaking. "I only ask because this lodging is so...large. For just one person seems a bit excessive, *no*? Or do you..."

"Beatriz," his deep voice carried the syllables of my name like a soft melody. The corners of his mouth lifted for just an instant, teasingly. "Why do you want to know? What is it to you?"

I scoffed, "Well, I have not seen you for half a decade, I would not be surprised if you have moved on, have a wife, perhaps a few children. 'Tis only...."

"*Che cos'è*?"

"Natural," I said. "We were so young. All those things we said..."

"Were they lies to you?"

Standing in front of him, with nothing left to lose, there was no escaping the truth of my love for him this time. Saving me from an answer, he walked over to me, this time his eyes piercing through mine. The corners of his mouth lifted for an instant as he brought his fingers to the pearled detail on the bodice of my dress.

"*Contessa*," I could feel his breath fill the air with intoxicating warmth.

"Oh, I—" I watched his finger trail my shoulder, caressing the back of my arm, sending shivers through me. His hand delicately reached up to my chin, pulling it up to face him.

"*Nella mia vita*, there has only ever existed a single woman. I have tried to forget you, Beatriz. To erase the moments we spent together in our youth. Your passion and character. The way a curl always finds a way out of the confines of your intricate hairstyles to sit in the middle of your forehead while you paint."

His hands pushed stray hairs away from my face now, observing the scars left from Niccolo's beatings. His pained expression reflected the spark of impotence and injustice. Finally, he used one hand to bring my body closer.

"*Prometto,* Beatriz, *ho provato.* I have concluded that I was right all those years ago, and now, now that you're here in front of me, there is no doubt. There is only one woman in this world for me."

He brought himself close to my lips, whispering before sealing them, "you."

33

A MIRROR INTO THE SOUL

Mar

Madrid, Spain – 2024

"Breathe deeply now, Mar. We're coming back. We will only spend a few more minutes in this lifetime, then we can return. Breathe into those feelings you have just described. Shame, humiliation. Notice them in your body now." Almaguer's voice felt distant as I navigated this regression.

I clutched my solar plexus.

"This is the same. I am starting to feel like I recognize who she is...we have been to this life before...there he is, Dante! She found him again."

"Can you move forward into her timeline? Is there anything else you see?"

"No, I'm not able to move forward at the moment...just. She wants me to know something, but he is coming back...No! No!"

"Who is coming back?"

"No, no, bring me back, I want to leave..."

"It's all right, Mar. It's all right. You are safe. It's time to gently return to the present moment, bringing with you only the sight, strength, and healing you have learned. Take a deep breath in and let it go. On the count of three, you'll become aware of your body, the room, the couch you are lying on, feeling clear, grounded, and safe."

I opened my eyes, returning to the room. "Wow."

"How do you feel? Different from the last time?"

"*Mierda*, Almaguer. That was fucking insane."

She chuckled in her fairy-like voice. "Were you able to return to the same life? I gathered you might have, but I wasn't certain."

I was still collecting myself after the session. "Yes, yes, it was Beatriz's life. BVR, it stands for Beatriz Velázquez de Rossi."

"Hmm, between this and the painting you found of her at the Prado museum, I think there might be a connection between you two. It seems like she wanted her soul to find out what happened...at least eventually. What about this life stands out to you?"

"I see so much of myself in her."

"Of course you do, you are the same soul...you just had different life experiences."

"I feel her anger. There's an element of jadedness to her that I also recognize. That defeatedness and lack of trust in the future. And to be honest, I thought maybe she could be..." I trailed off, thinking back to the curse.

"She could be?" Almaguer prompted.

"I just thought we would find out more about the curse... or at least get close to finding out how the whole thing started."

Almaguer adjusted herself on her seat, looking at me with her piercing blue eyes.

"Mar, let's say the curse *is* real. What elements of the curse concern you the most?"

I scoffed. "Isn't it obvious? The being doomed to have

horrible relationships, to not ever fall in love, to perhaps never be able to have a family…"

"Do you have a good relationship with yourself right now? In the present?"

"I mean, not right now."

"Are there any aspects of your life that you are in love with? Not just men, but overall. Are you in love with yourself?"

"No, obviously not. The only thing I'm sure about is that I love what I do…and I almost lost that too."

"So, even if there *is* a curse, why don't you look for the answers in the present with the information you've gathered from the past for now?"

"But—"

"Give it some thought, and we can discuss this next time you come. Unfortunately, I have to tend to another patient now, and you need time to process this. I look forward to hearing what you discover about yourself. *Piénsalo* and we can discuss this next time."

34

A SMALL FAVOR

Mar

Madrid, Spain – 2024

I left Almaguer's office determined to find out more about BVR. If we were the same soul, then perhaps she also lived under the curse, and it came before her time. She was experiencing many of the same feelings I was. I also wanted to know more about her artwork, and I knew exactly who to contact.

Lucas would be at Torre de Espadas. We were one week away from the soft opening for a few special patrons and guests, and one month before the official launch. I tiptoed through the front entrance, trying not to disturb his concentration.

"Jesus, Marisol," he placed a hand on his chest, visibly startled. "I wasn't expecting you today. Almudena isn't getting here until seven. I already had my walkthrough with you."

"Eh…it's 6:55, Lucas," I chuckled. "But, yeah, sorry. I came in because I wanted to see you…and my family gets here in a few days, so…"

"I'm in awe of the art we have built together," he clapped his hands, bringing them to his mouth like a prayer. His phone chimed with a message. "Ah, Almudena is running late. Want to stroll through the building with me and tell me what it is you came looking for?"

We walked back toward the front entrance, closed the door, pretending we'd never been inside the building. Lucas's bright smile headed toward the door, opening it like a true *caballero*. "After you," he said.

As if it were a portal, I walked into another dimension, even though I'd already been in the building minutes before. In many ways, it felt like a completely different space from the bare bones I helped restore. The sunlight, now fully casting its splendor on the foyer, revealed to me what I'd overlooked coming here every single day—the building had transformed, and so had I. I'd spent most of my heartbreak in this building, putting my heart back together with every stroke of my brush, in every corner, through early mornings that bled into night.

Occasionally, I'd even taken a little nap on the terrace when the weather was nice. To see it come to fruition was something I'd had on my bingo card for a long time that I'd now be able to cross off, allowing the next space in my life to open.

Lucas's vision was clear from the start. The building should feel like an ascent to heaven for visitors. They would walk into the splendor of water, first. Then, earth. Almudena sculpted various structures, from branches to a full-blown beehive from plaster and real pieces of recycled wood that intertwined with three of my murals. A giant Bougainvillea in deep purple and magenta whose flower canopy bled into Almudena's branches. Bluebells, orchids, wild rosemary, and red roses like the ones Flamencas wear on their hair lined the walls, swaying as I moved past them. Their smell filled the room with a concert of floral notes and the bitter whiff of herbs.

The second floor was reserved for heaven. In contrast to the colorful symphony of earth, the ascent through the ivory marble staircases welcomed guests to a wide space where high ceilings, cloud-like furniture and monochromatic walls allowed them to soar in their interactions. Instead of painting the walls on this level, my work was on the floor. Plastering the mural onto concrete, creating simple lines in a plethora of whites, golds, light blues, and the softest hints of pinks. It was a stark contrast to the basement, or the inferno, which would be a late-night speakeasy, where patrons would walk through the river Styx and reach the nine circles of hell.

Finally, the terrace, my favorite of all parts, was dedicated to the cosmos. Almudena, inspired by the former Victorian patrons, used the molding to create bulging planets that emerged from the ceilings. Between them, I delighted in creating constellations with the brightest stars. The cosmos came alive, a space where there was no present, or future, or past, just souls floating in stardust.

I stared into the mural I spent four months painting on the ceiling.

"This is my favorite of yours. Your quiet brilliance shines through it."

"My quiet brilliance?" I asked.

"Yes...that disbelief in your own talent."

"The disbelief...?" I raised my eyebrows, it seems like everyone was shooting indirect messages at me today. "You're the harshest art critic in all of Europe. I thought I had to prove myself to you."

"No, darling, I don't recall telling you that you had to prove yourself; that was your own perception. You never believe that people are choosing you for who you are, your talents, the immense creativity you hold."

I knew he was referring to how I valued myself both in life and at work. I felt like an idiot, allowing my own lack of self-belief and self-esteem to overcome me, when clearly, if I was chosen to do this, it was for a reason. Hearing this after my session with Almaguer, I realized Beatriz and I were similar in yet another way: our upbringing. I didn't grow up learning how to love myself or love my work. I always believed these kinds of jobs were for people with "a lot of talent," and they were difficult to make it in. My mother cemented this, and in some ways —she was right. I guess what neither of us realized was that I *was* one of those people who had enough talent and nerve to take myself to the next level.

"You're right," I said. "Thank you...for *seeing* me."

He crossed his arms, smiling with his eyes. "Not a problem. Now, what is it you wanted to ask me?"

"Oh, right! There is this portrait I found, at the Prado, a few weeks ago. I've tried looking for some information on it, but all I found is the name of the painter: BVR. It stands for Beatriz Velázquez de Rossi. But I don't know where I could find information about her, or more of their work. Do you have any idea of anyone who could know?"

"Hmm," he scratched his beard. "BVR....do you have a picture of the portrait so that I can share it in my circles, perhaps?"

I scrambled for my phone, "Yes! Yes I do." I had found a small sample of it online on the exhibit's website. I opened to the portrait of the woman who might as well have been me 500 years ago. "This is it."

His face blanked, his amber eyes closing in on the photo. "Uh—Marisol...this looks so much—"

"—Like me. I know. That's why I need to know more about who she is."

"Wow. The resemblance is just uncanny. Truly," he said. "*Bollocks*. Send me this, I will send it around. This is...wow."

I took my phone from him, putting it back in my bag. "You think there's hope of finding her, then?"

"Hell yes."

35

ESPRESSO MACCHIATO

Mar

Madrid, Spain – 2024

I got home to find a notification waiting on my Instagram.

"Friend request: Dario Messina."

I jumped up on the couch, startling the dogs. This is the guy from the art show the other day! I immediately recognized his boyish smile, accepting his request. Two minutes later, he slid into my DM's.

"*Ciao* Mar, I promise I'm not a creep. Lucas gave me your full name, and I decided to look you up. Your murals are incredible. Anyway, I'm in town for two more weeks...would you fancy a coffee with me? Maybe we can find out if we know each other from somewhere or not." He added a winky face at the end, giving it a touch of cheekiness.

I grinned from ear to ear. Huh. I didn't even think I was capable of doing that anymore. I felt nervous. The thought of dipping my toes back in. Even the idea of coffee with someone —sharing space with a man again—was terrifying.

I waited to text him back, texting Tania instead, giving her the details.

"*Tía, no seas tonta.* Who are you holding your celibacy for? Guillermo is *marrying* Silvi. Take the coffee from the hot Italian guy. IT'S JUST ESPRESSO! Also, don't forget we're taking that trip to Irati at the end of the month for my birthday. The rest of the group has confirmed. I'll send you the details later."

I hesitated for a moment, pacing around my loft. The warm, colorful lights I had installed when Guille still lived here bounced off the tall walls, bringing back memories of the nights we would play records and drink wine together. I was *just* starting to sleep through the night again, have an appetite.

I was still figuring out who I was on the other side of that heartbreak...but there was also something about Dario that called to me. That familiarity.

I closed my eyes for a moment, thinking about what both Almaguer and Lucas said. I could still look for answers in the past while living in my present. I opened the DM again, feeling Dario's warmth through his profile picture.

"*Hola* Dario. Sure! I know a place I think you might like."

We met at Norah Café just off Ortega y Gasset. It had a whimsical touch to it and an olive tree in the middle that took the edge off our meeting for me. Plus, the coffee here was fantastic. I picked a window seat overlooking the street that provided the right amount of privacy and escape options possible. He walked in minutes later.

"Mar!" He embraced me as if he'd known me his entire life. His charm made me feel guarded, as if letting his warmth in might lead to a dangerous path. Tania's words resonated in my head. *It's just an espresso.*

"I hope this is all right with you. I don't have many friends in Madrid...and seeing as you and I apparently already knew each other," he teased.

"Oh, no *pasa nada*. I know what it's like to be new in the city and not know anyone else. Is the school you work for closed right now?"

"University," he corrected me. "And yes, they are on spring break. Gives me some time to dive into my research, things like that. I've had a bit of a...rough year. Leaving Italy for a couple of weeks is helping."

I watched as he spoke, noticing the familiarity of his dark eyes, the coal black hair that framed his face like a painting. *Where did I know him from*? We ordered two espresso macchiatos, bonding over our love for art. Dario met Lucas years ago when he was putting pieces of literature together for him. Now, he'd be doing the same for our exhibit next week.

"I'm pulling some pieces from *The Divine Comedy* for him, to go along with the murals and the artwork. Dante Alighieri is one of my favorites."

Dante. DANTE!

"Oh my God!" I blurted out, startling him.

"Everything okay?"

Reel it in Mar. You don't want him to think you're insane.

"*Sí, sí, discúlpame.*"

What I really wanted to say was, "I know exactly where I know you from. And it's not this life."

If I was the spitting image of the painting BVR had done years before, Dario was the living embodiment of Dante, the lover I still didn't know if she ended up with. They held that similar kindness, the non-imposing chivalry and sturdy masculine energy. His face still rested in confusion, but I found a way out.

"I've also been through a lot this year. I was supposed to get married, and now he's marrying someone else, and well, I don't get to escape to another country, but I escape into my art."

He placed his hand over mine in solidarity. "I am really sorry to hear that, Mar."

By then, we were both done with our espressos.

"Me too," I sighed. "How about we go for a walk?"

36

FAMILIA

Mar

Madrid, Spain – 2024

A*buela*, *Mami*, and *Tía* Carmen arrived in Madrid for the opening of my murals at Torre de Espadas. I had painted and designed the murals. Almudena Castelló, an artist from Cadiz, sculpted more than twenty pieces. And Lucas was charged with bringing it all together.

I thought back to the initial controversy the city faced when bringing me on. Much of Madrid's upper class wondered *why* a Cuban muralist, an Andalusian sculptor, and a half-Spanish half-British curator were in charge of such a daunting task. But despite what the city wanted, the owners sold it under one condition: it must be restored by the youth to bring in the youth.

The Spanish aristocracy wasn't the only group up in arms about the decision. My very Cuban family also had a collective heart attack when I decided to move to Madrid for this project.

Before moving to Madrid during the pandemic, I was a tried-and-true Miami girl born to Cuban *balseros*, rafters. The first wave of immigrants in my family had moved to Miami in the 1980s during the Mariel boatlift; the rest came as they could. Some claimed by other family members, others on foot through the Mexican border. I arrived in my mother's belly in 1993, living happily in our home on Bird Road and 62nd Avenue until the day *Papi* went to Cuba to pick up his brother, Fernandito, and never came back.

Similar to how I felt now after the walls of my engagement had collapsed, art was my liberation. Back then, I had stepped toward embracing my creative spirit which I held hostage for the sake of survival for far too long. Now, I had to embrace it again as I searched for other missing pieces of myself, while facing my family.

Mis señoras, or the "Bermuda Triangle," as I liked to call three generations of women in my family, waited impatiently for me at the arrivals gate of Madrid Barajas's fourth terminal. Flights never arrived on time, and if they did, you had to pass customs *and* baggage claim. All which could take hours, but somehow, to my demise, it only took thirty minutes today.

"Since your *abuela* and *Tía* Carmen came in wheelchair service, we went right through," *Mami* told me after I finally picked up her call. "You should have been here, *tú sabías*. You knew we were coming."

"Yes, *Mami*, and I was on my way, but I didn't know that the *one* day I'm a little behind is the day the Spanish airport system works flawlessly. Excuse me."

Tía Carmen also gave me a piece of her grievances, but the true star of my life, *Abuela* Mariana, was just happy to see me. Sitting at the coffee shop just outside the terminal, she beelined toward me as I made my way through the airport doors.

"*Mi chiquitica,*" she said, holding me in her soft arms. "I missed you so much, *mi sol.*" Switching to a whisper, "I smuggled in some *pastelitos de guayaba y queso* for you."

"*Oye,*" I teased her. "But you're going to have to eat some of those *pastelitos* yourself, because you're a little *flaquita.*"

"Ey, leave some love for me, you two. I'm the one who has been doing all the hard work to get us here, and you are *my* daughter," my mom interrupted our moment.

"Come here, *Mami,*" I embraced her. "Don't get jealous."

"Jealous? Nah, let's go, *anda*. We all need to change and rest before tomorrow," she stared me down. "You're going to do something about your hair, right? It's a disaster."

My curls were wild today. Unruly, just as the rest of my life felt. Yet, for the first time, I was fine with it.

We arrived at my apartment to find a parcel at my doorstep.

"*Te llegó un paquete,*" *Mami* pointed out the obvious, carrying the box and placing it on the kitchen counter. It seemed small, but not too light. She didn't even bother wheeling in her luggage as she went straight to the kitchen for scissors. *Abuela* and *Tía* Carmen wobbled to the couch, leaving me with all their luggage to carry inside.

"This luggage is not heavy at all. I can take care of it," I joked. "I'll take a look at the package shortly. Does it say who it's from?"

"No," *Abuela* answered.

"Are you hungry?" I asked.

"Yes," *Mami* said. "But don't you want to open the box first? What if it's a gift for the amazing opening of the gallery tomorrow?"

"It's not a gallery, *Mami*. It's going to be used for events—it has a bar, a library, a restaurant," I said.

"Are you taking someone with you to the event tomorrow?" *Mami* continued. "What about that hot guy leading the exhibition?"

"Lucas and I have a strictly work-related relationship, *Mami*. Plus, I think he's dating someone. An Argentine model or something like that. I've never met her, but I've heard from Almudena rumors here and there. I'm currently on my healing journey after all that went down with Guillermo. No men for me right now."

I wasn't going to mention my semi-date with Dario.

"*Haces bien.* Men only bring you *dolores de cabeza*. God knows I loved your *abuelo*, *Dios lo tenga en su santa gloria*, but that guy required *lots of* attention," *Abuela* said. "And in our youth, *alabao*. I won't even get started on that. Pero, Mar, *mi bien*, are you going to keep us waiting here for you to open the package? The only reason we haven't opened it yet is because we know you get upset when people open your mail, calling it a 'felony.' But between the jet lag and hunger, we can't take it anymore."

Rolling my eyes, I sliced through the tape on the box. Immediately, I found a handwritten note in Lucas's elegant calligraphy. It was sitting on top of a set of wrappings.

Mar,

I hope this isn't too much of an overstep, but when you showed me the image of this portrait on your phone last week, I couldn't help but find her. It wasn't easy, but it turns out one of my friends at the Prado museum knew the curator, and they were just about to take her off the walls and place her into storage. The person who donated the work didn't want her anymore. I've taken the atrevimiento of

Retrieving her for you, as I believe this BVR some 500 years ago may have imagined you into being through her. Let's chat at the opening, and I'll tell you more of what I know.

Till then, enjoy your new roommate.
-Lucas

"Oh my God, oh my God, oh my GOOOOOD!!!!!" I jumped excitedly, scaring the crap out of *Mami* and *Abuela*. "Do you know what this is?! Do you!?" I went for the wrappings, revealing the minuscule portrait I'd seen weeks before at the Prado with Alberto. "AHHHHHHHH!!!!" I squealed, holding her up. "He even included the frame!!!!"

"*Niña por Dios,* what is going on?" Mami said, coming closer to take a look at the painting. "What is—" she gasped.

"*Mami,*" she called *Abuela*. "Come look at this. You won't believe this."

Puzzled, I took a step back, still holding the frame. *Abuela* stepped forward, taking the frame from me, focusing on BVR's portrait.

"*Ay virgen santísima,*" she let it go, passing the painting to me. She made the sign of the cross, horror painting her face. "Marisol, who sent that to you, *mi niña*. Put that down!"

"Lucas sent it to me. It's a painting I've been inquiring abo—"

"Who is it by!?" *Abuela* shouted. It was strange for her to get upset. Almost nothing fazed her. "Who is the painter?"

"Her name is Beatriz Velázquez de Rossi. This painting is over 500 years old," I said, still confused. "What is the big deal? It's just a portrait of someone who looks like me."

"That woman is a curse to our family and to everyone who touched her work, do you hear me? You need to get rid of that painting *right now!*" I was confused.

"Wait, *Abuela*, no. This piece of art is a relic. I have to talk to

Lucas first to see how much it is even worth or if it truly belongs to me now. Lucas got it for me because I asked about the painter. I'm not throwing this out. Are you insane? Can you please just explain to me what is going on…and how in the world do you even recognize her art? This is insane."

"That woman, her art, is the reason the women in your father's family are cursed, Marisol," she lectured, sitting down on the dining room table to ease her agitation. "She's the reason your father drowned, the reason Gretelcita was left at the altar, and the reason your mother never remarried."

"What? *Abuela*, what are you talking about? How come this is the first time I am even hearing any of this?" I said. "*Abuela* Cristina said the curse was started by one of our ancestors. Not a painter from the Renaissance."

"*Mira*, Marisol," she got up with the same look she used to give me as a child when I disrespected someone or rebelled against the family norms. "I curse the day we let that crazy American professor into our home in Miami and helped him dig into this woman's past. I curse it. I'm done talking about it, now please, take that back to where it came from. At least while your mother and I are here. And promise me, Marisol, that you *will* let this go."

I put the painting back in the box, covering it in its original wrappings, then I knelt at my grandmother's feet.

"A professor? I have no idea what you're talking about, but *Abuela*, I do understand your pain. I understand your fear. What I don't understand is how this painting, who is—"

"Marisol," *Mami* interjected. "Enough of this. Put it away for now before you give your *abuela* a heart attack."

"Pero—"

"*Pero nada.* I know this is your home, but we are your family, and you have to respect your *abuela's* wishes," she said sternly, taking the package and handing it over to me.

I felt my face get hot, rage bubbling from my core to my

mouth, waiting to erupt like a volcano. A deep breath suppressed it. I remembered now why I left. I was so eager to leave so early in my youth, to fly, to gather my wings and find my own path in the world. As much as I loved my mother, my grandmother—heck, my entire family—my voice would always be less than.

37

TORRE DE ESPADAS

Mar

Madrid, Spain – 2024

I met Lucas the next day, before we opened the doors to the building. It was right after the argument with *Mami* and *Abuela*, and tensions were high. I'd kept the painting in my storage closet to keep them from spooking. I'd set it up in my studio after they left. It was a warm day in Madrid, its iconic blue skies and breezy terraces inviting every soul in the city to come out and sip on a *tinto de verano* and munch on *gildas* at this beautiful space we had set up for them.

Lucas, as fashionable as always, showed up with vintage aviators, tailored pants, and a linen shirt open just a smidge to reveal a chiseled chest. It was simple, but just as sophisticated as he was. Knowing he'd show up looking like a Calvin Klein model, I'd tamed my curls and opted for a flowy dress and belt combination, rather than my usual jeans, white button-down, and comfy sweater ensemble. Now and then I knew how to clean up—and well.

We sat outside on the terrace, he brought over two glasses of Albariño.

"Heey," he said. "*Buenas tardes*. It's nice to see you not covered in paint from head to toe. This dress is great."

I felt my cheeks flush, "*Gracias*. Thank you so much for the painting. I don't have words to even—"

He put a hand up, as if to stop me.

"It's a beautiful day, *no*, Mar?" He asked, looking up at the tree-lined street that shielded us from the sun, then gave me a playful smile he'd never given me before. At work he was always so...serious.

"Yeah..." I nodded. "It's definitely nice."

"I'm fucking with you. I just don't want us to be all professional if our work here is done." He chuckled. "But let's talk about this BVR woman, because I think there's a lot here that could be interesting for you to explore. I also think there's someone you should talk to."

"Go on," I said.

"It turns out this woman, Beatriz Velázquez de Rossi, was born here in Spain. She was the daughter of a court arts dealer who worked closely with the monarchy in the late 1400s, right around the time of the Italian Renaissance. Since she was a woman, there's not much I know except she immigrated to Cuba later in her life, continued painting there, and some descendants of hers sold the paintings to a gallery in New York for showcasing."

Ah, this is what Abuela was referring to.

"I'm not sure if they ever did or what happened—there's very little information about her other than court documents, which I haven't looked through. However, the painting that you found, the one in the Prado, was given away by an anonymous patron who previously owned it. Apparently, it's a piece that hadn't been showcased before. It was found after the New York exhibit."

A bartender was setting up for the event behind us, waving at Lucas and letting him know we would be set to open in about fifteen minutes.

"Wait." I stared. "So...she lived here, then in Italy, then in Cuba?"

He washed his wine. "Yes, Cuba."

How on God's green earth had a woman from the Renaissance ended up in Cuba? It made no sense. Especially if she had money or a family close to the court. The only people immigrating to Cuba in the late 1400s and 1500s were peasants and colonizers. Why would a painter make that trek?

"This makes no sense, Lucas. I just can't imagine why, or how, a woman of her time would do this. I would assume she had a husband...or children? Is that why she left?"

I thought back to my last session with Almaguer. The last thing I had learned about BVR was that she had rekindled her romance with Dante and was trying to figure out a way of being with him. It just didn't make sense they would escape to *Cuba*. Was what I had experienced in my regression part of my imagination?

"Honestly, I don't know, Mar. But it sure as hell is interesting," he said. "I think you should look into this; maybe there's something here for you to explore. Either way, we're pretty much done here, and you don't start your mural at Casa America for another two months, no?"

He was right. I'd be living off the last of my royalties from the Torre de Espadas project and picking up a few commissions from fans who wanted specialty pieces. I had a few weeks before I started working on them, so looking into BVR seemed like an enticing alternative.

"I wouldn't even know where to start," I said, taking a sip from my glass.

"You don't need to worry about that, Mar. I know exactly who you need to get in touch with."

He pulled out a business card from his wallet, asked the bartender for a pen, and turned it over to write down a name, number, and email. "This is the information for Giulia Giordano. She is the descendant of a woman who ran a secret society of women painters back in Florence during the Renaissance. I learned recently about her through a friend that also lives there. I hope it helps. Keep me updated."

He turned, his focus now shifting to the opening.

"Wait, Lucas. One last thing—what do I do with the painting after all this?"

He looked puzzled. "It's yours. Keep it."

"What about taxes? Don't I have to report it or something?" I asked.

He walked back toward me. "Let's just say, it's been taken care of."

The doors to Torre de Espadas opened, welcoming over 100 guests to the experience that we so carefully created. Lucas charmed everyone, explaining each concept, and inviting them to hang around the rooms they felt the most comfortable in. After explaining the murals, taking pictures, and schmoozing potential patrons, I headed to the bar for a drink.

"We meet again, Mar," Dario said softly, coming up behind me. "Congratulations on these murals. They are incredible."

I turned to him, finding his boyish face replaced by a much more mature semblance. His hair brushed back into neat waves, his beard combed, his exposed arms revealing forearm muscles I hadn't noticed underneath the jackets he wore the last two times I saw him. He looked...*appetizing* today.

"Glad you like it," I said casually. "I put my literal heart and soul into this work. It has seen every facet of me over the last three years."

He cocked an eyebrow, then grinned. "What a beautiful soul to have if this is what it looks like. Imagine if this is what you do when you are heartbroken, what you create when you are in love."

His directedness took me by surprise, again. I was used to being the direct one when it came to flirting, especially when the person I was flirting with looked this good.

"I mean, some of this was done when I was in love," I said.

"In love with the guy who got back with his ex?" He scoffed, shaking his head. "That was not love."

"Wooow, I didn't know you were the expert on romance now." I grabbed a glass of white wine from a waiter making the rounds.

He leaned in closer. "I am not. Far from it. But I believe people think falling in love is something they have no control over. Loving someone is a choice, not something that just happens to you."

I took two steps back. I disagreed with him. If I had any control over who I loved, then I would have made better choices in the past. I would have been able to at least foresee what I was getting myself into. His approach also seemed so... cold.

"Here I thought *I* was jaded," I said. "It looks like I'm not the only one disappointed by love."

"No, nothing like that. I do believe in love. Just that the next time I love someone, I want it to be a choice. Not some random event that was fated or destined, or one of those lines, what is it that people say? 'When you know, you know.'"

I felt a familiar frustration rise within me.

"You don't believe in soul mates?"

He guffawed. "No, of course not. It is ridiculous to think that there is one person you are fated to meet and you will fall in love with and everything will work out."

I can't believe I saw this as the Dante that Beatriz chased

after. They may have looked similar, but there was no connection beyond that. His cynicism about soul mates was driving me insane.

"That's not how soul mates work, Dario. But either way, what you're saying is that if you met someone that you truly connected with, you wouldn't pursue it? You would just walk away without exploring it because it felt 'fated' that you met?"

"No, that's not what I'm saying. I would need to do more—"

"Do more what?"

"I would need to know that person more, get to know them better, make sure our purpose was aligned."

"You would make a decision on a partner based solely on logical thinking?"

He crossed his arms. "You know what, maybe."

Irritated, I finished my drink, leaving the glass on the bar.

"*Vale*," I said. "Well, I have to go. I have to see how my family is doing. Nice seeing you."

In my dream, I'm walking through a dark corridor. It's the middle of the night, and the smell of Jasmine fills the air. The street is quiet. In the distance, I hear people laughing and drunkenly singing. Then, she appears from the corner, her golden hair releasing a trail of golden dust and daisies.

Vieni, Mar, vieni con me.

She's giggling and skipping while wearing a long white robe.

She turns the corner, and I see the cupola of Santa Maria del Fiore peek its head.

Ah, I'm in Florence.

Suddenly, the woman from the painting disappears. Everything goes dark. Now, I'm in what seems like the forest. It's still nighttime. I can't make out anything other than tree trunks, and instead of singing, I recognize hooves, galloping horses, and shouting. Panicked, I run for cover, as if they're coming for me. But how could they? I don't even know where I am.

Run, Mar.

I hear a similar voice—it's the girl from the painting, except this time I don't see her, I can't find her.

Run before they catch you.

"Marisollllllll!" I hear the men now. I recognize my name. I try moving my feet, but they're stuck, heavy, glued to the foliage beneath them. Then, I see them, black horses headed toward me, a man with a red beard in the front. His evil smile was made even more evil by the torch. *Ciao, Marisol.*

I wake up screaming and panting. *Thank God.* It was just a dream. My bed is soaked in sweat, Sirius and Romina snoring as if nothing happened, as if I didn't just run through whatever wilderness that was and make it out alive. What the actual fuck was *that*. Then, I felt even more panicked when I realized the woman from the painting was in my dream. *Oh, fuck.*

38

MIRRORS

Mar

Madrid, Spain – 2024

I stormed into Almaguer's office, threw my things on the spare chair, and flopped onto the couch. She didn't say anything as I crossed my arms across my chest.

She stared at me through her spectacles. Today they were purple. "Hmm...Here I thought the soft opening had gone well."

I'd completely forgotten she had attended after I invited her. I hadn't even noticed her there.

"It's not about the exhibit. The exhibit went fine. It's other things that keep happening."

"Like?"

"My family is driving me insane. My *abuela*, mom and *tía* arrived, and I don't know why I thought things would be different, or that we may have grown out of old resentments, especially when it came to my work, but they're still there. And to make things worse, Lucas gifted me the portrait I told you about. You remember?"

"I do, we—"

I interrupted her. "And they freaked out! They say that the artist, BVR, is cursed. How can she be cursed, Dr. Almaguer? There's nothing from our diving into the past that has led us to believe this."

"Mar, it's alright to feel upset. You hadn't told me this about your family before. Is there something else you haven't revealed to me...maybe some fears?"

Angry tears pooled in my eyes. "I never feel like I'm enough for them. I always fuck up somehow, even though I spent most of my life trying to do what they wanted. Trying to make up for the fact that my dad died and that my family had sacrificed so much for me to have a good life."

She walked over to the teapot, pouring some into a mug for me.

"Does it remind you of someone? Maybe a part of your soul you visited recently?"

"Yes, it rings Beatriz everywhere. I see her everywhere now."

"Remember what I told you about soul families traveling together? About us choosing the experiences we have in this life?"

"Yes." I said, sulking..

"Your family is reflecting your wounds back to you. All that unhappiness, the feeling that you've sacrificed who you are for them—it goes back to what I was telling you the other day about the love wounds Guillermo mirrored back to you. The same goes for what you're living with your family. Every experience that still frustrates you, that takes away from your feelings of peace—that is where you need to dig in. These are things you are resolving now, in this life. You have the choice to change them."

Choice. Was that the word of the month?

"Arrggghhh." I pushed back further into the couch. "Let's just do this."

39

AMOR FATI

Beatriz

Bologna, Italy – 1491

I skipped breakfast, hiding away at the *bottega*. I could still feel the touch of Dante's lips imprinted on my own, his distinctive smell of bergamot and citrus vivid in my memory. Leaning against my makeshift workstation, I closed my eyes, tasting his tongue and the pleasure of it tracing my neck and bodice. My skin felt luminous and radiant, as if it had been opaque for the past five years. How had I lived without him? How had I survived?

"I will not lose you again, Beatriz," he said sternly. "Not this time, not anymore. I refuse. *Amor fati*. This is our fate, and we must embrace it. Are you with me this time around?"

I hadn't given him an answer, but I knew it was *yes*. I was ready to do everything necessary to ensure we were never separated again. Even if it meant living in a shack in the mountains or running away to Spain. Life was giving us another chance, and who were we to stand up against our destiny?

I rearranged the brushes and powders in the *bottega* by the stained-glass window I'd painted three months ago, the sun creating an explosion of color against their wooden bases and the space.

Little by little, ideas came to mind, a rebellion of everything I'd considered was the prophecy of my life: I wasn't going to live my entire life in the hands of a monster. I wasn't going to bury another unborn child or allow the darkness that lay deep within myself to engulf me. I realized the only thing I wanted from then on was to be myself again, with the man I always loved.

40

DOZZA

Beatriz

Bologna, Italy – 1491

"Come with me to Dozza."

I was being lulled to sleep by his gentle touch tracing the outline of my hips where a few stretch marks formed after my last pregnancy. It was the first time we laid together since our reunion.

"There is a place I want to show you…a place where we might…be alone for a bit. Spend some time together."

The arrangements were difficult, particularly given what was expected of me as a countess. Even in Niccolo's absence, I still had to attend banquets and act in his stead. Still, I wanted nothing more than to disappear into the countryside with Dante.

"How far away is it?" I asked. "Are we to arrive there by carriage?"

"It's not very far. We would not leave Emilia Romagna. There is a property there…belonged to my *nonno*, he left it to me. There is some land and a cottage with...provisions. It is not the richness of your palazzo, but it is livable. I would like to spend more than just a few rushed hours with you, *amore*. No one would know who we are there."

I rolled onto my stomach, taking his hand into mine as I looked deeply into his eyes.

"What of my husband? We must be wary of his rage..."

"*Oh, Beatriz,* I know one day both of us will die. Perhaps we already did. Somehow, we have found a way back to each other, to healing our wounds together. All I ask from you, *bella mia*, is a moment where we may be free...to live."

41

THE BIRTH OF VENUS

Beatriz

Bologna, Italy – 1492

Three months later, there were three heartbeats within me. My children's and my own. Daria and I had been staying at my brother's home in Siena after our voyage to Dozza. I knew from the weeks I had missed they were Dante's, which filled me with inexplicable joy and radiance I had not experienced in my previous pregnancies.

My skin shone, my belly grew larger than the previous ones, and my sense of purpose now doubled.

I was not surprised when the midwife announced she believed they were to be twins. My sisters were twins, as were my uncles. It seemed some people in our family liked coming into the world in good company. My pregnancy felt like I was living in another world. With each passing week, my belly grew larger. They danced together like fish in a pond, circling in the universe of my womb. I stepped out into the gardens of the palazzo barefoot, careful the servants did not see me, sneaking out one of Dante's letters or poems in my robes.

"Your *papá* wrote this for me. He will be so happy when he learns we are to be parents," I said. "We need to find our way back to him soon enough."

And that way found itself to us first. The courier arrived by carriage, not horseback, the parcel taking up most of the roof of the carriage. It was addressed to me, even though Enzo received it. He called me into his study, closing the doors, dismissing every servant around us.

"Do you know what this is, Beatriz?" He pointed to the covered parcel; he'd already opened it. "*¿Has perdido la cabeza*? Do you know what it is?!"

"No, but I am hoping you will tell me..." I plummeted onto a *sedia*. "I would also appreciate it if you calmed yourself."

He roared, "Calm myself?!" He pulled apart the wrappings, revealing the unmistakable painting I worked on so long ago. "How have you come into possession of the Birth of Venus?"

I rose from my seat immediately, walking over to it, tracing my fingers along the golden rim of the frame. *How, indeed*? Immediately, I thought of the letters from the *Fiori*, *Signora* Clarice's warnings that Sandro had become more and more radicalized by the friar's teachings. Could this painting of his beloved Simonetta Vespucci coming out of the water as Venus be in danger of his new beliefs?

I was sure no matter how much he embraced new beliefs, he would never stop loving Simonetta. I looked over at my brother. The vein on his forehead was pulsating, awaiting an answer. Bracing myself with a new kind of courage, I knew it was time he knew everything. More than ever, I needed an ally.

His mouth stood agape by the time I finished. The violence, the years, the twins that were not Niccolo's and would not take after his likeness. He paced the room, pulling on his beard in the same way our father did when he was lost in thought or didn't know how to move forward.

"*Hermana*," he said softly. "I think it's time for you to pack your trunk and go."

"*¿En serio?* You're kicking me out," I walked over to him, holding my belly.

"I'm helping you escape. I have four children to look after, Beatriz. I cannot be caught with this painting in my home, not the way things are progressing in Florence. Any paintings that resemble paganism or go against the church are being banned. There is talk of war among the kingdoms. I would be tortured. I will also not leave you to suffer any longer, even more with the forthcoming birth of your children. I will arrange your departure. I need you to hide as best as possible in a place no one can find you. Take Daria. I will provide you with enough coin to sustain you."

"What about Niccolo? What if he tries hurting your family?" I said. "I don't want you to be killed like *Papá*."

"I must journey to Milan soon with my family on business. I will leave you here with a carriage during my absence. The driver shall have specific instructions to protect you and take you wherever you wish. Do you understand? You have to leave the same day or the day after for this to work; it needs to look like you fled. You can leave your trunk...just take the painting with you."

I leaped into him, tears spilling from my eyes. "*Gracias, hermano.*"

"It is time you knew some happiness, *Beatriz*."

42

AN OATH ON BLOOD

Beatriz

Dozza, Italy – 1496

Matteo and Chiara came into this world *en caul* after nearly two days of labor. They were born on May 16, 1492, in their great-grandfather's home in Dozza. As if by my own hand, they were both born with one green eye and the other, brown. Exactly as I had painted Sol years before.

When I first looked upon my children's faces, I understood something I had never known before. The love I felt was unlike anything I had experienced, fiercer than devotion, stronger than duty. Carrying them had changed me, given me a strength I did not know I possessed. For these children, mine and Dante's, I would do anything. I would move heaven and earth to protect them, or burn the world if anyone dared threaten them.

Dante and I had somehow lived the life we never thought we could. I changed my name to María Lupo and we married.

Daria and *Signora* Clarice had come to live with us to escape the Florentine turmoil. We were happy.

Until Niccolo took it away from us.

Five years after we fled my brother's home in Siena, he found us. Dante left on the morrow to teach, and Niccolo took advantage of his absence. He arrived at our home armed, claiming he had come to take the twins and me with him to Siena, where he said he had waited for our return. When he realized the children were not his, he seized Chiara and took a knife to her neck.

"Come with me, Beatriz, and I will leave the child," he threatened. "You are *my* wife!"

"*Dai, Dai,* I will come with you. Just put the child down." I knew if he took her, I would never see her again. Niccolo's cruelty knew no bounds, he would end a child's life without hesitation if it achieved his ends.

Signora Clarice and Daria had thrown blue powders in the fire, hoping the town would see the smoke and come to our aid, if our screams had not already drawn them.

"Niccolo, give Chiara to me, allow me to say goodbye to her and we shall leave together, I promise you."

He put her down, and just as she came into my arms, he seized my hair, pulling me from her like a mutt. I screamed in pain.

"We are going." He dragged me toward the door of our cottage, the children screaming behind me.

"Not like this, Niccolo, wait! Wait! Let me say goodbye to them."

His eyes turned darker than their usual storm. "You did not bid me goodbye; you will not bid them goodbye either."

Dante darted through the door, coming face to face with Niccolo, who still gripped my scalp. Taking out the sharp knife he carried for carving, he pointed it at the man who had inflicted such great pain upon me.

"Let my wife go, you brute," he warned. "I will not repeat myself. Release her, or I will slash you."

Niccolo sneered, looking down at Dante. He was enormous in comparison to him and clearly believed Dante could never defeat him.

"I would like to see you try," he said.

His underestimation earned him a slash across the chest that forced him to release me, igniting a rage directed strictly at Dante.

"Take the children and run," Dante screamed at us. "Do not come back, Beatriz. DO NOT COME BACK!"

We were halfway through the field when I handed Chiara and Matteo to Daria and *Signora* Clarice. Planting a kiss on each of their foreheads. "I will be back for you. Be good to your nanas, *dai?*"

I had already lived without Dante once. I knew I could not bear to do so again. I would not allow him to perish at the hands of my abuser. I ran into the house, finding Niccolo bloodied on the floor. I searched for Dante until I saw him lying unconscious with a head wound in a corner.

Niccolo cackled as he watched me attempt to pull Dante from our home. Dragging him toward the field.

"Did you think I would let you get away with this, Beatriz? That I would allow for you to live your life as if I never existed? You took away my possibility of having a family. Now watch yours disappear."

He coughed up blood, staining his garments and red face. I looked at him with pity, knowing he would die from his wounds. I turned back to Dante and dragged him through the threshold, praying he would wake. Behind me, I heard rustling. Canvas shifting. Before I could stop him, Niccolo had set one of my paintings alight and hurled it toward the wooden beams that held up the cottage.

The fixtures kindled almost immediately, fire roaring from floor to ceiling, locking us within that hell.

"Dante! Dante! *Amore*, please wake up!" I pleaded. His eyes opened forcibly, washing in and out of consciousness. "I beg you, I need you to help me."

He struggled to get on his feet. Walking a few steps before falling over. Daria ran in, horrified by the fire. She aided me in carrying him into the field, as far away as possible.

The rest of the town gathered, attempting to extinguish the fire, ensuring the dry fields would not catch and take the town with it. Dante wheezed in my arms, his hand stretched toward my face, lowering it toward him.

"*No me dejes, no me dejes, Dante*," I wailed. "Please, restrain your abandon, my love. We need you. I need you!"

He smiled at me, as if remembering each time we had been separated by life and brought together. Every moment fate's cruel hand snatched us from each other. I felt all hope drain from my body, as if I were dying with him, my spirit broken from knowing this would be the last time I would love in this way.

"I vow to you, Dante, that I shall never love another. I shall never find peace in this life or in the next until I find you and recognize you. We shall find a life, my love, where we are not constrained by society or the rules of man, where our love may be free to choose. Until then, I will not love another soul that is not yours."

I looked up to find our children hiding behind *Signora* Clarice, clutching on to her skirts. How would they survive this earth with this pain? They could never. No one else in their lineage could live through something such as this, the pain I had endured in my life. The forced love. The constrained fate. No.

"And as for our lineage, I free you from the perils of

romance. From the perils of despair. From believing in a love as strong as this one I have lived. You shall never have it, so that you may live."

43

BREAKING A CURSE

Mar

Madrid, Spain – 2024

It's real. The curse is real. *Abuela* Cristina wasn't making it up. Now I just needed to figure out how to break it.

My eyes shot open to see Almaguer's office. The warm light, the lavender, and her half-moon glasses were all there as they were before I went under. Unlike other sessions, this one was intense, deep. I felt the relief at least at having an answer to this void, the frustration.

"Welcome back, Mar," Almaguer said, walking over to a teapot she had a few steps away from her chair to bring me a cup. "Do you need a minute? That was quite—"

"—intense," I interjected, sitting up. "But I think I'm good. I feel much better."

She squinted her eyes, inspecting me.

"Do you want to dis—"

"No, no, I actually have to go. My family is waiting for me so we can have lunch. I'll see you in our next session."

Unable to sleep that night, my mind spinning with ways to break the curse, I headed downstairs. To my surprise, my *abuela* was in the kitchen. She had the dim light of the stove on, probably to keep her eyes comfortable. It was 5:30 a.m., not at all her usual waking hour. While my *abuelo* was up every day at 4:45 to make *cafecito* and breakfast for everyone, my *abuela* was the go-to-bed-late-wake-up-late type.

"*Abuela*," I whispered as to not startle her. "*Buenos días*, are you okay?"

She was watching the *cafetera* closely for that first drop of concentrated coffee to make *espumita* with. "*Mijita,* yes, I just couldn't sleep. Maybe it's that—*¿cómo se llama eso?—jaylay.*"

"You mean, jet lag?" I giggled. "*Abuela*, there's no way you have jet lag. You've been here for three weeks. Plus, the jet lag here makes you tired in the afternoon, not this early in the morning. *¿Qué pasa?*"

She sighed loudly, pouring the drops of coffee onto the sugar before starting to cream them.

"As you get older, Mar, you're going to realize that life has passed, and you go back to being treated like a child. It is a circle. It's like you have no voice anymore, because your children and your grandchildren, they don't care about what you have to say. The life you lived is just an anecdote to them..."

This was typical *abuela* behavior. I knew me keeping the painting was something she took personally, a sign of disrespect. I looked at her closely, folding my arms and leaning against the kitchen counter. "That's not true, *Abuela*. You are still the *most* important figure in this family, and you know this. There's no question in my mind that you will *still* be that person until the day you die," I said.

She paused to ask me if I wanted the coffee *cortado*, or if I was going to drink it straight. I nodded. There was no way I'd be taking a shot of Cuban coffee this early in the morning without a buffer.

"*No sé*, Mar." We headed toward the living room to enjoy our serendipitous meeting, finding comfortable spots on the couch that left us looking at each other. Returning to her initial comment, I broke the ice about BVR.

"*Abuela*, is this about the painting? I know you're upset about it, but I need to understand a little bit more."

I knew now that the curse was real, but I wanted to know what happened that made my family so terrified of it.

She sipped her coffee. "It all started when Fernandito, your uncle, came in contact with a professor from Columbia University who used to visit Cuba occasionally for research. Fernandito and your father weren't from Havana. They were born in Trinidad, as was the rest of their family."

She paused, putting her coffee down. Then, she clapped her hands together to pick back up on her story.

"*Bueno*, during that move, Fernandito found hidden in one of his *abuela*'s closets a box full of paintings. Beautiful paintings. Some of them were properly stored, others weren't. All were signed with that name....BVR," she looked into my eyes, making sure I understood the importance of what was to come. "He thought he could maybe sell them at the *mercado de artesanías* and make some money. It was tough times already, and Fernandito was always looking for a way to *sacarle el agua al coco*."

She picked her coffee back up, taking another sip before continuing.

"*Entonces*, a friend of his who worked at *la Universidad de la Habana* helped him sort through the paintings, which to everyone's surprise were actual cultural heritage. BVR wasn't just a bored colonial housewife; she was a well-known painter, part of a society in Florence, who at her time had some sort of influence. It eventually made its way to this professor from *Nueva*

York and another guy, a young Cuban exile who was living and working at a gallery. I actually met him before he, *bueno,* I'll tell you about that later," she rambled on.

"The first set of paintings came with Gracielita in what must have been, 1985 or 86? The second set of paintings was supposed to come with your mom, but she was a doctor and her plans to go to Miami were halted for a few years. *Eventualmente*, after what seemed like *el Niágara en bicicleta,* we managed to convince *Tía Carmen* to bring the rest of the paintings, giving them to the professor and the exile."

"Okay, and what was so bad about that?" I asked. "From the story you're telling me, you all transported some paintings and made money out of it."

"The money we made was meant to bring Fernandito and your father to Miami. *Pero* that money, Mar, it became saltwater for us. Nothing good came out of it. Eventually you and your *mamá* came to Miami, but Fernandito and your father...they just"—tears flooded her eyes—"They drowned in those shark-infested waters because they used the money from that sale."

"*Abuela*, hundreds of people have drowned in the Florida Strait. *Papi* knew the risks, *Tío* Fernandito knew the risks. It wasn't anybody's fault other than the political systems that led them to make those kinds of decisions," I reasoned with her. "The curse *Abuela* Cristina had talked about was related to relationships, not political mishaps."

"*Hazme caso, mijita.* Stay away from everything that has to do with that," she pleaded. "It's already bad enough that you still haven't found a partner. You're 29, almost 30, and men are scared of you. It's the curse. That kind of love, the kind your grandfather and I had, it only came once for our family. I want to believe things will be different for you, but I don't think it'll come if you hold on to this painting."

44

PALATE CLEANSER

Mar

Madrid, Spain – 2024

Tania and I sat on the floor of my living room barefoot and drunk, decanting the bulldozing I received at the hands of my mother and *abuela*. Before they left, they made sure to deep-clean my entire apartment, bathe the dogs, make enough food for the apocalypse, and strip me of all hope of living.

"They just don't get it," Tania poured me another glass of Rioja. I was rolling a "grown-up," which was our term for a half-THC, half-CBD joint that would get us high enough without a panic attack. With a few bad trips under our belt, we had to take the right precautions.

She passed the glass to me. "It's the same thing with my parents after I broke up with Michel. My mom just wanted me to roll over and put up with everything he did. As if I weren't worth more. Then, she's all, 'Well, you have to give people a chance. You can't expect him to be perfect.' But, that's the thing —I don't. I expect kindness within our communication, not someone that yells at me every time he's frustrated."

"At least now you're doing great with Juan," I said. "I know exactly how you feel. I've been giving it a lot of thought, especially after everything went down with Guille. There were so many nights where I'd stay up thinking, 'Would he really rather be with his cheating ex than with me?' It took me a while to realize the problem was *him* not me. I have my own things to deal with, obviously. Oh, and the curse, because yeah, we blame it all on the curse."

Tania caressed Romina's chin, still holding up her glass of wine. "So, tell me about this guy you met at the art gallery. Didn't you kind of blow him off last time?"

"Dario Messina?" I asked.

"Mmhm..." She nodded.

"I haven't reached out to him since the last time I saw him. I'm feeling a little weird about it. What am I supposed to say? 'Oh, hey, sorry about the other day, I just thought you were this guy from my past life and realized you weren't?'"

"Or," Tania said, reaching over for some manchego cheese on the table. "You could say something super complicated like...hi."

Lighting the joint, I snorted, nearly choking on the smoke. "Stop!"

"Text him or whatever," Tania poked. "What's the worst that could happen? He tells you he doesn't want to see you again. Maybe this is just your palate cleanser, and then the real love of your life comes along later on, once you've had time to break the curse."

I took another puff, holding it. Then I thought about her proposition as I released the smoke.

"Yeah, but the curse from Beatriz said we had to find each

other in another life to be able to have the love we couldn't back in the 1400s."

Tania wasn't buying it. "I'm starting to regret giving you Almaguer's number."

"Fine, hand me my phone."

Her eyes widened. "Now?!"

"Yes, now. While I've got the nerve."

"Fuck, okay," she passed it to me. I'd already saved his number from our second meeting.

Hi Dario...this is Mar...Mar Varela. Are you still in Madrid, or did you go back to Florence?

I hit send, putting the phone down and returning to my libations. "Done." I laughed. It felt good to take control, act, and once again, rebel against my family's desires by keeping the painting. It wasn't out of spite. No one in this life was more important to me than my grandmother. But this was something I needed to do for myself.

Ping. My phone alerted me to a new message. My eyes wide, Dario's name appeared on the screen.

Shit, he's fast.

"Is that him?" Tania squealed.

"I didn't think he'd respond so quickly," I said. "Shit."

Ciao, Mar. I've been expecting your message. Yes, I am still in Madrid for another week. I extended my trip for work.

Oh.

"This is weird, Tania. We're talking like nothing ever happened," I said, holding the phone up to her.

She smiled, the joint between her fingers now. "Oh! He's typing." She threw her head back as she laughed. "This is good. Looks like we're finally going to know if this curse can be broken or not."

Would you be open to having dinner together? I wasn't happy with the way we parted a few days ago.

I felt nervous taking him up on his proposal, but I did want to see him again. Even if he wasn't Dante, something about him made me feel—intrigued.

Yes, let's do it.

We continued texting for hours that turned into the next day. Agreeing we would meet for dinner later that week, after I returned from Tania's birthday celebration in Irati.

45

IRATI

Mar

Navarra, Spain – 2024

L*a Selva de Irati* lies in the western Pyrenees at the border of Spain and France's Basque Country. Tania had planned this trip months earlier as a birthday present, to a forest known for its healing properties and quantum energy, hounding all of her friends to come with her.

If this year had been difficult for me, last year had run over Tania. That's when Tania found past life regression and Almaguer suggested she visit this place after her final session. Juan, Tania's boyfriend, drove while Tania, Raquel, Eli, and I picked out the music. We would spend the entire weekend here.

We arrived at the rustic treehouse hotel, dropping off our stuff before heading for our first hike in the forest nearby.

"They say there are fairies and other kinds of mythical creatures here," Tania shared as we walked toward the trail. "Who knows, maybe we'll get kidnapped by one."

Her laughter echoed in the cover of the tree canopy above

us. It was slightly chilly, but rays of sun poked through the leaves, creating a kaleidoscope of colors that led the way for us. The forest radiated an energy I felt in my bones. The fresh air, the sounds of birds, the detachment from our busy lives in Madrid.

Tania, who was walking ahead with Juan, waited for me to catch up to them. She put her hand around my shoulder, lowering her voice.

"The true gem of this trip happens tomorrow," she said. "Just wait until you see the surprise I have planned."

Tucked within the rolling green folds of the mountain range, we headed toward Harpea's Cave the next morning.

"Once you arrive at the mountains, you need to hike down the trail until you see the opening of the cave," Almaguer explained via voice note. "The cave is known for transforming everything we want to leave and giving us a new opportunity at life."

Tania had first planned this trip way before Guillermo left me. But now that I knew the curse was real, I figured this could be a good place to leave the curse behind and let the cave take over. Then I could see through my dinner with Dario and find out more about BVR's art.

We left behind the last signs of civilization, the landscape opening up to a pastoral dream of undulating hills and emerald grass. Wildflowers and horses led the path, until eventually, the only thing left to do was park and descend into the cave. Hidden beautifully by the surrounding mountains, the cave snuck up on me, carved by ancient tectonic forces, a natural stone arch with several layers like the pages of a book, appeared before me. The cool air pushed us forward and over a rustic bridge where a river flowed and all our energies shifted. At the hotel, locals of Navarra who worked there told us the cave was home to *lamias*, half-women, half-animals, and was a place of rebirth.

Tania edged closer to the river, taking a moment to address us all.

"*Amigues*, I'm so happy that all of you agreed to come with me and share my wild birthday plans. Thirty-six feels like a big number. It's that next step toward forty," she sucked in air. "Oof, that was hard to say! Anyway, I want all of us to do a little ritual here. I'll start, and the rest of you can join me. We're going to each grab a stone—or two—whatever your heart desires—and I want you to write down what you want to leave behind in this cave with this chalk I have here."

She broke it into several pieces, passing it around.

"When you're done, we can all meet outside the cave."

Following her instructions, I dipped my hand in the river, the freezing water taking me by surprise. I picked out three rocks and walked toward the opening of the cave. I took a second to look at the enormous, natural archway, sheltering myself in its shadow, feeling the wind brush against my skin and whisper.

A prayer began spilling from my lips.

Padre nuestro que estás en los cielos….

I pulled out my chalk and started writing on the rocks. The first, I dedicated to myself and the women in my family.

A mis mujeres, may all of us and our ancestors be liberated from generations of oppression, violence, and trauma.

The second, to Beatriz Velázquez de Rossi.

Beatriz, I liberate our soul. I heal our lineage. I see you and honor you. We will enjoy this life and all the others that come after. I liberate all our existence.

The third, to Dante.

Dante Lupo, I liberate you from the curse I placed upon our souls hundreds of years ago. Love who you want in your new timelines.

Live freely and happily. I release our descendants *and our souls. Our contract is terminated. I release you. I release you. I release you.*

I tucked each one of them deep inside the cave, the wind rising from the surface of the ground and all around me. Walking out, I stood at the edge of the river, taking in the towering beauty, at the power of healing. Ready for whatever came next.

46

SANGIOVESE SPELL

Mar

Madrid, Spain – 2024

Unlike the more formal coffee meeting we had before, Dario offered to cook for me tonight, giving me a "true" Italian experience. Even though he lived in Florence, he was Roman, so he opted for making me his grandmother's Amatriciana, which we would wash down with several glasses of Sangiovese wines—the intersection of Tuscany and Lazio, a perfect meal made by the descendant of Sicilians for a Cuban-American.

I arrived at the Airbnb he'd been staying at close to Retiro park to find he had lit a few candles and set the table. The pasta boiled on the stove. It was a refreshing change to the "dates" I'd been on over the years which mostly consisted of people taking you to their homes after you split a dinner bill and then expecting you to be turned on by their lack of romance.

Dario wiped his hands on his apron, moving toward the record player the owners of the apartment had left here, and picking out a jazz vinyl. John Coltrane filled the space beautifully.

"I wouldn't have pinned you for a jazz guy," I teased. He was back in front of the stove, stirring the sauce with a wooden spoon. He brought it up to his lips and licked it. The simple motion was simple enough to deepen my breath. *We are breaking old patterns, Mar.*

He put it down, checking on the pasta now. "I've been a fan since I was a child. My *mamma* was a fan of jazz. She learned to love it when she moved to New York to help my uncle out before I was born."

"Your uncle lived in New York?"

"Yes, he was a professor at Columbia University. They were very close, and he was going through a very difficult time back then. This was, I don't know—" he waved his hands in the air in thought. "Around 1985-88?"

"Huh! Interesting. That's the year my parents were thinking of moving to Miami, but they were stuck on the island because my mom is a doctor and they couldn't get permission for her to leave," I said.

He handed me a bottle of the Sangiovese and two glasses from a cabinet above him. I decided since he'd shown off his cooking skills, I should show off my *sommelier* chops. I knew my way around a bottle quite well.

"*Hmmm, mia mamma*, she loved New York, the time she spent there, even though it was in the middle of the AIDS epidemic, and my uncle was quite impacted by it." He leaned against the countertop. "She would escape to the jazz clubs to take rest from all the tragedy around her. I think that's what made the difference between them staying there or coming back to Italy."

I handed him a glass. We clinked and took a sip, looking at each other. "Your uncle came back to Italy...to live?"

"He did. He returned here after an art exhibition he was

helping a lover with. My mother says he became so involved in the process of it and curating the exhibition that it made sense he..."

"He what?"

The timer went off, startling both of us. "*O Dio, la pasta!*"

We dined casually, barely exchanging words, although it felt unnecessary since our eyes filled the space of our thoughts. The first wine bottle was more than done by the time we finished eating. He observed the wine stained rim of his glass, and I observed him. His hair was longer in the front than the back, shagging a bit over his nearly constant brooding expression. He reminded me of Mr. Darcy from *Pride and Prejudice*. In his private world, he was much more introverted than when I saw him out in public.

And God, did he have to be so divinely attractive?

It had been months since the last time I felt attracted to anyone, and my body was reacting viscerally to his presence. I hadn't realized I was biting my lip when he looked up from his wine-induced trance. I shot up, starting to clear the table. He joined me, quietly picking up the plates that housed the pasta and the salad. We bumped into each other, causing him to drop the dishes while I still held the wine glasses. My heart beat forcefully against my chest as I looked up at him, awaiting his reaction. John Coltrane was now just background noise.

Without lifting his eyes from my face, he took both glasses from my hand, placing them on the table. He put a hand on my waist, pulling me closer to him, then smiled as he tucked one side of my hair behind my ear.

"*Stai attenta.* You could cut yourself," he released me. Every part of me still pulsated at the memory of his touch. *Gather yourself,* Mar. *You came to ask for his help on BVR.*

He handed me the remaining bottle of wine, noticing my obvious discomfort.

Composing myself, I cleared my throat. "I wanted to ask you something about Florence."

"Sure, tell me."

"There is this painter, Beatriz Velázquez de Rossi, I'm not sure if you know who she is. But I want to know more about her life. I have this number for someone in Florence who appears to have known something about her....there is also a town... Dozza. Does any of it ring a bell for you?"

"Mmm yes, I know about BVR," he said. "I also know where Dozza is."

"Oh, great," I said.

"What do you want to know specifically?"

I hesitated to tell him the *exact* reason. Instead, I just went for the proposition.

"I mentioned it since a while back you told me to come visit you in Florence sometime...is that offer still open?"

He chuckled, seemingly amused by the question.

"It is. I don't start summer courses until July, so you have about eight weeks. Do you think that would be enough time?"

"Yes, I think that should be plenty, maybe just a week or two would be enough to find out what I need."

"Stay as long as you need to," he said. "I'll be happy to be your tour guide."

I perked up. "Awesome! I'll look into a hotel or an Airbnb to stay at, then." I gazed intently at him, watching his reaction.

He shook his head, throwing his hands up. "*Ma, che*, absolutely not. You are coming to stay with me, at my place."

The combination of the wine and his reaction made heat rise through my body.

He edged closer to me once more, this time I could feel his energy radiating between us, and I leaped, wrapping my arms around him and sealing the night with a kiss.

We lingered there for a moment, and a sense of peace overcame me. The kiss wasn't forceful or rushed. Instead, it felt natural. Like I'd been kissing him my entire life.

He pulled away gently.

"You are very interesting, Mar," he held my hand. "But for right now, I don't want to complicate things. If we are to ever have something, I don't want you to think I am the kind of person to disrespect you. Especially if you are coming to Florence..."

My heart shrunk with disappointment. The flutter of emotions that had bloomed with our kiss now closed back into the familiar pang of rejection.

"Right," I said, fidgeting. "Maybe opening that second bottle of wine isn't the best idea, then. You know what they say, '*Liquor goes fast. And it's a magic trick. It makes everything come true.*'"

"I'm sorry," he said.

"Nothing to be sorry for." I shot him a fake smile. "I'll look into the tickets for Florence and let you know when it would be a good time for us to meet there."

47

RESACA

Mar

Madrid, Spain – 2024

"I kissed a guy yesterday, and it was disastrous." I looked up at the ceiling of Almaguer's office. "Ugh, I think instead of breaking the curse, it's gotten worse. Now guys won't even look at me."

"Oh, well, this is new and exciting...who is the guy?"

Almaguer and I were starting to develop a friendship beyond our meetings. During my trip to Irati, we'd been texting back and forth as I updated her on what our group was doing. I also felt our energy lighten from the initial sessions.

I turned to face her. "His name is Dario. Dario Messina. I met him at an exhibit at the Juan March Foundation. He knows Lucas. Anyway, I had dinner with him last night after asking him if he would give me the grand tour of Florence and help me find out more information about BVR."

"...And?"

"And after he said yes and way too much wine, I kissed

him." I pulled a pillow over my head, feeling like I was seventeen instead of 29.

Almaguer chuckled. "How did he reject you?"

"He pulled away from me and said that he didn't want to ruin the chances of building something real by making it intimate so soon."

"I'm confused," Almaguer said. "How is what he said negative? It seems like he is being respectful, setting boundaries, and letting you know that he doesn't want to fall into shallow patterns with you."

"I also don't want to fall into negative patterns, but maybe he just doesn't like me. He says he wants to take it slow. Come on, Almaguer. Who wants to take it slow in 2024? He's obviously just letting me down gently."

She shrugged. "Or maybe he is someone who, like you, has been hurt in the past. It seems to me like he wants to connect with you on a deeper level. What is your usual pattern when you meet someone you like?"

I hated that she was so good at her job sometimes.

"Before Guillermo and the other serious relationships I've had, all I've had were situationships. Or men I would just sleep with without any real connection."

"Aha," she said. "What do you want to do with Dario, Mar? Is he someone you want to connect with just sexually, or do you want something more?"

"I want something more. I think. I just don't know what that looks like with the physical connection first. How will I know if there's sexual chemistry? "

"Well, that's part of why you're here now, isn't it? Let's see what you learn about yourself, or perhaps impatience during this regression."

48

EL JARDÍN DE LAS DELICIAS

Luciana

Madrid, Spain – 1808

The carriage rattled to a halt on the side of *Calle de los Estelos,* delivering General Humberto Roca in front of *El jardín de las delicias*, Madrid's most exclusive brothel. I stood behind the satin curtains of the second-floor window of my bedchamber, pulling them to one side to see his thick frame exit the carriage as a guard greeted him discreetly at the door.

Madama Magdalena knocked on my door three times, her signal that the general was on his way up. His heavy footsteps were the greatest announcement of his arrival. He burst through the door, unbothered to knock. His eyes held a desperate, consuming hunger—a passion so raw it bordered on rage. He fixed them on me.

He had spent several weeks tending to military business in Barcelona, and I could tell from his gaze he was famished for pleasure. He shut the door with a thud, moving toward me, gripping me with both hands as he brought me into his sturdy chest. I caught my breath as his fingers dug deeper into my hips, and he leaned in, kissing me hard. His touch was never gentle. I'd first lain with him four years ago, after which he'd decided I was the only prostitute he would visit.

"Luciana..."

Chills crawled up my spine as I heard my name uttered in his raspy voice. A mixture of disgust and detachment brewed within me.

"I could think of nothing but this," he breathed in my ear. "The fire between your thighs—I nearly killed my horse racing back from Catalunya." His rough hands proceeded to strip me of my silk robe.

Like countless encounters before, he ravished me—and I let him. It was easier to exhaust him before taking control. There were beasts such as him who thought control came from brute force, pain, and invoking a feeling of helplessness.

I knew the opposite to be true. Pleasure was a much more effective bargaining tool for achievement than pain. As his desperate thrusting weakened, I used my thighs to guide him underneath me, mounting him. Distracted by the weight of my breasts on his face, I began my subtle interrogation.

"Was the voyage what you expected, *mi general*?"

I moved my hips around his member in a circular motion, ensuring his mind was truly elsewhere. His eyes rolled back as he moaned, but still he spoke, always he spoke. Even now, he loved for me to know of his own importance. "*Sí*....We almost got 'em. Those bastards. We are growing close.....I feel it."

"¿*Quién*? Who are you closer to?"

"Those propaganda-spreading ruffians. *Els Artistes.* They have been smuggling pieces of propaganda against the Inquisition across Spain...pieces of art with nude women...defamation of our government...they are indecent..."

Said the man who had stopped at a brothel before arriving home to his wife and three daughters.

"They—They believe we are unaware of them, but we are... we are."

I rode him faster, aiming to keep his cock occupied while I peeked into his mind. "Is that what you were doing in Catalunya, then? Chasing artists? I do not like it when you are away for so long..."

"*Sí, sí, Luci.* Do not pause."

"I shan't, *general.* Will you be gone for long again?"

He groped my ass firmly with one hand while reaching for my hair with the other.

"Miss me, didn't ya?"

His clasp on my hair pained me. The only way to release it was to release him. "*Sí, general. Mucho.*" Like sorcery, he finished.

I stared back at my reflection in the dim lighting of the room, brushing through my long black hair. The general lay snoring on the bed like a sleeping lion. It felt satisfying to know I had been the one to tame him. He had a few minutes before I needed to let in my next visitor. Despite his status as a general and honored patron, *Madama* Magdalena forbade the gentlemen from remaining longer than they paid for. But I still had information to extract from him, and breaking the rules was one of my talents.

He stirred with a groan, stretching his beefy arms. The air stiffened with his mercurial temper. I lifted myself from the chair, handing him his uniform.

"When will you return from Catalunya?"

He furrowed his brow, his tone serious. "Why do you wish to know?"

I widened my eyes as I looked up at him. I needed to pace myself to keep from revealing my real intentions. My eyes always captivated him, one green and the other brown. It was one of the reasons he had been drawn to me initially. Other patrons were afraid it was a sign of witchcraft.

"Oh—only curiosity *mi general.* I thought perhaps we could have an outing," I said.

He relaxed, buying into my ruse of a harmless woman of the night.

"I am afraid I will be gone for some time, Luciana. My platoon has been tasked with eradicating the group I mistakenly mentioned to you during our *coito*. I cannot share with you how long. *No te preocupes*, I will be back. That I promise."

49

ELS ARTISTES

Luciana

Madrid, Spain – 1808

A carriage retrieved me from *El jardín de las delicias* at sundown. Under the cover of night and the thick, swirling fog that painted Madrid after a day of endless rain, *Madama* Magdalena shut the door of the carriage, sending me away to another patron. Inside the humid carriage, I swayed to the rhythmic clatter of the hooves on the slick cobblestone.

The only light came from the occasional streetlamp, each one casting enough glow to momentarily reveal shadowy hooded figures as they headed hastily towards their homes. We plunged through the concealing darkness, coming to a final halt. The carriage driver opened the door, extending his gloved hand to me. I held on to him with one hand and lifted the bottom of my gown with the other, keeping it from getting wet. As I stepped off, I saw a figure waiting for me at the door.

"Luciana, *bienvenida*," Renato Álvarez said.

I took three steps toward him, curtsying. He was a prominent lawyer who would fetch me once a month for our gatherings, telling *Madama* Magdalena he could not afford to be seen at establishments of ill repute, given his father-in-law's position within the Spanish court.

He led me through the door, ushering me down a long, narrow hallway that made way to a staircase. Candlelight flickered off the walls, revealing a circular basement with stone walls lined with bookcases on each side. Clouds of cigar smoke obscured a small group of men and two other women gathered around a portrait on the long wooden table.I took one step forward, clearing my throat.

All, except one man, Diego Morales, dispersed as soon as they saw me.

Diego pulled away from the painting slowly, folding his lorgnette into the pocket of the green velvet vest he wore. It contrasted well with his copper hair and the mustache he'd grown since the last time I saw him a few weeks prior.

"Very well, *señores* y *señoritas*, Luciana has arrived at last. Let us find our seats and proceed with our gathering."

He came toward me, finding my hand and leading me to the top of the table, where I took my seat. He sat beside me.

Roca had been wrong. *Els Artistes* were not in Barcelona.

We were here, in Madrid. In Diego's *librería*. In the very body of the woman he just lay with. The one he so often underestimated.

"First order of business. I believe you have all heard of the trials currently in place for the painter Don Francisco de Goya over the findings at the Prime Minister's home. He could face interrogation and torture, exile, or have all of his paintings and property confiscated if the trial results do not go in his favor. We pray this does not happen."

I breathed in evenly before continuing, remembering the

screams of others being taken by the Inquisition. Begging for mercy.

"The Inquisition continues to persecute dissent despite its waning power. Though weakened, it remains dangerous which makes our efforts more vital than ever. The very purpose of our group is to defy the Inquisition and bring justice to a new Spain. We have created the following pieces for disbursement. Our campaign must be one of silent protest, but protest nonetheless."

Diego laid out a series of pamphlets calling on villagers to stand against the Inquisition and information on Goya's predicament, maps, and a list of names for the lawyers and judges we knew would be involved. Many of them were customers at *El jardín de las delicias* with *peculiar* tastes that their wives and the church would not approve of.

"The pamphlets must be delivered across the following towns. The locations are on the maps provided; you must *not* miss the marks. Diego has made them specifically to match our contacts in those regions."

The volunteers would leave Madrid in four days, where they would be met by a cell of *Els Artistes* in Segovia. Then, the pamphlets would be delivered across the towns in Spain, hoping to rouse enough support to have Goya acquitted by the Inquisition. This groundswell of popular favor, combined with the quiet advocacy of Goya's influential patrons within the royal court, could be the force powerful enough to compel the weakened church to yield.

"One more item of note," I added. "As of yesterday, we have also been tasked with delivering a rare book of Jewish parchment scrolls from the medieval ages. They are illuminated manuscripts with a wealth of detail. It shall make it across the same route as the pamphlets, but it is to be delivered to León."

Diego shot a look of bewilderment in my direction. I

ignored him. "Ambassador Prieto sent word last night that it would arrive here in the morning. His homes are being searched, and he requires our assistance."

"He knows of our existence?" Diego's freckled face became red, the sudden rush of heat making his ears burn. He despised it when I withheld information from him. The muscles in his jaw tightened.

I pretended not to take notice, responding calmly. "We require allies, and he will not betray us. Especially if we deliver this as promised."

He shook his head in disbelief, removing his spectacles to pinch the bridge of his nose with two fingers, which I knew meant we would discuss this later.

"Is there a reason why we are to transport this scripture in such short notice?" Alfredo Gutierrez asked.

"It is a precious piece of art," I said. "Not only are these pieces nearly nonexistent in Spain, but they are crafted from the finest parchment, bound by thick, carved wooden boards faced with polished gold that has been hammered into intricate filigree. The ambassador tells me it is one of the only volumes left with true gemstones added to the pages."

"How do you know of this?" Alfredo continued.

"I have seen it. The ambassador keeps it in his *casona* and has shown me his private collection in the past."

Diego gazed around the room, avoiding eye contact with me, eager to move the meeting along.

"Who volunteers for this mission?" he asked.

No one responded.

"Say, Diego, this is a rather dangerous mission, no?" Gaspar, an architect from Andalusia, shouted across the table, stirring the rest.

"Yes, it is. As are all of our missions."

Gaspar narrowed his eyes.

"*Dime*, why is it that neither Diego nor you go on

missions? We fetch you from the brothel; you are the intelligence behind *Els Artistes*." Gaspar stood. "Yet we are risking it all on missions based on information she gathers from patrons."

"*Sí, sí,* Luciana. We believe in the work, *pero*, this is turning perilous with the military on our tail," Pablo added.

I became inflamed. "Is it, now, Pablo? When was the last time you had to extract information from the military? Imagine having one of their general's hands around your throat, knowing they could find out you are behind the operation and execute you. You say Diego and I do not expose ourselves, yet we are the ones consistently exposed."

Pablo scoffed. "It is hardly exposure if you are already a whore."

Diego stood, fist pounding the table. "RETRACT YOUR STATEMENT, YOU BASTARD!"

I pulled him back down into his seat, attempting to maintain composure in the room. "That is enough from all of you! Pablo, you are finished." Diego said firmly. "Whoever is not in agreement with the way this group functions, you are free to leave. Nothing has been written about cowards as far as I know. So be it. Take your leave."

Pablo stood at the bottom of the stairwell. "I could have you all arrested, you know? I could have you all taken by the Inquisition."

Diego, still sitting, pointed to the door. "Then do it! The rest of us would be happy to tell them of the missions you have been on. I'm sure you would look darling hanging from the *Plaza del Sol.*"

"Diego." I locked eyes with him, then flickered briefly toward Pablo before sweeping the rest of the room. "Anyone else with a grievance?"

The rest of the group remained silent, yet I could tell they stewed in Pablo's words. Their heads down, fidgeting hands tapping on the table, not a single comment or response from an otherwise opinionated lot.

"Diego and I will go on the mission," I said sternly.

Diego turned toward me, eyes wide.

"Luc—"

"That is all."

50

BORN FROM ART

Luciana

Madrid, Spain – 1808

While a reportedly ruthless *general* known for spurts of military brilliance, Roca was unaware that two years ago, when I founded *Els Artistes* alongside other members of the art and literary world, he had become an involuntary informant. The Inquisition could not fathom a woman in prostitution—and the artists who visited her—had successfully achieved the smuggling of dozens of pieces of art through the northern border. It was unthinkable.

We had given the group a Catalan name to throw off military informants. Dropping innocent knowledge in establishments we knew they frequented—bars, brothels, and markets, their wives or servants would surely visit. While they tortured folks for information, we delivered traps in places of pleasure.

Rumors swirled that the Inquisition was nearing its final days of torture and harsh punishment. They were grasping at the loose cords left that they could pull. They were ridiculous old men who knew nothing of the real world. Their riches made them ignorant and petty. Even with Napoleon's army already within our borders, the church and military were still more concerned with naked bodies being painted or lovers exposed in portraits than in resolving an impending invasion.

Just a few months ago, it was rumored that the Inquisition questioned Prime Minister Manuel Godoy's art curator, Don Francisco de Garivay, about one of Francisco Goya's paintings. It was said Godoy had a room of naked portraits, and Goya himself would soon be questioned.

Apparently the Catholic church fears it will be toppled by a pair of painted breasts. They should be afraid, but not of Goya's nudes. Art has power within society. Words influence thought. Whispers ignite rebellion. Brushstrokes topple kingdoms. That is why they should fear *Els Artistes*. Once a mind is touched, action follows.

I had become enamored with the world of art through the same establishments I aimed to destroy. The ones that placed art only in churches for the lower classes to admire yet kept special pieces for themselves. Ambassadors, royals, generals, they lusted after me just as they lusted after their precious art. *Madama* Magdalena charged double when patrons wanted me to escort them to private gatherings. My mismatched eyes made me a novelty among the upper classes - fascinating to some, unholy to others who refused to meet my stare. I was fortunate that the Inquisition was past their hunt for witches by the time I was born.

Ambassador Prieto was the most generous of all my clients. Showing me each art piece he kept in his *casona*, explaining where they came from, who the artist was, and what each element of the piece was like.

"This one is from M-Moorish t-t-times," he would stutter nervously as he pushed his spectacles onto the bridge of his nose. "*Y esta*...more from the Renaissance....t-t-this is a special gift from my friend Marcello from Italy. It is by-by an artist known as BVR."

It was a small painting in comparison to the others around it. Its golden frame had flowers of different kinds carved around it. The eyes of the woman in the portrait were the same as mine. We looked very similar, except that where her hair was the color of honey, mine was dark as coal. Hers flowed freely. The painted woman's gaze held a feline intensity, growing more pronounced as one moved around the canvas.

"BVR," I repeated, still enthralled by the piece. "He did not want to be known?"

"She," he corrected me. "*She* was part of a clandestine group in the late 1400s known as *Casa dei Fiori*. This is a unique piece."

He trailed off while an idea formed in my mind.

A clandestine group. Born from art.

This could be just the thing to collapse the Inquisition once and for all.

Diego paced around the library with his arms crossed. Every so often, he paused to raise a finger and address me, but would stop himself, not finding the right words.

"¿*Estás loca*?" he asked. "You are the leader of this group, but these kinds of actions cannot be made on a whim to prove a point, Luciana!"

I stood firmly in my decision. Leaning back on the chaise, I would sleep in his library tonight before the carriage retrieved me on the morrow. "I apologize I did not consult you first, but we cannot look weak in front of the others."

He stopped pacing, placing his hands over his mouth and taking a deep breath. "Did you stop to think that if our lives are lost, *Els Artistes* will also perish?"

The truth was I had not. My decision was made on an

impulse to preserve the group, not the people who led it. Only now did I have the luxury to consider the ramifications.

Over the past three years, Diego had become my most trusted ally and friend, ever since he'd arrived at the brothel seeking news of his sister after the Inquisition apprehended her.

He'd stumbled into the brothel. Holding up crude sketches of her likeness to *Madama* Magdalena, asking if she had seen her. Maddened by spirits and desperation, he collapsed upon the polished wood floor, consumed by lamentations.

"If he stays, he pays," was all *Madama* Magdalena had said. She was not keen on having a man occupy one of her ladies if it did not make her any coin. Knowing the feeling of losing a loved one all too well, I hoisted him up, dragging him to my bedchamber. I knew I risked a beating, but I had been in his place not too long before. I gave *Madama* Magdalena my own coin, saying they were his, almost depleting my reserve.

I never touched a single hair on his body, allowing him to weep as he told me the story of a cardinal who had been obsessed with his sister Zoraida, taking her in the middle of the night. No one knew of her whereabouts from that day. We had turned our losses into our cause.

I diverted his worries. "Nothing will happen to us. Segovia is not where they are seeking us."

"Oh, and where are they seeking us, then?" Strands of his red hair poked wildly from his head, making him appear mad.

"Barcelona. He believes *Els Artistes* is there."

His interest piqued. "Did you retrieve information from Roca?"

"I did."

He stroked his chin. "You mean to say he does not think that you simply use him for information."

"He does not. Women, Diego, are the most underestimated

creatures on this holy earth, and perhaps right now that is our greatest power."

"How is that our greatest power? You are a lady of the night at one of the most prominent brothels in Madrid! How are you going to even get away from there long enough for us to make it to Segovia and back without *Madama* Magdalena being suspicious?"

My resolve wavered for a moment. My hasty decision had blinded me from considering the journey's time. But what was most important was for Diego to believe I had it under control.

"Do not worry yourself on how we will do that, Diego. It will be resolved. I have a patron in mind who could help us without *Madama* Magdalena putting up resistance."

He crossed his arms. "And what of this scripture book? Have you truly seen it?"

"Yes, of course I have. Prieto has been very generous with showing me his art. Which, now that we are on the subject of..."

He raised an eyebrow. "What?"

"There is a painter I want you to look into: BVR. She is from Moorish times, or at least it is what Prieto believes. He owns one of her paintings and told me she used to run a clandestine group in Florence. It haunts me like no other piece of art has. I don't know why I feel like it touches my soul."

His eyes glistened with this information. "Is that so?"

I stood from the chaise, walking over to him. "Yes. See, even before our existence, other people were risking their lives as we are for the love of art. Do you forgive me now? Can we move forward with the journey?"

He breathed deeply. "I have not yet forgiven you, Luciana. You have placed us both in grave danger. But there's nothing left to do now other than carry on."

51

MAJAS

Luciana

Segovia, Spain – 1808

This mission was my first time leaving Madrid.

Diego was correct in worrying about *Els Artistes* being exposed through me. And if we were found with propaganda against the church and state, we would be executed.

My very presence did endanger the mission even more so. If I ran into any of the men I had been with, and they recognized me, it would raise suspicions. What would a prostitute be doing outside the quarters of the city? Most of the women also relied on the brothel for lodgings—it was our home.

The farthest I had ever traveled was from my place of birth in La Latina to the brothel and the homes of the men I served. But for most of my life, opportunities were afforded to me because of my beauty. This mission was afforded to me by my wits and a bit of personal pride. I had volunteered us, not thinking of what it could cost, as Diego had pointed out. Not just my life, but Diego's and the identity of *Els Artistes.* Yet, this needed to be done. I could not ask others to take risks I wouldn't take myself. Disguised, I was safe enough. The real danger was our group fracturing at this critical moment, jeopardizing everything we'd built. And if Spain were truly invaded, it would either render us obsolete or make our resistance essential. I believed the latter.

The details of the mission came together flawlessly. A recurrent patron of the brothel who was also part of *Els Artistes* paid *Madama* Magdalena a hefty sum for my presence for four days. While she did not know of our existence, she owed him a favor, therefore, she could not refuse. He ensured my delivery to the wagon where Diego awaited me, then left. Traveling in this way diminished suspicions.

"We are husband and wife visiting your grandmother in Segovia. I have hidden the pamphlets within the hollows of these books." Diego paused for a moment, stretching his neck. His eyes scanned the front of the wagon, ensuring the rider could not hear us. "The scrolls Ambassador Prieto sent are hidden in the jars meant to be olives, the ones you are sitting on top of. You will deliver the pamphlets while I deliver the olive jars. Do you understand me? If at any moment we are caught, you run. You better than anyone understand that during this mission, our lives are more important than the delivery of these pieces. Do not throw our life away—or take unnecessary risks —for a piece of art. Your life is worth much more."

He was right, but he was also wrong. Art was life, emotion in raw form. Was that not worth the price of a life, to convey something that will live so much longer than we would? Even then, despite my belief, I was sweating beneath the tight wool robe the others managed to borrow from a seamstress in Madrid. I would never admit it, but I was petrified. In the brothel, I could control the outcomes. If a patron became violent or unruly, I knew exactly how to react. Outside, there were too many variables to consider. All of it was foreign to me. Diego could not know this, of course. He was ready to wrap the noose around me after I impulsively made this decision on his behalf.

"The benefit of having you along is that women are rarely stopped, rarely even looked at, unless you stand still for too long or do something out of the ordinary."

"Do not fuss over yourself, Diego," I said. "I know very well what being a woman feels like in our society. We are desired by men, just not seen by them."

He cocked his head. "I do not take your meaning."

"Men only look toward women when they wish to impose their desires on us; at all other times, we are ignored. They do not fuss over how we feel or what we believe in. Take *Els Artistes*, Pablo's own words on how I do not risk enough for us as our leader, yet this is all I do. Every day. Holding such a position during our time is nearly impossible. I am still not seen as the leading figure capable of moving this group forward, simply because I am a woman."

Diego frowned. "This is not true, Luciana. It is also not the time to discuss this. Focus on the plan now; we'll discuss this further later."

I opened my mouth to speak, but his sudden, intense focus shook me. The seriousness in his eyes was undeniable.

"When we arrive, I shall stay with the wagon to deliver the olives. You keep walking past the aqueduct to the meeting point beside the cathedral. It is one straight walk. Drop off the books after delivering the code word, and you shall be fine. Meet me at Aurora's Inn as soon as you have finished."

We arrived in Segovia in the afternoon. The air was crisp, the town silent in comparison to the bustle of the Gran Via.

We separated at the entrance of the aqueduct that the Romans had built centuries prior. For an instant, I was captivated by its simple architecture, how it towered over the town, creating doorways of light. I walked on through the cobblestone streets with a history that came before anything we knew today. Romans, Jews, Christians, and Moors all shared this place at some point before the Jews and the Moors were exiled. I forced myself not to get distracted by the scenery. My mission was first.

Initially, I was afraid I would miss the cathedral where I was to meet the other members, but it was impossible. I walked up to the plaza, and its grandeur robbed me of my breath. A patrol of royal guards marched past, their eyes sweeping the crowds with chilling indifference. I pulled the thin wool shawl tighter around my head, hunching my shoulders. My heart pulsed in my ears as I crossed the plaza, avoiding contact with others who paraded with their families.

Living within the walls of a brothel secludes you from the outside world. It is a prison without iron bars. Every face I saw could be a potential informer, my contact. How would I recognize them?

Stick to the plan, Luci. As I passed the cathedral's entrance, someone whispered my code name. "Fernanda."

Two young men sat on a bench overlooking the cemetery beside the church. One of them leaned forward, wiping sweat from his brow with the back of his hand. His gaze fixed on me. The other leaned back, eyes on the mountains in the distance. I took a seat on the bench next to them.

"*Código.*"

"Francisco Goya. Yours?"

"*Majas.*"

I placed the books beside me, wrapped in a gray cloth. My fingers dipped into the wrappings, brushing the rough binding, confirming they were there. I leaned forward, pretending to adjust the heavy wool of my skirt, and stood, leaving them on the bench between us.

My retreat felt agonizingly slow. I could feel the weight of their eyes on my back. Bracing for the potential sound of alarm, a guard's hand on my arm. The borrowed boots felt like bricks on my feet. I walked, slow and deliberate, until I disappeared into the crowd. When I looked back, they were gone.

52

OMNIA VINCIT AMOR

Luciana

Segovia, Spain – 1808

Diego was already at the inn when I walked in. He sat in front of a steaming bowl of *judiones*. I was startled when he stood and walked up to me, kissing my cheek tenderly.

"*Esposa, ¿qué tal la abuela*?" he said joyfully, the pretense already in play.

I smiled, noting the keen, observant look of a woman behind the kitchen counter. "*Muy bien.* She sends her regards and hopes next time we will spend more time with her."

The woman, whom I suspected to be Aurora, walked over with a plate of *judiones* for me, setting them on the table next to Diego. He still held my hand as I sat down to eat, his thumb tracing a small, gentle circle on my skin. His behavior was a stark, bewildering contrast to this morning, when he could barely look at me.

I knew we were simply acting out the roles of husband and wife for the mission, yet the effortless tenderness of his touch provided me with a deep, unexpected warmth within. Something new and unfamiliar. I shook it away. *Focus*.

"Were you able to deliver the olives to the merchant?" I inquired, pulling my mind back to the mission. "Will they be useful for making oil?"

"Yes, yes. He has promised to send a bottle for us back in *el pueblo* and that he will happily purchase more olives if these prove satisfactory."

I sipped on the delicious, warm broth. "Mmm, that's marvelous, *querido*." The endearment slipped out easily, naturally, and I was grateful for the steam that hid the sudden rise of color in my cheeks.

The night went on under the ruse that we were married. We were given lodgings with just one bed. I was used to sharing my bed with other men, but it was profoundly different with Diego. He walked back into the bedchamber, taking off his mask of husband and pulling out a piece of parchment from his satchel. He began speaking, the sudden shift in his demeanor snatching me from my spell.

"Tomorrow, Luciana, we have to remain in town to negotiate a route for upcoming deliveries. Toledo and Segovia are the cities closest to us from Madrid, and we require allies. I understand Ambassador Prieto has a home here, no?"

"Yes, he does. He has spoken of it previously, but—"

"When we return to Madrid, it is important we reinforce that connection. What are your thoughts on this?"

My stomach tightened. "Sure, we could consider tapping into that connection further. Perhaps it is time that we push past our current priorities and onto a greater purpose for *Els Artistes*."

The flames from the fireplace reflected on his spectacles, flickering. We had been successful, but this notion of a greater purpose would require me to return to my life at the brothel to extract information from the ambassador and others in the same way as before. Give a bird a taste of liberty, and they will never want to return to their cage.

"What is the matter?" Diego asked, his tone softening with concern.

"*Nada*. It is nothing. I had not left Madrid before today, did you know?"

He closed his book, his face softening as he realized the true significance of the day for me. "I did not. You have never told me much about your life before the brothel. I only know you were born in La Latina to a printer."

"When I was younger and my father was still alive, I used to pester him about taking me to the ocean. The closest I had ever been to a body of water was the Manzanares."

We both chuckled softly at the pathetic nature of the comparison. The Manzanares was just a sliver of water that was nearly dry. In the gentle light of the fireplace, the harsh edges of our real life were softened. He moved closer to me, his voice a low, intimate murmur.

"Luci, you did very well today. I must admit I was nervous when you volunteered us for this task. Do not misunderstand me, I believe you are an incredible woman; this movement was started from your brilliance. But I did not expect today to go as smoothly as it did."

He leaned forward, his lips briefly brushing against my cheek, mirroring his earlier "husbandly" kiss, but this time it was purely him. My breath caught. I did not pull away. He did not move any closer, yet the silence between us stretched taut with unspoken feelings.

"We make a good team, Diego," I whispered, realizing the depth of my reliance on him, not just as a colleague, but as a sanctuary. "Your planning made it easy. The detailed instructions you gave me on our journey here, how you knew the precise timing of it all. Even the code words. Without your foresight, that half of the burden wasn't nearly as heavy as it could have been."

His eyes, usually shielded by his intellect, were utterly exposing his soul now. He gazed at me with a tenderness that stole my purpose, my resolve, and my very breath. I did not only feel desired - I felt seen.

"You are the one who makes everything possible. And...I want to make things possible for you too," he said, his voice husky.

He gently removed the spectacles from his face, placing them on the bedside table. Without the lenses, his eyes seemed larger, more honest. Our eyes locked as he leaned in. I did not —could not—move. His lips brushed against mine, a delicate, exploratory press that asked a question rather than demanding pleasure from me. It was nothing like the brusque, transactional ones I was used to. His was a slow, beautiful confirmation of the warmth that had been building between us all day—or perhaps—over the last two years.

When he finally pulled back, he rested his forehead against mine.

"I do not wish to make you uncomfortable. I only just realized I have been in love with you for a very long time," he confessed, his voice trembling. "I never thought I would confirm it like this. I had kept those feelings at bay."

I leaned back, away from him, my heart thudding in my chest, my stomach turning as his words sunk in. I could not allow myself to imagine a world where our love could blossom. At least, not at the moment.

"Diego, w—"

He took my hand in his, pulling me closer again. "Do you not feel the same way about me?"

I closed my eyes, feeling the warmth of his touch on my palm rise to my chest. "No, *no es eso.* I have not been physical with someone I care deeply for before. You know of your importance to me."

"I do not lust after your body. It is your heart I seek refuge in," he said.

Tears welled in my eyes and began cascading down my cheek. He wiped them away, pulling me into his chest. For that moment, I felt at peace.

Tomorrow, we could return to our mission. Tonight, there was only us.

53

ET NOS CEDAMUS AMORI

Luciana

Madrid, Spain – 1808

We returned victorious to Madrid, showing the rest of the group we were capable of not only leading *Els Artistes* but delivering the scripture and our own literature with ease to neighboring towns. Now, no one questioned our authority.

Diego had come to the brothel several days in a row, knowing I had to resume my duties as a courtesan, something neither of us could ignore given our realization of the love we held for each other in Segovia. On occasion, the feeling of caring for someone was overwhelming. The act of care was not a burden, but the potential for pain that came with it was. I considered letting him go. I would tell him I was enchanted by our passion, but did not truly love him. However, he had known me long enough to see through that pretense.

"I do not care what we must do; all I care about is that we

find a way to be together, even if it is for short periods of time outside here," he said.

I paced around my room. "How? How would we convince *Madama* Magdalena of my leaving for days at a time once more?"

"There is something I wish to discuss with you. It regards another mission for *Els Artistes* that could grant you—us—another opportunity. This would be a challenging one, though, Roca's platoon being considered."

I leaned in, intrigued. "What would that be?"

"Word has come that a piece Ambassador Prieto holds in his *casona* will need to be moved to France. He reached out to Renato directly while we were away and I met with him yesterday. It is a rare portrait by that Moorish painter from the Renaissance you mentioned to me."

"Wait. Is this a piece by BVR?" I said.

"Yes, it is."

Joy pulsed through me. "Is it the piece we had discussed? Or another?"

"Yes, the one we spoke of."

"Beatriz Velázquez de Rossi, that is her name. That is what BVR stands for."

I stood in awe of this information. Ambassador Prieto had told me there was not enough known about her, but Diego had done as I requested and found out. I couldn't explain it, but I knew preserving her work mattered as much to me as defying the Inquisition itself.

"Where did you learn this?" I asked.

"One of our contacts at *Els Artistes*. He was the person who gifted it to the ambassador. Prieto also provided me with a list that the Inquisition has created—the artists they are targeting. She is among them. They want to burn it, due to the fact that Velázquez was not only a woman, but a Moor."

Diego continued laying out the plan. Once there, the mission was simple. The portrait would be separated from its frame and rolled into a carpet. We would deliver the carpet to Portbou, where it would be mounted on a ship to Marseille. There, one of our cells would collect it and take it to a safe house for remounting. Once restored, they'd deliver it to our contact's workshop, where the ambassador's people could retrieve it.

The ambassador would pay a hefty sum for the smuggling, including a substantial amount to *Madama* Magdalena for my services for an entire month.

“This could be our chance to get you out of the brothel. We could run *Els Artistes* from Barcelona.”

“What of your life here?” I asked.

“I have long considered closing the *librería*, moving it elsewhere.” He moved toward me. "Napoleon's army has already moved in to support the invasion of Portugal, but there is word that the French army is going to take over Spain. Rumors are saying they are going to invade Madrid first. It will be best for us to be far from the chaos of it all.”

“Where would we go?” I said.

“There is a contact of mine who could give us lodging once we are finished. We could finalize the plan then. Think about it. Both plans.”

After tasting the bit of freedom the last mission awarded me, I had slowly come to learn something of myself. Art was a way for me to see the world beyond my cage.

As far as the painting...

I remembered seeing it at the ambassador’s home all those years ago, being captivated by the freedom that woman exuded in the painting, one of her breasts exposed while the other was covered by a robe. She was stepping out of a bathtub in a seemingly rural home. She also deserved to be in a place where she was worshiped, not destroyed.

"Diego, yes. We *must* do this. Deliver this painting."

His eyes gleamed. "You know what else is in Portbou?"

"What?"

"The sea."

54

THE PRINTER'S DAUGHTER

Luciana

Madrid, Spain – 1808

I filled my trunk with the few possessions I owned. Gowns that were gifted to me by prominent visitors. A bit of coin I had earned that could allot me safety if necessary. A locket that had been my mother's before she passed. My father's last letter to me from jail.

Before *Madama* Magdalena found me, I was the printer's daughter. It was a title I carried proudly throughout my childhood, watching my father work his printing press. He taught me how to set the letters and how to read. He also taught me how to read between the lines and the secrets people exchanged within stories. We lived in small lodgings above the printing shop, and everyone knew him. He would come up for *a siesta,* and we would laugh while making plans to visit the sea.

All of that went away when my mother died.

The disease took her slowly, consuming most of my childhood with it. It began with a sharp pain in her back, then her chest. By the time death came, she could not walk or talk. I often wondered if her soul had left long before her body gave out.

Upon turning fifteen, the Inquisition took my father in the middle of the night. He was printing pamphlets secretly, books that were considered "immoral." He sent letters from jail, urging me to stay inside the home and not step out. He warned me about the dangers that lurked outside the safety of our walls. Eventually, the Inquisition took that too. They left me on the streets to fend for myself without a single coin. I searched for work, telling others I would do anything to make ends meet. Mend their clothes, clean their floors, cook their meals. But their wives were afraid of me.

I knew from early on that my appearance was different from others. My breasts were big, my hips wide. I came from a working-class family, but I did not possess working-class features. My teeth were not chipped or rotted, and I did not have children, my body untarnished by the perils of lost nutrition.

When *Madama* Magdalena found me, she found a pot of gold.

"The things we could achieve with this face." She held my chin between her stubby hands. "You have good curves. My clients would love ye."

I was starving, searching through the trash for scraps. "I will give you a life you have never had, *hija*. You will be surrounded by money, men, and power. First, you will learn from the other girls, then you will have your trials."

The early days were the worst I endured. The harshness of the touch, the feeling of being powerless underneath the fury of men. Feeling used. When you first start at the brothel, you get the slim pickings. It all changed when Roca took a liking to me; then all the other generals and ambassadors wanted me.

They were no longer put off by my eyes—they were enticed by them.

"It is as if you are with two women at once," one said after leaving the room one night.

Madama Magdalena had given me special privileges for the clients that word of mouth brought in. I had found power in my position. If I could not change my fate, I would find ways to become useful to society outside male pleasure. My lot in life had been the Inquisition's fault. They had taken everything from me. I knew one day I would take it all back.

After tasting life beyond the confines of the brothel, the time had come for this all to end.

I understood now that *Madama* Magdalena had known no other life, and had built one for herself on the exploitation of others. All of us, in some way, exploited others to achieve what we wanted. I exchanged pleasure for secrets and coins. I exchanged my knowledge to help topple a system that no longer worked, within a society I did not wish to be a part of. Not in this way.

I would never stop fighting until I saw the last cardinal stripped of their robes. But it would not be from here. Not from this reality. Starting tomorrow, my life would change. It would stand on the strength I discovered, the power I learned to harness, and with luck, love.

55

PORTBOU

Luciana

Portbou, Spain – 1808

It took us a fortnight to reach Portbou by carriage, stopping only for rest and sleep. The scenery of the Spanish terrain was impressive, changing each day. Leaving Madrid's imposing mountains, crossing through desert canyons with plains in hues of reds and oranges. Arriving in Catalonia, the air changed. Diego told me the heaviness I sensed in the air was the salt from the sea.

I saw the sea for the first time as the carriage trailed along the coast and through the mountains. I imagined it tasted of tears—salt and sorrow—as the dream I had always shared with *Papá* returned to my mind.

"*¡Mirad! ¡Mirad!*" I tugged at his shirt each time the ocean came into view.

"You will have more opportunities to see the sea," Diego said, his voice measured. "You can come at any time you want.

Provided, of course, that we see this venture through to its conclusion."

I felt a sudden chill. A fear that settled deep in my stomach.

"Let us go over the plans for the delivery of BVR's painting," I said, my voice hardening. "The information the ambassador relayed the last time I saw him was that his contact would collect the piece in Marseille."

"We will arrive at Portbou shortly, delivering the goods in the evening. The vessel that is to convey the carpet across the Mediterranean to the port in Marseille is not available until then. They must ensure we are not seen. I have brought other garments for you to dress as a man come morning. I have been thinking of General Roca as we traveled. Where did he say his platoon would be stationed?"

"In Barcelona." I had not seen him since our last encounter at the brothel. With Napoleon's army impending, and Roca's platoon focused upon chasing the crumbs we had left for him in Barcelona, it was likely he was occupied with military matters.

"Good. Then he should not be of our concern," he furrowed his brow slightly, pausing before looking over at me. "Say, did you ever take a fancy to any of your patrons?" Diego asked.

"No," I said without the slightest hesitation. "The only one I felt I could trust was Ambassador Prieto. And that is because his interest in me was for company, not intimacy."

Diego raised his eyebrows. "Is that so?"

"Why do you appear so dumbfounded? He has been an agent of aid to *Els Artistes,* trusts me. Trusts you." My tone was verging on anger.

He put his hands up. "I understand. I just thought everyone who paid for a..."

"Paid for a woman of the night? Thank you for the blunt reminder, Diego. I was under the impression you regarded me in a different light. Your questions demonstrate a possessiveness. Now tell me, what is the real pretense of your bringing me along on this mission? What rest will there be for *me*?"

He looked confounded by my sudden interrogation. "Why, the rest is your freedom. A life away from the—"

"A life away from the brothel is only the beginning," I said abruptly. "Let me remind you that my role here is to deliver the painting and use the connections I secured with *my* body and wit to ensure its safe passage. I did not come all this way for my freedom to be defined as your mistress. I came for the freedom of being my own woman. I will not trade one gilded cage for another. Is that understood?"

He stared at me for a long, anxious moment, knowing my resolve was absolute. I could tell, he too had been wounded by my choice of words, but I would not retreat them.

"I apologize. I do not see you in that manner at all. You have my word."

I turned to face the window. "Good. Then let us keep our eyes fixed upon our plan."

56

THE FRENCH

Luciana

Portbou, Spain – 1808

We trod in unbroken silence through the harbor's sprawl at nightfall, the tightly rolled carpet girt upon our shoulders. This mission required every measure of concentration from all engaged, for the dockside was a place of notorious ill-repute. A truth doubled for any woman, although disguised as a young sailor, I felt shielded against the worst perils.

In the distance, I spied the wretched assemblage of prostitutes clustering around the vessels, beseeching a patron. A cold, clammy shiver ran down my back, conjuring the indignities and brutalities they must endure in a place such as this, where men debarked from the port. These patrons were not of high rankings; they were mostly unlettered sailors. Diego forewarned me that many were former prisoners.

We were almost upon the dock where our vessel awaited us when a high, piercing whistle sliced the thick air.

"*¡Alto ahí!*" I squeezed my eyes shut, uttering a silent prayer that it was not meant for us.

Diego quickened his stride, whispering to me, "Anon, we are near, hold the pace."

"*¡Dije alto!*" A soldier galloped toward us on horseback, cutting off our access to the port. We froze.

"Forgive us, *señor*, we couldn't quite hear you." Diego said in a friendly yet reassuring tone, pretending to be of a simple background. "What seems to be the trouble?"

The officer's eyes, hard and suspicious, conducted a thorough inspection of us. I buried my face behind the rolled carpet.

"What burden is this you are carrying?" He remained on horseback.

"We are delivering a carpet, sir, to a vessel nearby that will transport it upon the tide. I hold the documents of purchase with me, should you require review."

The officer gave a dismissive wave. "No need. The port is shuttered. The nation is gravely compromised as Napoleon's army has seized Madrid. Other platoons are anticipated to cross the border this very night. Portbou will not be directly affected, yet we are braced for it all. The sea is a treacherous mistress giving way to land."

A paralyzing dread seized my throat and heart, turning my blood to glacial brine. The carpet, our means of passing this precious secret, suddenly felt like a coffin of lead upon my shoulder. My breath caught in a gasping rattle as the full, awful truth of his words struck home: we were trapped. Madrid was compromised, as was our safety.

"Oh—is there no other means of reaching the vessels? Perhaps on the morrow?" Diego's voice cracked, echoing my own fears.

The officer's face grew dark. "You must take leave of Portbou at once. Seek shelter and *do not* stir from your homes.

After this evening, Spain will no longer be the country you have known."

57

LA ENCRUCIJADA

Luciana

Portbou, Spain – 1808

We sought shelter to no avail. Each home in Portbou shuttered by its citizens as they prepared for the impending war. We took refuge in an abandoned barn, hiding the rolled carpet as we devised a new plan for escape. It was not just the painting that needed to make it to France. We required shelter as well.

I imagined the turmoil in Madrid, Napoleon's army leaving no soul untouched. The pain of knowing the city I was born in was overtaken sunk me, yet a ray of hope was born within me. Would the French accept the Inquisition? Was there a possibility they would take down the church?

My father had taught me about Napoleon's reign, the secularism that rose with his power in France. I was not for the death of my people or the loss of our Spanish identity, but if this meant the Inquisition could be toppled, a part of me wished this would be the only result of the war. Suddenly, a thought came to me: France could be our answer.

"Diego, what if we make our way to the French border ourselves?"

He considered my proposition. "Do you mean taking the carpet to the border and crossing along with it?"

"Yes." I searched for the map he had brought along with us. The moonlight provided just enough light to illuminate what we required. "We are not far. With the town asleep, we could manage to steal horses and arrive at the border by dawn."

"What of the army? There must be more of these soldiers around, Luciana."

"What do you suggest we do, then? They will find us come morning if we stay here."

Diego shook his head; he was far beyond his academic knowledge. "What if we attempt returning to the port, to the vessel that should have taken the carpet? Perhaps they will know a way."

Something deep within me told me no, but in the desperation of the moment, I agreed to accompany him. We tiptoed out of the barn, leaving the carpet rolled behind the hay. I took off my hat to release its pressure from my head, exposing my locks to the night.

The streets were so empty that the town felt abandoned. Every shutter closed.

"This way." Diego pointed to a side of the dock we hadn't crossed previously. "This is it."

We turned onto the street when I felt a familiar hand on my shoulder. Then, his voice. "Where do you think you are going, Luciana?"

I turned to find General Roca towering over me.

58

BOOTS ON THE GROUND

Luciana

Portbou, Spain – 1808

"DIEGO!
RUN!"

I slithered from Roca's brutal grasp with the desperate fluidity of a serpent. My only thought was the dire necessity of hiding myself. I ran aimlessly, seeking shelter, my lungs burning through my body. The overwhelming blackness of the night I once held as my ally now betrayed me.

In the chaos of my flight, I lost all sight of Diego. At first, I had heard his boots retreating from where we were, stomping against the ground. The only sound that traveled through the night now were my shallow breaths. I scrambled past several barns, my fingers scraped against the rough, splintered wood and latches, attempting to pry open each door to no avail. They were sealed tight with the warning of the French encroaching upon Spain.

Roca's shouts were immediate behind me, cutting through

the silence with a baying sound that chilled me to the marrow. He was upon me, near enough for me to hear the clatter of his sword against his uniform. The smell of his furious sweat reached me, returning me to the memories of his violent touch back at the brothel. I could not allow him to inflict that kind of pain on me again, let alone destroy my purpose.

I rounded the harbor, pausing for a moment to inspect my options. The slick stone of the quay appeared underneath my feet, not a vessel in sight. My only hope of escape was to plunge in the water.

The smell of saltwater and muck reminded me that I had to decide quickly.

Piensa, Luciana. *Piensa.*

Then came the chilling realization that I could not swim. My fate lay in the unknown depths of the water or with Roca. And in that crippling moment of doubt, he caught me.

The crushing force of his body slammed into me, seizing the breath from my chest with a thud as I fell against a rock. I felt the warmth of fresh blood dripping from my forehead, but I could not reach it with my hand to wipe it away.

"*Te tengo*, Luciana. Let us see your pretty face again, covered in blood," he cackled, then his face turned serious. "What are you doing outside so far from *El Jardín?* Surely, she does not know you are here..." His voice trailed as realization crossed his face. Roca was a brute, but no fool. He wrapped his hand around my neck. "I hope you are not here for the reason I think you are..." he breathed into my face. "I made myself clear. Our secrets were meant to be kept between us."

59

ART OR LIFE

Luciana

Portbou, Spain – 1808

The screaming outside my cell awoke me from my forced slumber. Following came the shots and dull tramp of boots as a person was executed. The pain emanating from my forehead served as a throbbing reminder of my capture. *No, no, no, no, Dios, no.*

I could discern the nearness of a window, just not its precise location. It was not until I attempted to shift my body that I realized I was fettered to the wall. *Roca.*

"*¡SOCORRO!*" My cries were drowned in the tumult of the outer world. He had shackled me so firmly I could scarcely reach my face.

"*Nadie le escucha,*" a raspy voice coming from a man declared. The darkness was so profound I could not tell if we were in the same cell. I stirred in panic, causing myself more pain. "*¡Eh, eh, no! Es peor*. I assure ye. Hold yer peace or the rats will come for ye. They have a taste for blood, the rats."

"How do you know I am bleeding?"

"Every soul dragged in here by the soldiers comes in bleeding. They are not known for being the kind or gentle lot, I assure ye."

In this, he spoke the truth. Roca was a particular brute of a man; I was surprised he did not hurt me further.

A few hours passed, the clamor outside subsiding, when the door to the holding cells was thrust open. Three thuds followed, then a candle-lit lantern that came pointed directly at me.

"Luci." Roca smiled eerily. "We meet again."

I drew in a breath, spitting at his face. "Why am I confined, general?!"

He wiped the spit away, casting his gaze to one side. "That, my dear, I know not. You are about to inform me."

I whimpered. I had to maintain my composure for the sake of my own safety. I needed to protect myself.

"There is nothing to tell. I am here on business for *Madama* Magdalena. I am attending a patron."

"Then why did you flee? You know me far too well."

"I did not recognize you at first, I took you for another...I feared you were a French soldier. I believed you to be in Barcelona."

"Pah! A French soldier? You hold me in utter derision!" He inched his face closer. "You look far less pretty with blood on your face than you do in your brothel rouge. Now tell me, who sent you to this place? Are you an informant?"

"No."

His eyes turned savage as he slammed his hand against the wall beside my head. I winced. "Do. Not. Offer. Me. A. Lie. Luciana. Who was the man you were with?"

"I know not."

"Why are you here?"

"I know not."

"Very well. Have it your stubborn way, whore."

The soldiers dragged me down a narrow stairwell to a cold cobblestone floor. The room was lit by a single, guttering oil lamp. Roca was lighting a fire in the stone fireplace. I could smell the iron and rust of caked blood on the floor. In the middle of the room, a heavy wooden block surrounded by chains and rusted metal tools threatened me with its force. I had heard of this tool before. The Garrucha. It was used by the Inquisition to torture their prisoners. One swift pull and your shoulder would be dislocated.

"Do you not have better things to tend to, Roca, than torturing a poor woman of the night?" I spat.

"I always have time for you, Luci, you know this," he said with a cold, thin smile. "You have a choice. You may rest here until the rest of the town is ransacked and the soldiers have moved on toward Madrid, or we may begin with the methods. I am aware your tongue is stubborn, but believe me, the joints are not. I am well acquainted with every corner of your body."

I confirmed what I knew from the first time I lay with him: physical pain was the only form Roca knew how to achieve what he wanted.

"*Vete al diablo*, Roca."

He laughed. "A spirited answer. Would not have expected less from you. Let us have a bit of fun before we break you. Emmanuel, would you do the honors of bringing the young lady to me?"

The soldier seized me roughly, binding my arms behind my back with a coarse rope, then threading it through the pulley on the ceiling ring.

"I only ask for one name, Luciana, of the person you are

working with." He stepped close enough for me to smell his breath. "Who do you spy for?"

I clenched my teeth, shaking my head. "I do not spy for anyone. I am a free woman."

"Are you now?" He gestured toward Emmanuel, who gripped the winch handle.

A searing pain shot through my arms as I was lifted a foot off the ground.

"A mere taste of what is to come," Roca said, watching me struggle. "Your arms will begin to give way shortly."

I gasped, unable to scream as the pain compressed my chest.

"The name. You can either choose to save yourself or choose to die." He paced around me, but all I could muster was a sharp cry. "Drop her, Emmanuel."

The short release sent my body plummeting through the air, a loud crack muffling all sound around me.

"This is only the beginning. We can continue with other methods if you're enjoying this too much," he said. "Save what's left of your beauty, my dear, you will need it for when you return to the brothel."

Rage flared through me as I found my voice through the pain. "I—will n-n-ever return to the brothel. After tonight. After I escape this hell, you will never see me again!"

Next came the irons, which he clamped on my feet. Then his fists. The blows had the pleasure of leading me towards pools of unconsciousness. When he began to undress, I fought to stay awake. This, I would not allow.

"No!" I groaned. "No."

He paused, surprised that I would refuse now what I'd sold for years. Lying there broken and bloodied, death so close I could taste it, the truth became clear: I had survived by giving myself away. Not anymore. I had wielded pleasure as power. I would not let him make it my prison.

But what had it all been for?

The French had arrived. Their army would ravage through Spain, taking with it the church and the monarchy with a new wave of violence.

Diego was gone. Our bond as allies and lovers was an illusion of a destiny that was not meant for us. But it did show me the power *to* love existed within me.

Everything I had fought for, the freedom for artists to express themselves—for Beatriz, and those women like her—would eventually succeed, with or without me. Did I want Roca to decide whether I lived or died? Was he the last face I would see?

Life or art. Art or life.

Life.

Art.

But weren't they the same? Wasn't Beatriz sharing pieces of herself through her painting? Pieces of her soul that would outlive her body by centuries. Art was the only immortality we had.

My mind turned back to the carpet left rolled behind the hay. If Diego couldn't return for it, what would happen to the painting? They had tried to silence Beatriz during her time so she would be forgotten, but she wasn't.

I would not allow Roca to force me to choose between life or art. All this time, I attempted to topple the Inquisition for the sake of the freedom of others, I had bargained with my own. But even now, what I could bargain for could gain me more than just my life back at the brothel. It could allow me to even continue this fight. Allow me to save BVR's legacy. Give a bird a taste of liberty, and they will never want to return to their cage.

"I will tell you the name," I said weakly. "With one condition."

He drew his pants up. "What condition is that?"

"You will not ravish me. Not now, not ever. You will take me to the border with France, to a hospital. I will tell you when we arrive. The locations. The informants. Where to find what you require. I will tell you everything. And you will disappear from my life."

I had been willing to die for art before; now I was willing to *live* for it. Isn't that what art inspires-raw emotion, unadulterated life? Diego had been right, however. It was not worth dying for.

Roca looked at Emmanuel, considering this truce. My heart raced, hoping the bargain would suffice.

"Wrap her in the potato sacks and throw her into the wagon. I will see to the rest."

60

THE ART OF LIVING

Mar

Madrid, Spain – 2024

"Bring me back! Bring me back!" I screamed.

Almaguer's voice was distant. "Mar, we haven't resolved what happened in this lifetime. Move to the next important event and I'll bring you out."

I resisted. "No! No! Pull me out now! I am being tortured, please!"

"Move to the next part of this life, you are very close..." Almaguer urged.

Remembering the rules of hypnosis she told me during our first meeting, I opened my eyes and returned to the room.

I lay in a pool of cold sweat on the couch in Almaguer's office, frozen in place. All I could feel was radiating pain shooting from my feet to my head in waves. I closed my eyes again.

"Mar, are you alright?" Almaguer said, her tone alarmed.

My mouth was too dry to answer. I tried to lift my arms to

push the imaginary restraints away, but they felt impossibly heavy. My muscles seized up, mimicking the agonizing breaking of bones I had lived through in a past life.

She stood from her chair and walked over to me, noticing I was shivering. She covered me with the wool blanket and sat at the edge of the couch.

"Try to close your eyes and take three deep breaths, Mar. Pulling away from a past life regression can be harsh on your body and your psyche. But you're safe now. You're back. You're here in my office. Look at me when you are ready."

I followed her advice, my body relaxing as I opened my eyes again and stared at the ceiling.

"I—I was a prostitute," I stammered. "They tortured me because I was smuggling art pieces. I was strong, though, mentally. But it was so...painful. It was a different pain than the other one, with Beatriz. This was *physical* in every sense. The pain felt so real."

I dragged my eyes toward Almaguer, still sitting on the corner of the couch. "What else did you feel in this life?"

"She had a confidence in her...she knew how to use her body to get what she wanted."

"Sex, you mean?" Almaguer said.

"Yes. She was using it as a tool. She didn't *allow* herself to be a victim of her circumstance," I said.

Almaguer stood, walking toward her chair and sitting once more. "That's an interesting statement. Do you see how this theme reflects in this life?"

"Yes. The detachment. That pattern to completely remove myself emotionally from men and go straight for sex. To the physical. But what does this mean? I ended the session before we could know how her life ended."

"We're here now. Everything happens for a reason. Perhaps your soul didn't want to, or didn't need to know what happened next. You got everything you needed to move forward in *this* life."

"And that is?"

"Your experience with past life regression is curious, Mar, because for most people, they don't remember a thing or have these reflections outside the brief moments when they return. Yet, you almost relive them completely. They are very present in your unconscious. I don't know what the way forward is for you. That's up to *you* to decide. Now that you know the root of your pattern, it's up to you whether you want to continue in that direction or not."

Dario came to mind, our kiss. The absence of anything more physical might have made space for something more.

"I think I know what I'm going to do."

61

FIRENZE

Mar

Florence, Italy – 2024

In 1817, French author Marie-Henri Beyle visited Florence and fell in love. Not with a man or woman, but with a city so beautiful it involved him in an array of emotional responses. Fainting, confusion, a racing heartbeat. He considered he was dying, but no, it was just his body reacting to the immense beauty of the art and architecture of the Tuscan city. Years later, the term "Stendhal" or "Florence" Syndrome became well known as contemporaries flocked to the city and were absorbed by its sublime beauty.

In 2024, I was falling under the same spell.

Dario and I sat on the steps of Santa Maria del Fiore, eating focaccias to the sound of bells marking the time. Dario sipped his *limonata rossa* as he shared the itinerary of our first day around the city.

"I've dug up some stuff about BVR, and I think today we can visit the places where she grew up. The palazzo is close to here, actually. There was also the studio of Sandro Botticelli, where she completed her first work, and well, I believe she started the portrait you told me about in your email there."

I swallowed a piece of sun-dried tomato, nodding in agreement with everything he said. In the midday light, the buildings glowed in rich ochre and faded ambers. The Duomo's round outline stood out against a cloudless blue sky. I'd never been to Florence before, but I still felt incredibly connected to it. I knew what the city was like when Beatriz walked through it, when it was at its prime during the Renaissance. Florence now had a special place in the story of my soul. Dario's company wasn't a bad addition either.

"Would she have spoken Italian back then?" I asked, taking another bite. "How would she have even met Sandro Botticelli?"

"It was at a party, or at least that's what she wrote in her journals later in life," he started. In the two weeks since he'd returned to Florence and I had come, he had met with Giulia and gathered information about BVR. She had lent some of the diaries to Dario for research. He also found out through his mother that his uncle had worked on an exhibit by the same painter in New York back in the 80s.

"And no, she wouldn't have spoken the Italian we know today. Probably Tuscan Italian, which later became the base of the current Italian. She spoke Spanish perfectly, probably a little Latin since she was well studied."

"It's insane to me that a woman of that time has this kind of history and no one has shared it before. I know so little of her. Why isn't she being studied in art schools?"

He pushed his eyebrows together. "*Certo*, but as you'll learn when I show you a bit of her background and go through the documents I've put together, she was a very important part of the art in some of the smaller towns around Tuscany and Emilia Romagna, even if her identity was kept secret. Dozza, that town you mentioned back in Madrid, is where she lived."

We finished our focaccias, taking advantage of the low number of tourists to enter Santa Maria del Fiore, where the tour began. The cathedral's imposing scale was just as impressive on the inside as it was outside. Soft lighting illuminated the vast but spare interior, a stark contrast to the elaborate exterior. Then, on Brunelleschi's dome, Vasari and Zuccari's *Last Judgment* swirled above us. I gasped, imagining the intense work it must have taken for them to finish this, especially such a long time ago.

"How are you going to top this?" I joked with Dario.

He looked down at me from his towering stature. "Oh, Mar, just wait until you see the rest. This is only the *aperitivo*."

We stepped out of the cathedral onto the sunlight spilling into the piazza in long, golden brushstrokes. Putting his sunglasses on, he tucked his hands in his pockets, guiding me along Via dei Calzaiuoli toward Piazza della Signoria. We stood underneath the Loggia in the presence of Perseus holding up Medusa's head, the Sabines contorting toward the sky, and of course, Michelangelo's David standing watch.

"*Allora*, just down this corridor over there, you see that palazzo all the way at the end of the street?" he asked. "That is where Beatriz lived with her family when they first moved to Florence. This *piazza* wasn't this way when she was alive. Most of these artists weren't even born. Michelangelo was just a child during that time. Her father, working for the Medici court, needed to be close to them, and they were given this home."

I recalled the scenery from my visit to that past life, feeling the *déjà vu* in my bones. Even if it had been 500 years, the soul remembered.

He pulled me toward the other side of the plaza, leading down another street where another palazzo now turned into a hotel was tucked in a corner. "And here is where she lived later on, when she married Niccolo de Rossi."

Niccolo de Rossi. His name gave me chills.

The tour continued, crossing the Arno on the Ponte Vecchio. The water shimmered beneath streaks formed by ducks and kayak riders in the quiet bustle. Buskers, street painters, and musicians lined the river as we crossed and the city softened. The towering buildings were replaced by old, pale houses covered with climbing ivy, leading us to a hill.

"We're climbing now?" I asked.

He led the way, "Yes, this has nothing to do with Beatriz, but it's a good place for us to stop...maybe get to know each other better."

The path climbed gently, then steepened. Cypress trees marked the way, casting their long shadows on the cobblestone. We climbed quietly, our footsteps marking the tempo. By the time we reached Piazzale Michelangelo, the light had changed. Florence glowed in a golden mantle straight out of a film. At that moment, I knew how Stendhal felt. The out-of-body experience, the cosmic grandeur of a city that was built to be worshiped.

"*Bellissima, no*?" Dario smiled widely. I hadn't noticed we stood at the railing, shoulder to shoulder. The warm breeze caressed my curls, and in the distance, church bells tolled again. In all the beauty, my body still couldn't shake away the touch of his shoulder on mine. I realized then, he was looking at me.

"Now that we are both here in Florence, I am having that feeling you had before...the first day we met. Like we have known each other for much longer." His words echoed in the wind.

I looked up at him, catching my reflection in the pupils of his dark eyes.

"If only you believed in soul mates."

62

GALLERIA DEGLI UFFIZI

Mar

Florence, Italy – 2024

We woke up early, focusing on the task at hand: finding out what led BVR to move to Cuba. And who her inspiration was for painting that portrait that looked exactly like me. I tiptoed toward the kitchen, where Dario was already pressing coffee into a moka pot.

"*Buongiorno*. Coffee?" He flashed his boyish smile.

"Yes. Please. *Grazie*," I yawned.

We sat through breakfast silently, got dressed, and headed to the Uffizi Gallery, where most of the notable works BVR had contributed to were housed. The day promised rain, with intermittent clouds tinting the city with medieval sadness. We passed the tourists snaking around the semi-enclosed courtyard where the two long galleries were connected by the long passageway Vasari designed centuries ago. Dario snuck me in through a back door and up the stairs. His work in the art world permitted him these kinds of luxuries. Our rushed footsteps were muffled by the polished stone beneath us, leading us eventually to the gallery itself.

He started by sharing bits of the story of the gallery with me, how the Medici commissioned the construction of the gallery as a way of showing off their claim to power in the 1500s. Cosimo de'Medici had entrusted the architect Giorgio Vasari to create the formidable structure for Florence's judicial and administrative offices. Little did they know back then that 500 years later, it would be home to some of the most renowned painters in all history. We strolled through the galleries, observing the evolution of color, form, and how each artist told a different story through their work. Eventually, we reached the early Renaissance period, the time when BVR would've been around.

"She didn't paint all of these exactly, but she worked on bits and pieces here and there. Apparently, she was quite good at the details, particularly botanical ones," Dario explained.

As an artist and a woman, I imagined what risks BVR must have taken to partake in this type of work. Most, if not all, of the names on the plaques were of men. Even if her life had impacted and shaped the work of artists we know of today, her name was unknown.

"Look at these, right here," he pointed at some of Raphael's early work. "Among my uncle's findings was that she taught at the same studio where he learned to paint."

I was in shock.

"*Vieni,* Mar," he extended his hand, leading me to another room. We passed the vaulted and frescoed ceilings, walls lined with the faces of saints and forgotten nobility. Then, we turned a corner and the air changed, as if the room was holding its breath. In contrast to other parts of the gallery, the lighting resembled moonlight—filtered and diffused by the high tinted windows protecting the paintings from the harshness of the sun.

The painting was remarkably large. Venus rising from the sea foam, standing statuesque on her shell. Realizing I'd been holding my breath, I exhaled, finding a spot in the front of the crowd watching her to observe. "She painted the flowers and modeled for Botticelli...or so Giulia tells me."

I remembered. She was posing as Venus when I returned to my life as her. I kept looking at the painting, admiring the attention to detail in every brushstroke, feeling the connection to the art, the freedom of the paintbrush creating something new.

Edging closer to the painting, Dario pointed toward the flowers. "You see the flowers—that's her work. The detailing of the costume. He didn't let any of his other students help him with this, but she was allowed. He trusted her."

Suddenly, I was shaken by a vision, and an incredible surge of grief washed over me. I stumbled slightly, grasping for Dario's arms as my knees weakened. An image came to me, a room full of windows, the smell of nacare oxide. Painters know their tools. I closed my eyes, pinching the bridge of my nose, finding my breath, but the flashbacks kept coming.

"Dario," I whimpered. "We need to go. We need to go now."

He shuffled toward me, "Mar, *tesoro,* do you want me to find you a doctor?" His voice changed. As did his face. I jumped from the chair, shaking my head and adjusting my vision, returning to the person I knew. *What in the actual fuck.*

"What do you feel, Mar? Maybe if we go up to the terrace, grab something with sugar for you—"

I wasn't hungry; this was emotional pain. Crippling, creeping, rising in my chest, and leaving me without air or hope to live. Tears flooded from my eyes until I surrendered to the grief. That's what it was, it was grief. I saw a vast ocean, a boat. A garden with potted flowers...or was it a cemetery? Flowers flying toward Venus. Images kept coming as I struggled to make sense of them. The pressure in my ribcage. *Whose pain is this? Am I reliving Papi's death? Beatriz's?* I couldn't tell the difference, but perhaps there was no difference.

Finding my breath, I rose and found Dario's arm, "That's it for today. *Basta*. Take me home."

I spent the rest of the afternoon in a feverish sleep, my body aching. Scenes from my past lives flashed before me. And in between all the physical pain, the unshakable grief that I carried, which I knew deep down, wasn't only mine. It was similar to how I felt when I traveled back during the regressions in Almaguer's office.

By the time I rose to consciousness, it was 7 p.m. I could hear Dario humming in the kitchen, the smell of broth traveling through his apartment. I grabbed my phone, finding a notification from Tania with a picture of the dogs at the park, "We miss you, *Mami*!" I responded with a smiley face, scrolling through my contacts until I found Almaguer.

Normally, I'd text her first, ask if she was available for a consultation, but this felt urgent and necessary. The phone rang twice until her clear voice answered on the other side.

"¿Hola? ¿*Mar*?" I felt the concern in her tone.

"I'm sorry to call you so randomly...it's just that something really strange happened today. I have a feeling that it has something to do with a past life. Not just the ones related to Beatriz. I'm here in Florence and I feel...*haunted*."

I detailed the events of the day, how connected I felt, not just to Dario, but the painting and the feelings rising thereafter.

"Hmm...it does sound like there could be a past life connection there. We just need to figure out what it's trying to illuminate for you. Aside from that, how are you feeling? Is everything okay?"

I groaned. "Ughhhhhh, I didn't think this trip was going to be something this intense. Why can't it just be easy?"

She chuckled. I could hear her rummaging through something in what sounded like a kitchen. Outside the office, she was much more animated.

"Oh, Mar, because then you wouldn't learn. Love and pain move us forward in life. Remember that dark rooms remain dark until you flick on the light switch. Try to enjoy your time with Dario as much as possible right now. Don't worry about the lessons or being perfect with your healing. Have a glass of wine, loosen up, and we'll schedule you for a regression next week."

I got up from the bed, tying my unruly hair into a messy bun, and walked out into Dario's apartment. It was a quaint two-bedroom facing an indoor courtyard. Walking in, a long hallway led all the way back to an open living space that housed a tiny kitchen with a wooden table and two chairs, and on the other side, what was meant to be a living room. Two floor-to-ceiling windows framed an almond tree that grew in the middle of the building's courtyard. The bedrooms were right next to each other, facing the living space.

He leaned over a boiling pot on the stove, humming something he was listening to on his headphones. I edged closer, placing my hand on his back, so I would not startle him.

"*Ey!*" He smiled. "I am making you *brodo*. I hope you like it. I have been worried about you all afternoon."

"Thanks, I'm feeling better. The nap definitely helped," I said. "I'm excited about this soup. It smells great!"

He served dinner, and I downed the broth, which lulled me into a dream-like haze.

"We can skip tomorrow if you're not feeling up to it," he said between slurps.

"No, no, we're going. We're here for this, and I'm not going to miss it because of one bump in the road."

63

GIULIA GIORDANO

Mar

Florence, Italy – 2024

Giulia Giordano lived in a colorful apartment on Via Sant'Antonino. She was in charge of the building owned by her family for centuries. The back of the property housed what used to be Sandro Botticelli's studio.

"My *bis bis bis biiiiis nonna*, Clarice, owned the original home with her husband," she said in her thick Italian accent as she gave us the short yet grand tour of the space. "It used to be a palazzo, but also a space where a secret society named the *Casa dei Fiori* met. She was quite close to Botticelli during that time, building the women in the arts back then. Before the religious revolution and all that."

The building was now inhabited by foreign students from all over the world who came to study abroad. Some of the apartments were rented out for Airbnb, with very few Florentine tenants in the space. Similar to Dario's apartment building, it had a tree in the middle with a courtyard. It was so tall, it reached above the entire structure. I gazed up at it, admiring its resilience through centuries of changes, wars, conquest.

"You like the tree, *no?* It's an almond tree, about 800 years old, *io penso*. There is another similar one, close by to 'ere, in another building. It's where the residency of the poet Dante Lupo was," she shared, walking us to the space where the studio used to be.

His name was like a punch to the gut to me. I clutched my chest as I felt the grief from yesterday returning.

"Dante Lupo?" Dario asked.

She lifted her chin affirmatively at him, "*Eh,* his fame has faded over the years. Italians...we have so many great artists, but he was prominent during the early Renaissance."

"*Bene, ma*, which street did he live on, particularly?" he asked.

She fumbled with the keys on a heavy metal door. "*Ah, caro,* that I have no idea. There was a residence where a lot of artists of that time lived, Via del Giglio. Maybe there."

After several tries, she opened the door. Dust clouded the air, and we stepped in. "*Ragazzi*, here it is! Not as glamorous as we could have expected, but this is where Beatrice started her painting classes. Where the *Birth of Venus* was painted."

The studio was now the storage room for forgotten furniture.

"Giulia. Do you know why the *Fiori* were started, why Botticelli was even interested in investing in women artists?" I asked.

She looked at me quizzically. "They were always interested in women. They just never gave them the credit they deserved. Mar, do you think we do any better today? How many women artists do you know that get the recognition they deserve? That are as well-known as their male contemporaries and not thought of as 'cute' or 'inventive?' What the *Fiori* did was give the women of this time the opportunity to *at least* get to work on what they wanted, not just be housewives or objects to their husbands and society."

I looked around the studio's tall walls tinted with age and humidity. Even in my own work, I constantly struggled to compete with male muralists. I'd lost count of all the times people told me women shouldn't be hoisted on cranes, let alone holding cans of paint in their hands. Whenever a piece was done, they were impressed, as if they were expecting me to fail the entire time. No matter how far we'd progressed, there was still the idea that men could probably do the job better. For me, it had never been about gender. I painted my experiences, my inspiration, the stories that screamed to be told through my hands. That was it. Why couldn't it just be about our unique artistry, rather than what sex we were born into or where we come from?

I also knew these weren't questions people like BVR had the luxury of even asking themselves. She could consider herself lucky enough for being born into a family that allowed her an education, let alone the chance to practice what she liked. My generation could ask. That alone was a huge advance.

Before leaving the studio, Giulia asked us to wait while she retrieved something. She returned with a large manila envelope filled with letters and correspondence between *Signora* Clarice, some of the *Fiori*, and BVR. She hadn't felt like she could trust us with this until she saw how invested we actually were. We thanked her for the help, ensuring her we'd return the letters as soon as we had answers. Taking one look back at the studio, we stepped back into the busy Florentine streets, walking back toward Dario's apartment in silence.

"Would you like to have a coffee?" Dario asked, sticking one hand inside the pocket of his jeans. "It's almost six o'clock. The birds you liked the other day will be starting their *danza*."

I could feel his smile, even though I wasn't looking at him. Ever since the night we nearly hooked up at his place in

Madrid, I'd been ignoring my feelings for him. Whenever I'd catch the sun in his eyes, or find myself smiling at his humming in the morning, I'd remind myself he wanted to take things slow.

"*Sí, dale,*" I said. "I could use some caffeine, and I think we can sort through some of these."

We picked a spot at a piazza nearby, taking out one letter each, sifting through the information. Dario's uncle never got this far on his research with BVR, finding himself lost in a Florence of the early 1990s, with no phones or Google to help him find his footing.

"*Guarda, Mar!*" Dario said excitedly. "This one is for BVR from Clarice."

Dearest Amapola,

My warmest congratulations on your wedding. I pray it brings you every happiness. I eagerly await our next afternoon of needlework together—a courier has brought beautiful new threads. I shall see you next Tuesday.

Your friend,
Clarice

In my regression, BVR had snuck around to paint, and she couldn't tell her family what she was doing. I continued sorting through others, all cryptic. Although we figured out a few repeated patterns. All the letters mentioned flower names and were directed to Amapola, not BVR, leading us to believe this was her hidden name. At one period, some letters mentioned specific deliveries, inquiries. And finally, we confirmed my memories of Dozza.

"I wonder *why* she went to live in this town..." I said. I

couldn't remember many details of it from my regression.... except that's where Dante had died in her arms.

Dario was focused on a specific letter, his eyebrows drawn together. "Dario," I poked. "Did you hear me?"

He held his hand up as he scanned the page. Then handed me a letter. "Look at this. It's a poem from Dante Lupo. The poet Giulia mentioned at the studio."

I scanned through the page, blushing at its contents. Not only was it a poem. It was an *erotic* poem.

"Do you think it was about her? BVR?" I asked, still thinking of the verses.

He laughed. "Of course it is. It wouldn't have been about Clarice!"

"You never know!" I shrugged. "He could've liked them older. I don't judge."

We found several more. Opening yet another Pandora's box. I knew she hadn't married Dante. I just couldn't find a way of telling Dario *how* I knew this. The sun was already setting, the birds forming their intricate patterns in the sky before returning home.

"Let's wrap up. We can continue after we make dinner," I said, pulling out two euros and setting them on the table. Dario handed them back to me.

"Allow me," he said, paying for the macchiatos. "I was going to ask you if you would like to have dinner somewhere else tonight. There is a place in the city, authentic Florentine food, that I'd like to take you to—none of these *eh,* tourist trap places. What do you say?"

Surprised yet relieved we wouldn't have to tiptoe around each other back at his place, I accepted his invitation.

64

DINNER ON THE ARNO

Mar

Florence, Italy – 2024

We returned to the apartment, each retreating to our rooms silently. I considered throwing something simple on, but I found a blue silk dress Tania snuck into my luggage "just in case" an occasion such as this popped up.

In contrast to the comfy outfits I usually opted for, the dress hugged my curves, a slit on the right thigh revealing the result of years of ballet. The plunging neckline outlined my plump, firm breasts, and my fine-line sternum tattoo. An open back, where a tattoo of a paintbrush and three poppies decorated the middle of my shoulders. I giggled, thinking of my past life as Luciana, owning the confidence of my body and looks.

"She's Latina, all right," I sighed, looking at myself in the mirror. I could hear my mother's conservative voice resounding in my subconscious.

"Eso es para muchachas de pechos chiquitos, Mar."

Ya, Mami, shut up. I can wear lo que me dé la gana.

I picked up my hair into a messy up-do, put on a little lipstick, and stepped out into the living room. Dario was waiting for me, scrolling through his phone. He did a double take when he saw me.

"Oh, wow!" He stood up and straightened his black shirt. "You look, eh...*bellissima*."

I blushed. "Shall we go?"

Once on the street, he offered his arm as we walked toward Ponte Vecchio. The touch of my arm against his sent a rush of warmth through me. Clear skies lit the way to a quaint restaurant on the bridge with just a few tables inside. A short, thin old man with a giant gray mustache stepped out to greet us.

"Dario!" He embraced him warmly, nearly toppling with the weight of Dario's giant stature. "And who is this? *Tua ragazza?*"

Dario blushed, tapping the old man in the back, "No, no, *una amica*, Mar." He turned to me. "This is Maurizio."

"*Piacere*," I said in my broken Italian. Maurizio led us to the inside of the tiny restaurant, where a table for two awaited us by a window overlooking the Arno, the Florence Eye shining behind us.

I noticed Dario observing me as I took in the scene. Maurizio approached us again, this time with a bottle of wine in hand.

"Brunello di Montalcino, from the Tuscan region, for the lovely couple," he said, before we could correct him. "*Per favore,* let me bring out the dishes tonight; you will not regret it. Will give you our specialties."

The meal arrived like a symphony, each dish crescendoing toward the next with precision. First, *crostini di fegatini* and a mixture of cured meats like prosciutto, *finocchiona*, and coppa served with pecorino cheese and olives. The wine kept pouring as we passed on to the pasta, *pici caccio e peppe* and *pappardelle al cinghiale.* Wild boar was a common delicacy in these parts.

Every sip of wine and bite of food relaxed us further, putting the awkwardness of the previous nights behind us. By the time the *bistecca alla Fiorentina*, a massive T-bone steak, arrived on the table, we were tipsy discussing the intricacies of BVR's love life.

"How European of Beatriz to have taken a lover," I laughed. "No wonder her creative juices were flowing."

He snorted into his glass. "*Ey,* don't judge her. Her husband could've been gone for a while. She needed her desires met. They didn't have dating apps back then, you know."

"Good. It's not like they're doing us any favors these days." I spooned roasted potatoes with rosemary onto my plate. "Back then, you didn't get to choose who you loved, and now you have so many choices, you end up choosing nothing at all."

"Or choosing too many people," he laughed. "It's a sign of the times, *no?*"

"More like fear of commitment and love. We are so afraid of getting hurt, we don't even try." I reached for my wine glass. "Is that why you don't date?"

He looked down at the table, picking at a breadcrumb before looking up at me, "No, it's not. I was seeing someone before. She was lovely. Not the right fit for each other, though. We were going in a different direction. As I told you, I want to feel like I have a choice in how I enter a relationship. I don't just want to stumble into one."

He took a sip of his wine. "Do you still believe in soul mates? You never told me. "

"I'm not sure. I think I do, although most days I'm not convinced I believe in that kind of love anymore," I said. "Maybe I'm not made for the kind of love that these times offer."

I made no mention of the family curse. Or that I had gone back to my past lives to figure out why I felt so disconnected from my relationships.

"If you could describe the kind of love you want, how would you?" He poured the rest of the wine into our glasses, emptying the bottle.

"I want a vibrant and liberating love. The kind that makes you see the world in color because it deepens the way you experience life. I want it to be sturdy. Safe. Not the kind that quits at the first sign of turmoil or intensity. I'm tired of companionship so dim, you tiptoe around it, rather than run toward it. I don't want a love that possesses someone. I want to leave behind the dull hues of superficial caresses and empty sex to build something so bright and hopeful it feels like a rainbow," I responded, my clarity surprising me.

By now, the wine had removed any trace of a filter from me.

"So, what you're saying is you want a love that is unconditional," he said.

"Yes."

Dario observed me quietly. My monologue was enough to send anyone for the hills, but I didn't care anymore. He'd been clear from the beginning about his desire to take his time, and to not be influenced by others when it came to love.

"*Torta della nonna* and two glasses of *vin santo*. The meal, it was good?" Maurizio broke our seriousness.

"Oh, *maravilloso,*" I said. "I wish I had more stomachs!"

Dario smiled politely, looking back at me, waiting for Maurizio to step away.

"I think we should take a trip to Dozza," he said. "It'll be a turning point for your research. It's mentioned so often in the letters and is where she lived."

"When?" I stuffed my face with dessert.

He took a spoonful, letting it hang in the air. "The day after tomorrow I think is a good time."

"Sounds like a plan," I said, reaching for the sweet wine.

"Mar," he started, his eyes widening like two pools of coffee. "You deserve your rainbow."

65

THE GIANT MURAL

Mar

Dozza, Italy – 2024

Two days later, Dario picked me up at the front steps of his apartment on a black motorcycle. My jaw dropped.

"We're riding in this?" When he stepped out this morning to pick up "our ride" and told me to wear pants, I didn't expect we'd be on a motorcycle for two hours.

"Mar, I'm Italian, what were you expecting? A Chevrolet SUV?" He dismounted the bike, handing me a helmet. The brooding poet of the last week had transformed into a fearless bike rider, and I could see now what Lizzie McGuire, my childhood television pop icon, meant by "this is what dreams are made of."

Growing up in Miami, motorcycles were synonymous with death and organ donations. If you owned a motorcycle, you were a reckless person with a death wish.

"Are you sure you know how to ride this thing?" I said, still putting on the helmet.

He scoffed. "Of course, I know how to ride a motorcycle, Mar. It is like the second thing they teach us how to do in Roma after making gnocchi with our *nonnas* and walking."

"So it's the third thing." I approached the bike. "Those were three things."

He threw his hands up in the air, rolling his eyes. "*Madonna mia,*" he sighed. "*Dai,* get on the bike and trust me. All you have to do is hold on and enjoy the beautiful countryside of Tuscany and Emilia Romagna."

I clung tightly to his body as we left the city behind, the Duomo becoming a tiny red hat on the hand mirrors of the motorcycle. Soon enough, we'd left the bustle of traffic and were out in the rolling Tuscan hills, washed with green vineyards and olive trees before us. Wildflowers and poppies sprinkled the fields, serving as vibrant guides to our next destination. I began to relax my grip, letting the hum of the motor calm me, as the Apennines appeared like sleeping giants before us, with little medieval villages rising with the morning. Every now and then, we'd stumble across abandoned churches, stone farmhouses, sheep grazing lazily in the pastures. Until, finally, the roads shifted, leading us through cherry orchards and up a hill that revealed a small medieval village.

It's so hidden, you might miss it, except for the giant fortress towering above the hills. We found a spot to park the motorcycle, making our way toward the few streets of this tiny village. Immediately, I stumbled across a giant mural the size of a building, stopping me in my tracks.

"Dario! Look! There are murals *everywhere!*"

He smiled. "Yes, I know. The town is known for this..."

"What?! And you're telling me this now?!" I pushed him playfully and ran off in front of him like a child. "How could you have kept this information to yourself?"

He put his hands in his pockets, walking bashfully toward me. "There's a thing called Google, Mar. You should try looking up the places you're going to before you decide to hop onto motorcycles with random strangers."

I opened my mouth, speechless, then rushed toward a square surrounded by murals. One caught my eye in particular, painted above a clock—a mother perching her child onto the curve of the circular structure. Behind them, an explosion of colors reflected their pure bond.

"They host an event here every two years. It's called the Biennial of the Painted Wall," Dario tells me as I continue taking in every piece of art. My kind of art. "They invite artists to come and paint the walls of the city. Maybe someday you could come."

I shoot a look at him. "Oh my God, can you imagine?! That would be *amazing!*"

The town was silent, perhaps because it was a Sunday, with the murmurs of families dining within their homes singing through the stone walls as we walked through, like intruders. There were other tourists, taking out their phones to snatch photos of the murals. There must have been at least two hundred of them, each one unique and beautiful in their own way.

"So, she lived here," I offered Dario as we strolled through the streets. "A painter living in a city that would later become a breathing piece of art suspended in the countryside of Emilia Romagna."

I also remembered Dante died here. The memories of it were coming back to me.

"Do you think anyone would know about her here?" I asked.

We reached the edge of the town, watching the stunning views atop the green hills. I stopped for a moment, taking in the scenery, breathing in the fresh air you can only find in the countryside.

"Mar!" Dario shouted my name. "Mar, *vieni—affrettati!*"

I ran toward him, his face pale with shock as he stared up at the wall of a home facing the outskirts of the village. There she was. Or should I say, there *I* was. The same tiny painting that started all this towered over us like a giant. My green eye and brown eye looked out at the matching landscape. Dario and I looked at each other, then stared back at the mural in silence. Who was the artist? Who knew of this painting and placed it here? Could it have been the same person who gifted it to the Prado museum and then me?

Dario's face was in shock as the same questions crossed his mind.

"Dario, there's something I have to tell you."

66

CONFESSIONS

Mar

Dozza, Italy – 2024

I told him everything. From the first past life regression to the thoughts I had about him being Dante.

"Have you lost your mind, Mar? Do you hear yourself?" He walked away from me hastily, heading toward the motorcycle.

Flustered. I trailed behind, trying to catch up.

"Hey! Are you just going to be upset and not talk to me? It's not like we knew this would happen," I said. "Where are you going?"

He didn't answer me, continuing his pace. I reached for his arm, pulling him toward me. "Dario!"

He groaned, looking at me with a pained expression. "You don't actually believe everything you're saying, right? That suddenly we are these people from 500 years ago, and we had this contract and blah blah blah. *É un cazzo!* You have to be crazy to believe that stuff, Mar! It's the same thing I've been telling you all along about this fated love thing. It isn't real.

Love is when two people make it work. It doesn't just work like magic."

I took a step back, throwing my arms up. "Well, I also didn't believe in that stuff, but now that I've lived through it and have seen evidence of my past lives, I can't just ignore YOU or how I feel about you."

"All of this stuff is in your head, Mar. You were hurt by someone, and now you want answers because none of your relationships have worked because you're still in pain, and you hate to admit to yourself that you made a mistake and don't trust yourself or anyone else!"

His words reopened wounds from months before. Exposing my sadness as a tool against me.

"I know what I've lived through, Dario."

"And what are you going to do? We're going to marry each other because we didn't get the chance 500 years ago? That's some incredible matchmaking."

I felt frustration bubbling within me. I'd finally found answers to who BVR was, only to realize the connection I felt with her came from something deeper—we shared the same soul. No matter how nonsensical it sounded, it made sense. The inability of women in my lineage to love romantically. My own devotion to art. The way I had returned to her home and *found* the portrait waiting there. The inexplicable connection I felt when I saw Dario. For the past year, I'd been searching my past lives for answers. Now I had found them. The only problem —I wasn't the only one implicated.

"Let's go back to Florence, Dario. This was a lot for one day. I think we both need to process all this."

Without saying a word, he turned around and kept walking.

67

WHY THEY CALL IT THE BLUES

Mar

Florence, Italy – 2024

The ride back was long and silent. The scenery seemed less poetic. Dario dropped me off in front of his apartment, handing me the keys while he went on to park the motorcycle. I walked into the now familiar saffron-colored building, passing the staircase to his apartment toward the almond tree in the middle of the building courtyard. Its fresh leaves were a bright green against the fading blue sky. I leaned against it, finding my phone to text Tania back. She had sent a message earlier asking how the trip was going.

"I miss you and the pups so much. I wish you were here so we could talk. See you soon," I wrote.

I could finally pin down the strange feeling of familiarity I'd experienced since arriving in Florence. The dreams where I roamed around the city in Medieval times. My body's reaction at seeing *The Birth of Venus* in person. I wasn't imagining it. My soul was remembering. It had always been me — in a different body, at a different time, living a different life that led me again and again to the same corner.

Dario opened the door to the building, spotting me by the tree as he turned towards the staircase. He redirected, walking in my direction while running his hands through his dark, messy, helmet hair.

"You think this is where Dante lived, and that's why I chose this as my apartment?" He looked at the fallen leaves on the ground, lightly kicking them with his foot.

I sighed. "I don't know, it's hard to verify. Sometimes you just have to trust."

"Mar, *mi dispiace.* I'm sorry for the way I reacted..." he started. "I just don't trust these things. My family...they were led by these kinds of ideas their entire lives, and it didn't take them anywhere other than...I feel like it's manipulation. You see what you want to see."

I peeled myself away from the tree, leaving my hand on it for a second longer. "It's fine, Dario. I understand," I walked toward him, leading the way back to the apartment. "Let's put it to rest for the rest of the day, ok?"

Four hours later, I woke up to darkness and the sound of Dario whipping something up in the kitchen. I'd knocked out the minute we walked in through the door, plopping on the couch to look at the crown molding on the ceiling and drifting away into a dreamless sleep. I tiptoed around him, walking into the shower to disperse the happenings of the day. Everything felt so heavy, it still didn't feel like it happened that morning. My time in Florence was coming to an end soon, giving me an escape back to my own timeline, my own life. To process it all on my own terms.

Dario was waiting for me with a glass of chilled white wine when I stepped out of the bathroom. His mood had shifted from brooding to chipper, all in a matter of hours.

"I made *cena* for us, since we skipped *pranzo*." The wine was like a peace offering. "I hope you like *tortellini in brodo*."

I sipped from my glass. "Oh, *grazie*. I don't think I've ever tried it."

"It's a typical dish from Bologna...I thought it appropriate for the day we've had. Plus, you didn't get to try any of the foods from Emilia Romagna."

I sat in the same seat as our first night together. He served the broth with the ring-shaped stuffed pasta, sprinkling fresh parsley on top, then took his place across from me. The warm broth served as a balm, relieving the heaviness of the day and turning it into comfort. Occasionally, our eyes would cross, and a soft smile would form at either of our lips. Neither of us wanted to break the ice. That would mean having a difficult conversation we weren't ready to have: what do we do about us? What happens next? Is this all too crazy, or is it crazy to not give into the impulse that was calling to us both?

On paper, he was everything I was attracted to. We came from a shared world of art and literature, the very things that nurtured my soul. We'd known each other for centuries, apparently, even though seeing him in front of me now, I felt the reality: I barely knew him. He was a fresh canvas. And his behavior today showed me a side of him that made me want to run in the other direction.

"Are you ready to go back to Spain?"

I let out an involuntary sigh. "I think so. I definitely have a lot to talk about with my therapist."

We both laughed.

"Do you like the blues?"

"As in the music?" I mocked.

He seemed shocked as the sarcasm set in. "No, as in the period in art history."

I let out a chortle, "I love Etta James and Mamie Smith...and if you'll allow it, Amy Winehouse."

He raised an eyebrow. "I don't consider her a blues singer per se, but I'll allow it because she was amazing."

He pushed away from the table and took my hand leaving his napkin and the remains of the broth behind. He gestured toward a seat on his couch, then walked over to a small wooden cabinet where he took out two small grappa glasses and poured a green, herbaceous liquid in them, handing me one.

"This grappa is homemade," he said, clinking his glass to mine. "A *nonna* in the building makes it. She gives me some in hopes I marry her *nipotina. Salute.*"

The strong alcoholic liquid made me cough. He kept pacing the room as I pulled a blanket over myself.

"Sometimes, when words aren't enough, the best thing we can do is borrow someone else's."

He grabbed the banjo resting against the wall, taking a seat next to me. The notes played softly at first, like a whisper, his fingertips barely grazing the strings. I closed my eyes, feeling the vibration all over my body. There was a sadness, a melancholy in the air I couldn't shake, but also the same electricity I'd felt all over my body the first night.

His eyes were also closed as he played a tune I couldn't quite make out. "When I was a child, we moved a lot because of what happened to my uncle. He died before I was born, and my family used to say I was his reincarnation. *Immagina quanta responsabilità.*"

"I'm sorry, Dario," I said. "Maybe we should've never opened up this can of worms."

"It's open though, Mar," he strummed. "Now I know, and I can't stop piecing things together, or thinking about them, and even worse..."

He looked at me intensely, with a mixture of longing and desire. "The worst part is I've been trying to avoid the feelings I have felt for you over the past weeks. When I hear your roaring laughter, or watch the way you play with the ring on your middle finger when you're observing something. *Mi sento come se stessi impazzendo.* I fear I may lose my mind."

I could feel my face flushing, the alcohol unveiling my vulnerability as his words flowed as if accompanying the music. He put the banjo to the side, edging closer to me until he found my hands. Then simply looked at me.

"What do you want, Dario?" I asked, terrified his answer may not be me.

He put his hand gently on my face, and I saw them all. Every life we'd found each other in, the pain of losing each other again. In one, we only passed each other. In another, we never met. Tears spilled from both of our eyes. He leaned in closer, his eyes meeting mine, the herbs from the alcohol in his breath.

"*Adesso,* I just want to kiss you," he whispered before joining my lips to his. My body gave in to his, finding the warmth my soul had searched timelines for. He kissed my neck gently, returning to my mouth as if it were an oxygen mask. My heart thumped loudly against my chest, as I impatiently took off his shirt, trailing his chest with soft kisses. Pushing aside the blanket still resting on my legs, he carried me to his bedroom, where vaulted ceilings and peeling frescoes nestled a four-poster bed. He laid me on it gently, stripping me of my pants first, then my tank top. He spread my legs, pressing himself against my center as he kissed my mouth. I could feel his hardness through his clothes—I needed more. He moaned softly, cupping my breasts with his hands, then moving his head down toward my thighs. In bliss, I dug my hands into his hair, leading him toward my center. He looked up at me, smiling, as he peeled my underwear off, throwing it to the side, sending shivers down my spine. His tongue felt soft against my clit, my wetness running down my legs. My body trembled.

Sensing my satisfaction, he rolled over next to me. My desire pulled me to my knees, and I straddled him. My hands moved slowly down his chest, before my fingers found the zipper of his pants, working faster. I paused at the sight of his perfectly sculpted dick. I raised my eyebrows.

His laughter filled the room as he pulled me over him, growling with anticipation. My body wrapped around his while he fumbled to open a condom, giving it to me to put it on. "Wait, wait," he grabbed my face in his big hands. "Mar, are you sure you want to do this? I don't want us to—"

"If we fuck it up, we fuck it up," I said. "Now, I just want to make love to you and forget about everything else."

"*Dio, amore*," he moaned. "Now I'm really going to lose my mind."

I slowly lowered myself onto him and began to ride him, guiding his face to my breasts. "Don't lose your mind," I said softly. "Just lose yourself in me tonight."

We spent the rest of the night discovering every corner of each other, until we finally fell asleep hours later. Our appetite didn't subside with sleep, it rose with the dawn. We paused only for short meals, some of which ended with me on the dining room table, his mouth between my thighs. Outside, the cover of rain gave us permission to lose ourselves in each other without thinking of a meticulously scheduled agenda. There was only one thing left to discover on this trip: each other. Everything else would unfold eventually.

68

THE FINAL REGRESSION

Mar

Florence, Italy – 2024

I shut the door behind me in Dario's room while he was out as I met with Almaguer over Zoom. "Are you alright?" Almaguer asked. "You look a little..."

"Sad—I'm sad. Drowning in it, really. The last few days have been *a lot,*" I said. "It feels like I'm finding the answers to my wounds but opening new ones. We need to sit down and have a coffee and chat when I'm back in Madrid. There's so much to... unpack."

She took off her spectacles, looking at me for a moment with something that resembled pride. "This is good. You've come such a long way. Actually, I think this should be our last regression, at least for now."

"What, really?" I felt a combination of fear and relief.

I thought about the past few months, all the progress I had made. Even opening myself up to Dario again was a big step. Being vulnerable. Trusting myself enough to push through the pain. All that was left to do was find out the last piece of my depression and why the sadness wouldn't go away.

"It's going to be different from the other ones you have done, but it might be the missing piece in helping you feel better."

"Are you ready, Mar?"

"Yes."

69

THE AMERICAN DREAM

Miguel

New York, New York – 1985

They say the second year after you immigrate is the easiest. For me, it was the fourth. Over the last year, a lot had changed. *Mami* and I managed to move to our own place, even if it was small. She got another job. And I left a shitty bartending job at a bar, Tito's, for a dream position at Galerías Macondo, where I could cultivate my passion for art.

Galerías Macondo was a world apart from Tito's grimy bar. Gone were the sticky latex sofas, the crusty menus filled with questionable items, and the endless parade of drunk patrons. My new workplace had clean white walls, vibrant canvases, and the hum of whispered admiration.

As its name—inspired by Gabriel Garcia Marquez's masterpiece, *100 Years of Solitude*—suggested, Macondo aimed to create an entirely new world for everyone who stepped inside. And who was there to ensure they left with lighter pockets and beautifully adorned walls? *Yo, por supuesto.*

While the neighboring galleries peddled Jackson Pollock knockoffs, half-baked Cubism, and installations that looked like a fourth-grader's weekend project, Macondo had a mission: to champion Latin American art in New York.

The gallery's owner, Ariana Martí, embodied that mission. Daughter of a Puerto Rican beauty queen and a Cuban exile, Ariana came from old money. Yes, sugar mills, sprawling estates, and mythical *wealth*. She also had a long queue of *pretendientes*, eager to make her their *mujercita*. Ariana? She wasn't interested in diamonds or devotion. Her singular passion was shining a light on Latino art, especially the kind women could create.

Recently, I'd thrown myself into a special project—something unprecedented: uncovering the work of women artists from the colonial period. Most of them were poor and invisible to history, but a lecture at Columbia University changed everything for me. I'd been waiting for my ex to finish class, killing time, when I stumbled into a talk about a secret society in Renaissance Florence that somehow connected to Cuba in the late 1530-1550s.

After the lecture, I practically jumped the professor—probably scaring him half to death—with my flood of questions. Who was this mysterious woman who documented the horrors of slavery? What was her name? Were there records to prove her story? Could I create an exhibit with her work? And most importantly, could I somehow bring her pieces to New York?

The professor, intrigued by my enthusiasm, gave me his number, and thus began months of negotiation. But Cuban bureaucracy moved slower than molasses. We finally got a response from a distant relative of the painter, who had been dead for nearly five centuries. Like so many still on the island, the nephew was strapped for cash, and pretty much everything else. And I get it. I've been there. When you live on the island, you're too busy figuring out *how* you're going to survive to be vaguely interested in an ancestor's legacy. Even then, he told me that she had arrived in Trinidad in 1530 with her two adult children and a maid, continuing her art in secret.

Yes, there were pieces we could acquire. *Yes*, they could be sold. But there were two conditions. First, one piece could never be sold, only preserved and passed down. Second, her full name could never be revealed. Only her initials: BVR.

When I pitched the project to Ariana, her excitement was palpable. "Do whatever you want, I trust you!" she said, her hands fixing her voluminous afro. "When do you think you'll have it ready? I'll need time to get my parents on board with this whole colonizer-art narrative, ya know."

"*Esquiusmi?* She wasn't a colonizer," I said, shaking my head. "Nuh-uh. She came on her own, with her children and maid, on some random ship. There's so much about her story we still don't know, but from the sketches her nephew sent, she vividly documented the lives of Yoruba and Taíno slaves. It was unheard of for a woman, let alone—"

"Do we know if she was white?"

I paused, stunned by the question. "I mean, I assumed," I admitted. "Now I'm even more intrigued."

"What's her name again?" she asked.

"Beatriz Velázquez de Rossi. But we're only allowed to call her BVR."

Ariana leaned against her desk, arms crossed, her expression a mix of curiosity and calculation. "It's interesting that no one aside from the professor had heard of her before. All right, if we're going to do this, we're going to need all the facts, and make sure we verify them. I'm not diminishing the work you've done and the negotiations over the past couple of months, *pero* we can't put the gallery at risk."

I took a deep breath, gathering my thoughts. "I get you. But from what her nephew told me, BVR wasn't just some hobbyist or a housewife who painted to pass the time. She had formal training in Florence before coming to Cuba. He mentioned her connection to a secret society of artists—women who worked under pseudonyms because it was the only way to get their art noticed back in Florence. In Cuba, she painted almost exclusively about slavery. There's not a lot that we have from her time in Italy. Probably she couldn't travel with paintings on a trans-Atlantic ship in the Renaissance. *Pero* these paintings she did in Cuba are *radical*. I saw them in the pictures the professor shared in his lecture. They're not just scenes, but emotions—the anguish, the resilience, the sheer humanity of the slaves. Apparently, she used pigments no one had seen before, made from native plants and minerals. Even in the portraits, her colors have this vibrancy that's unreal. I think this could be a huge turning point for us."

Ariana raised an eyebrow, intrigued. "Okay. Okay. I just want to make sure this isn't some myth someone cooked up to sell some art and make a quick buck. We're building a reputation here."

I laughed, shaking my head. "Trust me, Ari, I'm skeptical by default. But the details are too specific to ignore. Plus, the professor vouched for the pieces. A Columbia professor wouldn't stick his neck out for a scam."

Two days later, a letter from BVR's nephew arrived. I found myself pacing the narrow library of the professor's apartment. Shelves stuffed with aging books loomed around me, their musty smell mixing with the faint tang of tobacco from his ever-present pipe. The latest twist in this saga had shot my nerves: the nephew now insisted on accompanying the art to ensure its safe passage to the United States.

"This smells like *gato encerrado*," I muttered, throwing my hands in the air. "Who the hell does he think he is? The King of Spain? And how does he expect us to pull a visa out of thin air?" I raised my voice without a care. The absurdity of it all was infuriating.

"Now, Miguel," the professor said, puffing on his pipe with maddening calm. He sat in a worn leather armchair, looking every bit the cliché of an aging intellectual.

"I know what this is! And now I want to see the art before he sets foot here. What if it's all fake? A scam?"

I felt frustrated for several reasons. I knew leaving the island was a priority for many Cubans. I myself had left in the Mariel boatlift years before.

"It is not a farce," the professor said, his voice steady but tinged with offense. "I've seen the pieces myself. Where do you think I got half the material for my lectures? But tell me, Miguel—wouldn't you do the same in his position? If you were stuck on that island, wouldn't you take every opportunity to get out? We've all heard Cuba is worsening under the current political climate. Unless he is a revolutionary, there's a big chance he may be trying to use this as an opportunity to leave. The problem is we may not have the means to help him, and that would put our project at risk."

His words landed like a sharp slap. I hated it when people were right. Especially when their correctness called my own morality into question. Of course, I'd do the same. Who wouldn't? This man wasn't just holding his great-great-great-aunt's artwork; he was holding the keys to his escape, and he was playing the game flawlessly. Perhaps at one point he thought these pieces were just the random hobby of a woman who lived centuries ago, that they would never amount to much, or he could sell them at a street market in Havana and make a buck. There were many artists rising to prominence on the island—Roberto Fabelo for one, with his dreamlike portraits that leaped toward spectators.

I sighed, letting the anger dissipate just enough for clarity to creep in. "*Bueeeno*," I said at last. "Let's figure out what we can do and offer him a solution. But he sends some pieces upfront first. I'm not risking everything we've worked for without proof. If we're investing in this, then so is he."

The professor nodded, a faint smile curling under his pipe. "Fair enough, Miguel. Let's draft a response and make the call."

70

DELILAH

Miguel

New York, New York —1985

I stopped by the post office near the Hudson River to send Fernando's letter. Spring had enveloped Manhattan in a spell, its magic unfurling in blooms I'd never seen before. Some flowers were small and white, with golden-yellow centers that radiated like tiny suns, their pointy petals reaching outward like an artist's brushstrokes. Others stood taller. Flaming tulips in bold reds and oranges and strange, spherical bulbs with spiky heads that reminded me of giant dandelions caught mid-wish. I knew orchids, sunflowers, and roses from home, but these felt foreign, like secret codes from a world I was still learning to decipher. Even now, four years removed from Cuba, the seasons here still surprised me.

The air was a contradiction. Crisp with a whisper of warmth, carrying a myriad of scents: the sweet tang of river water, the heady aroma of blossoms, and the ever-present undertone of Manhattan's grime, garbage, and faint traces of danger. It was a perfume as complex and bittersweet as Alessandro, my long-lost lover, who haunted my thoughts even though he was an ocean away.

Ever since he left, I quickened my pace when I walked through the city, even though my leg had been hurting for months. It was as if speeding up could outrun his memory, could outpace the love—or whatever remained of it—etched into me. But today, I slowed. Today, I let the wind carry me back to him: the piercing blue of his eyes, his dark beard shadowing a face sculpted by sun and sea. The scent of espresso lingering on his breath mingled with the occasional sharpness of a cigarette, lit only when he woke up poetic about Neruda or Montale.

I wanted to tell him about BVR, the letter, the professor. I longed to share my fears about having it all fall down like a house of cards before me. He'd know exactly what to say or how to shake this anxiety away. But he was gone.

Six months had passed since he left for Sicily. "It's my *mamma*. I can't explain, but I have to go," he had said on a Wednesday, and by Monday, he was a ghost. "I will write, I will explain," he promised. But the mailbox had stayed empty long enough to teach me not to wait anymore.

"*Así son los italianos*," my friend Carmen declared back when he left, her voice tinged with both authority and the slight slur of cheap wine. She poured it into a chipped cup, the kind we always used when the budget was tighter than the dresses she wore to the club when we danced salsa. Carmen, ever loyal and brutal, was determined to fill the silence with her truths. "They are masters of deception."

She paused just long enough to deliver *la pullita*—the little barb Cubans wield like knives wrapped in silk.

"He probably met someone else, Migue," she said, her dark eyes narrowing as if daring me to argue. "And he didn't know how to break it to you. *Olvídate de eso*."

Forget him. Move on. She made it sound so easy.

I only let a single tear escape, hoping her words would fester, poison the love I still carried for him and transform it into something bearable, like anger or indifference. But here I was, sitting by the riverbank all this time later, and the venom hadn't worked. All I felt was sadness.

Her words hadn't stuck because I didn't believe them. Not really. Our love was so pure, so real, there was no way he was the man she was referring to.

But maybe that was the problem. *Los humanos somos así de complicados,* aren't we? We carry love and betrayal in the same hands and mix devotion with deceit like a poorly measured cocktail. Maybe he *had* met someone else. Or maybe his words about Sicily and his mother had been true. I looked out at the river, its surface shimmering with the bright light of day and let the question linger unanswered. Wherever he was, my only hope was that he was safe, that he was well, and that perhaps one day, I'd be able to walk through Manhattan without hoping his voice would catch me by surprise.

A painting arrived on the doorstep of Galerías Macondo three months later. The postman knocked on the glass window of the gallery with the package wrapped in worn-down muslin, yellowing copies of *El Granma,* and a makeshift tube that held it all together. I brought the package inside carefully, as if holding a newborn child. The Cuban newspaper gave away where it came from. My past came flashing back, sending shivers down my spine. I could suddenly taste saltwater in the air, even here in the safety of my job.

I unwrapped it with the gentlest of care, though it seemed determined to free itself, flying out of its confinement as swiftly as a butterfly from its cocoon, wings spreading wide. The painting was small, taking only about a fourth of my desk, but the gray eyes of the woman in front of me were bigger than the room I stood in. Her skin, the color of rich cocoa, seemed to glow against the palm leaves in the background. Her braids were wrapped neatly in a white cloth, leaving only her hairline visible. I traced my fingers gently on the edges of the canvas, noticing a name written on the back: *Delilah.*

The portrait was more vibrant and stunning than the paintings I'd seen at the professor's lecture at Columbia. My stomach tightened, and a wave of grief washed over me as I looked deeper into it. Even though this painting had been finished nearly four centuries ago, somehow I felt connected to it. It was as if *Delilah* and I had known each other, like her pain was mine. The contrast of her skin against a radiant blue sky and palm trees in every hue of green was insignificant in comparison to the reality of her life. She had once more traveled across the ocean against her will to a land she didn't know, to a place where now she would be seen to give others a glimpse of what it was like to be a prisoner of an unfortunate fate.

The wrappings had one more surprise: a letter from Fernando. He had sent *Delilah* as part of our official deal. She was proof that his word was good. The timing couldn't have been more perfect. We were on the verge of abandoning the project altogether, Ariana pushing me to redirect our attention to other artists.

I opened the envelope, unwrapping several pieces of paper stuck together with a single staple.

La Habana, Cuba
April 1985

Estimado Miguel Ángel,

I apologize in advance for the delay in responding to you regarding the paintings of my late ancestor, Beatriz. As you know, my family has safeguarded the paintings for more than four centuries, honoring her wishes. My aunt escaped to Trinidad when Spain's colonization of Cuba began. In short, the paintings go beyond what she saw—a testament to what she lived. She lived her last years here, saw her children build families, and left every piece of art she owned—with few exceptions—here, in Cuba.

As I have told you in our earlier correspondence, there are only a few blood relatives in connection with her still alive. I am one of them, her great-great-granddaughter is the other. Before confirming my agreement with you, I had to receive her permission to have Beatriz's work sent to a gallery in New York. As you should know, trust is not easy to come by these days, especially with outsiders. But that's beside the point; due to your insistence and our research of your gallery and the professor, we have decided to send you the paintings in the hope that Beatriz's work will survive as it has all these years.

Given the current situation on the island, our family plans to leave soon, and the paintings won't make the trip with us. We cannot risk them being seized or held by the government. Attached with this letter, I am sending you the legal conditions of our agreement, who will receive the payment for the pieces in cash in the United States (it will get to me through

A trusted person), and where you are to pick them up in Miami.

Once I receive the first part of the payment, you will receive the initial 20 paintings. After the final payment, you will receive all the rest, and I will even send you letters we found taped to the back of some of the pieces.

As a token of our trust, I have sent one painting as a gift: Delilah. She was a Yoruba slave brought to Trinidad in 1515. She stayed in the same house as Beatriz, where they eventually became close, even though this was unheard of at that time.

All we ask is that you care well for BVR's work, give her a name, and ensure you raise Cuba's position in the art world.

Ashe Pa'Ti,
Fernando Varela

I hadn't noticed until I finished reading the letter the smile forming across my face. *¡¡¡¡¡ESOOOO COÑOOOOOOO!!!!!!!* I had never conquered anything, but this felt like the world was in my hands, within my reach, and I could do anything. The man who a year ago was serving tables in SoHo was now curating his first art show in New York.

I made it, *Diosito!* I. Made. It.

Rushing toward my phone, I dialed Ariana's home number, but she didn't answer. Then, I called the professor. His balmy voice answered on the other line. I could tell his pipe was in his mouth.

"*Profe,* we did it, *meng*!" I yelled excitedly.

"Wait, what?" his tone picked up. "What do you mean?"

A cackle escaped me, "*Ay*, professor, you need to come down to the gallery. There's someone here I want you to meet. Her name is *Delilah*."

71

THE GAY CANCER

Miguel

Union City, New Jersey — 1985

M*ami* sets a plate of white rice, black beans, and *pollo empanizado* in front of me on the square table of our apartment in Jersey. She's not looking at me when she does it, or even at the plate. Her gaze glued on the television newscast playing across the room.

News of AIDS or "the gay cancer" as they're calling it, spreading across the States is playing on one of the few Hispanic television channels in the country. The stern voice of the reporter bounces off the walls of the tiny apartment, filling every square inch of it with dread and fear.

"Mami," I call to her, but she's too far gone into the tragic world the news is painting for her. "*¡Mami!*" I shout.

She jumps. "*¡Ay,* Miguel Ángel! *Me vas a matar del corazón.*"

"*I'm* going to give you a heart attack? Not Pepito the *amarillista* and his sensationalist reporting you keep watching all day?"

Mami, like many other Cubans of her generation, watches the news and her *telenovelas* religiously. On days when she doesn't work, she catches every forecast, and when she's out of the house, she tunes in on the radio.

She storms back into the room, her plate in one hand, a bowl of lettuce and tomato salad on the other. "I need to stay informed on what's happening with this illness, *mi amor.* I worry about you, about Ale..."

The curtain of vapor emerging from her beans disguises my scoff when she mentions my ex's name.

"*Mami*, there's nothing to worry about." I reach for her hand across the table, covered with a tablecloth she found discounted at a dollar store. It's decorated with sunflowers, which she thought was a favorable sign from *la virgencita de la Caridad*.

Cuba's patroness requires *un cariñito* every now and then, and since the cost of sunflowers was too high for us to afford an *ofrenda*, this *mantelito* would do. Let's hope the *virgencita* understands shit's rough in this economy.

"Ay, *mijito.*" Tears form in her tired eyes. Yesterday, she worked all day at the factory and spent all night caring for Mrs. Metz, who had hip replacement surgery. "*Te imaginas*, we've come so far to have you get sick with this awful disease. *Dios tiene que ayudarnos, protegerte.*"

"*Mami*, just because I'm gay it doesn't mean I'm going to get AIDS. It doesn't work like that. It's not like it's got some sort of radar in the air that's like, '*Oh mira, un maricón*,' and then we get it." I chew before continuing. "We don't even know for sure how it happens, and by now, gays aren't the only ones getting sick from it. *¿Me entendiste?* You can't believe everything you watch on the news all the time, or what you hear from Caridad. *No te preocupes más.*"

I knew telling her not to worry was useless. She worried about me from the moment she realized I was more interested in Manuel than Camila in primary school. When they told on me to the principal and one day took me to a camp where they beat the *maricón* out of me. For years, she wouldn't look at me when I walked around the house shirtless, afraid she would stumble across the scars on my body. Wondering what she could have done so they never ended up there.

But it wasn't her fault. It wasn't a fault. Even on my darkest days and the moments when I thought perhaps my homosexuality could be "cured," I knew deep down that the problem wasn't me—it was the society I was born into. Not only was I already *mulatico* or *jabao*, on top of it all, I liked men. And no amount of beatings or forced labor or dating women would change that.

It took me years to come to terms with it. To accept myself. To embrace who I slept with wasn't anyone's business. Still, the AIDS epidemic struck the world like a curse from the gods. Just as we thought the gay community, at least in the States, was finding their place, the disease made us *persona non grata* again.

Diseases reminded people of their mortality and stripped away their morality when survival was at stake. The curious thing was that no one, sick or healthy, could save themselves from it.

We ate the rest of our lunch in silence as the newscast turned into reruns of an older *telenovela*. When we both finished, I got up and headed toward the kitchen to make a *cafecito* before heading to work. *Mami*, tired from the day before, stayed at the table fumbling with a little piece of rice. Most days she would fight me if I washed the dishes and made coffee, but today, a combination of worry and tiredness won her over.

"Emilia, *mira*," I tease her, calling her by her first name. "Drink your *cafecito* and take a nap. You work tonight?"

She sighs. "No, *mijito*. I'm meeting with your *Tía* Teresita, and we're playing dominoes at a friend's house."

I lean in to kiss her forehead when I start coughing uncontrollably. *Mami* gets up, rushing to the kitchen to fetch a glass of water. I've had the cough for a while now; it was like a tourist who overstayed their visa.

"You need to go get that cough checked, Miguel," she argues. "You've had it since you returned from the hospital months ago."

"Ya, *Mami, no exageres.*" I try calming her nerves. "I feel fine. It's just a little cold and the changing weather."

The truth was I'd been feeling like shit since I left the hospital. I was tired, even when I slept for what seemed like days. Every part of me still ached, which the doctors said was normal.

"Call the doctor today, *mijo*. Tell him to check *everything*."

By everything, she meant HIV.

72

MIAMI

Miguel

Miami, Florida — 1985

For the next couple of months, my life became Beatriz Velázquez de Rossi. Since tensions were high between the United States and Cuba, taking the paintings out of my native island became a Herculean task. It wasn't as easy as putting them all in a box and sending them over. I also learned that although her paintings were of enormous historical value to us, her family had thought of her paintings as merely a hobby. "*Cosas de mujeres.*"

Somehow, Fernando and I found a way of getting them across the Florida Strait to Miami, where I was flying to pick them up. Mami was excited for me to visit Miami, since everyone said it was like visiting a little piece of Cuba. It was the place with the largest Cuban population in the country. She was also a little hesitant, since *Scarface* had come out two years before and everyone thought all refugees on the Mariel were cocaine drug lords.

"*Ay Mami, por favor,*" I said while packing my suitcase. "I'm not going to be going to any parties or to anyone's house *ni nada de eso*. I'm staying with your friend Tamara, meeting up with Fernando's brother's sister-in-law who has the paintings, to pay her, and then I'll be back here. *Ay Mami, pero* they told me there are *cafeterias* there that have *batido de mamey.* I'm going to come back with at least ten more kilos from all the milkshakes I'm going to drink. And of course, I'll bring you some too, *pa' que te pongas gordita.*"

She nervously folded socks at the edge of my bed, placing them next to my underwear inside my luggage.

"*Dios mío santo,*" she sighed, speaking to her god. "Where did I get this child from?"

I rolled my eyes. "*Mamiiii,* you get so dramatic. Why can't you just be happy that I'm finally getting opportunities to do things that I love, that I don't have to be a bartender and come back on the latest bus, only to wake up at 6 a.m. and catch the *earliest* bus back to Manhattan."

"No, *mijito*. I'm happy. And I'm happy that you are doing things, but I get nervous. You know I'm an old lady—and that you are the only thing I have in this world, *mijo*. I hold my breath every time you leave this house. If something were to happen—"

"*Mami*, nothing bad is going to happen to me, ok? I've survived horrible things. This is all beautiful. Don't you see it? *Alégrate por mí*, don't put all that anxiety out into the world, because then you attract it." I wiped a tear from her face. "You don't want to do that, right?"

"*Claro que no*," she whimpered. "*Solavaya*."

The following day, I flew to Florida. If the air in New York was still chilly, Miami's humidity brought me back to Cuba. From the plane, we saw the coastline, where flatlands awaited me underneath burning sunlight. I'd forgotten how much I missed this weather. Tamara, a friend of *Mami*'s who had come with us on the Mariel, picked me up from the airport. Her hair had been dyed a Kool-Aid red. *Ni Celia Cruz se atrevería a tanto.* After I was done with figuring out this entire BVR situation, I'd figure out a way of telling her we should go more copper with her hair. "*No te preocupes*. I got you. I've been dyeing *Mami's* hair for years." Nothing melts a Cuban *vieja's* heart more than a *mulatón* giving them hair advice and pampering them. *De nada.*

We reached Hialeah, where I would pick up the paintings. It seemed like I'd been transported back to the island. Elders hung out on their porches playing dominoes. Women swept their front doors while chatting with their *vecinas*. For many Cubans, most of our conversations centered around our families on the island, our families here, complaining about something trivial, or boasting about our successes.

Tamara pulled over in her red "transportation"—what she called her 1962 Chevrolet— to a little blue house with a yellow fence. I could tell from the outside that the house was divided into different apartments since, from the side, there were several doors with letters labeling them.

"I'll be just a few minutes, Tama. Do you want to come down?" I asked, hoping she'd say no.

"No, no, *mijito*. I'm going to stay out here and smoke a cigarette while you go in there and do your business. *Aquí te espero*."

After getting out of the car, I pushed through the yellow gate, which screeched as I slid through it to the other side. Fernando's letter said it was apartment "B," and I should ask for Gretel. To my dismay, the apartments weren't labeled in order, with apartment "B" being at the end of the row, rather than right up front. I knocked three times, and an older woman opened the door. She could've doubled as Maria Callas, the famous Soprano, her pale skin and elongated neck looking up at me.

"*¿Sí?*" She was confused by my presence.

"*Buenas,* my name is Miguel. I am a friend of Fernando's. I am looking for Gretel."

Her dark eyes still examined me, but a light bulb went off when I mentioned Gretel's name.

"*Gretelcitaaaaaaaaaaaa,*" she yelled, still holding the door frame. "*Te buscan. Un tal Miguel.*" This was as Cuban as this interaction was ever going to get.

From the end of the hall, a tall young woman with a similar frame to the one holding the door came into view. She had soft waves pinned away from her fully freckled face. Her black hair made her hazel eyes and plump, heart-shaped lips stand out. She held a plum in her hand, which she put away in the apron covering a yellow dress with tiny flowers underneath.

"*Gracias, tía,*" she said. "Don't worry, Miguel is a friend of Fernandito's."

With a paused grunt, the aunt walked away into the apartment's kitchen.

"Come in, *por favor.* I'm sorry my aunt can be a little intimidating sometimes, but there are a lot of *bandoleros* in Miami. *Tú sabes.*" She chuckled. "Sit, sit, please, sit."

Guessing from her behavior, she could only be about 20 or 21 years old. Her face was so innocent that had I not been an honest man, I could have fooled her and run away with the paintings here and now.

"*¿Cafecito?*" She let out a big *Mammiiiii,* summoning her mother. If the aunt who greeted me could be categorized as the moon, then this other woman was the sun. Contrasting what I guessed was her sister's demeanor, she was shorter and plumper, with beautiful salt-and-pepper chestnut hair and warm brown eyes. She walked over as if she had known me my entire life, giving me a giant kiss on the cheek.

"*¡Ay,* Miguel, we had been waiting for you!" she said. "Oh! I almost forgot to introduce myself, *qué loca*. I'm Mariana, Gretelcita's mother."

She was off into the kitchen to prepare the coffee before I could answer, leaving me with Gretel again.

"*Entonces*, Gretel." I grabbed the satchel where I brought the money. "Here's the money, exactly as I promised Fernando. I know we said we'd divide it into two, but if you have all the paintings, I'm willing to give you all of the money today."

Her face turned serious, looking in the direction where the aunt had retired before speaking.

"Miguel, I'm not sure if you know this, or if Fernando told you, but I brought the paintings over myself."

I was elated at the news.

"There are twenty paintings. I just got here a few weeks ago after my mother was able to get me out. I couldn't bring the rest because Fernando was worried about you. He was worried that you'd back out of the deal, and then he would be left without anything and—"

Mariana brought *cafecito* and *pastelitos de guayaba* to the table.

"*A ver,* Miguel," Mariana took over. "We have the paintings here. I want you to see them, but we have to bring them out to your car because my sister would have a heart attack if she knew that Gretelcita brought them from Cuba in her suitcase. She's very conservative, you know, and she's not okay with that kind of thing. I don't know if Gretelcita told you, but my other daughter is going to bring the rest of the paintings. She is supposed to be here by the end of the month. We are using some of the money you paid us with today to buy her ticket."

"*Bueno*." I sighed. "I was hoping to leave with all the paintings today since coming back to Miami is very expensive for us at the gallery, but if this is the only way, then this is the only way. Let me see them."

We brought the suitcases back to Tamara's transportation, where she was jamming to disco on the radio. I laughed. "*Eso,* Tama."

There were twenty individual paintings carefully rolled into cylinders. Some were bigger than others, but most were large enough to be carried without suspicion through alleys and cities as a young woman, which I imagine is what BVR was doing with these. I opened each one to ensure the merchandise was all there. Pieces from as early as 1493, brought over from Florence, lay revealed before my eyes. There were also some from the 1500s, apparently during her time in Cuba. My heart leapt as I held them in my hands.

"*Muchísimas gracias*," I said to Gretel and her mother. "This is such an unbelievable gift. We will do her justice at the gallery."

They held hands and smiled. Tamara joined in the moment of kismet that held us all in that front stoop in Hialeah.

"I will see you at the end of the month," I said, hugging them both.

By Cuban standards, at this point, we were family.

73

UNWRAPPING

Miguel

New York, New York — 1985

After three days in the Florida sunshine, I was greeted by summer rain and balmy weather in New Jersey. I called the professor and Ariana from Miami to give them the good news, and they eagerly awaited my arrival. The professor even gave me a ride from the airport straight to the gallery in his Jaguar that smelled like the inside of a box of cigars.

Ariana was at the door of the gallery, anxiously smoking a cigarette.

"Oh my God! Are they all in there?" We squealed and bounced together while holding hands before wheeling them into the gallery. In less than five minutes, all the pieces were rolled out, and we started sorting them by date and type.

"These are exquisite!" Ariana yelped. "This opening is going to be unparalleled. I feel it!"

The professor had brought his magnifying glass and was inspecting each painting in detail. Sporadically, he'd let out a "hmm." We didn't think anything of it, until the "hmms" turned into "aaah" and by then we were *really* curious.

"Okay, enough, what's up? The suspense is killing us."

"I'm just noticing. It's quite peculiar, really. I hadn't noticed this before when I saw them on my trip to Havana, but one can miss things, you know," he babbled. "Look closer there, into the looking glass. Do you see the writing that's on the painting? Very delicate, quite sneaky of her, actually."

Ariana looked first. I tapped my feet, hurrying her. She handed it over to me, and then I saw it, the scripture on the painting. It was in Latin.

"Is it only in this painting, or all of them?" I asked.

The professor chuckled. "It's in all of them. It seems like our lady Beatriz Velázquez de Rossi was more than we gave her credit for. Now, we're going to need someone who understands Latin—and the time period— to figure this out. I think I know the exact person that can help us. I'll make a call."

He tapped his cane twice on the floor and walked out of the gallery with a grin.

Eventually, Ariana left. Beatriz Velázquez de Rossi and I sat alone in the gallery. There were many faces behind this enigma of a painter. So far, of the paintings, *Margarita* was my favorite. Her long, dark face with sharp, elegant features, all broken by a smile and slanted eyes. I could almost feel her warmth radiating in the Caribbean heat. Despite all the paintings we managed to acquire from Fernandito, we hadn't found a single one titled after the author's name. Many of them were named after flowers, especially the earlier ones.

I wonder what she would have looked like, or how we could even describe her. In just a few weeks, we would pick up the last pieces, and the exhibit would premiere months later. For an instant, I forgot I was heartbroken, I forgot my cough, and it seemed like life was finally straightening itself out.

Ariana and I started setting up the show as soon as we received the paintings. There was a lot to organize, from finding the proper frames to figuring out if any of the pieces needed restoration. They had been closeted for centuries. Something I knew a thing or two about.

We wanted to honor the origins—Spanish, Italian, and Cuban—of the paintings, without angering either side. There was very little information about her, but the professor promised to dig deeper. He had brought her into the limelight, and now he had his chance to see her shine. It was insane to me that until now, she'd never been mentioned. It was as if history had erased her, and no one bothered to give her the praise or place she deserved.

"Migue, I feel like we are on the edge of something big," Ariana said.

"Me too."

"Isn't it insane to you that this woman spent her entire life hiding her true self, her talents?"

"She didn't have much of a choice. Even today many people still hide behind a mask, a last name, an identity. We still have a long way to go."

"Mmmhm" she said. "Especially in these crazy times. By the way, did you ever call the doctor about your cough?"

"I did. I'm sure it's nothing, but I'm going next week."

74

THE PARTY

Miguel

New York, New York —1985

The professor invited us to a party some of his friends from Columbia were throwing. He thought we could "make great connections and perhaps catch one or two patrons" for the event. He knew Ariana's pockets were deep, but the gallery could use fresh patrons, especially in the middle of creating a new installation.

I dusted off the nicest clothes I owned. A navy suit I'd brought over from Cuba, and a white shirt *Mami* spent the day before dipping in and out of bleach to make as white as possible. I gelled my curls, spritzed as much cologne as possible, and headed to the professor's *soirée.* The event was on the Upper East Side, so I already knew I'd be confused for one of the waiters. Regardless, I brought my edge and my charm, ready to give it all to ensure funding for my show. Ariana was waiting for me at the door of the building, dressed to impress, rocking a perfect blowout.

"You went to that Dominican salon two blocks away from the gallery, didn't you?" I laughed.

"You know I only let Altagracia roll and set my hair. You thought I was going to show up to this white, rich people party, not looking like the heiress I am? Miguel, people are getting progressive, but they're not *that* progressive yet. And you know, for some reason, white people don't know what to do with themselves when they see textured hair, so let's just go with it. *Además*, I look stunning."

She did. You couldn't turn away from her. Ariana was one of those women that commanded a room. It wasn't only her beauty, even though she was gorgeous. It was her energy that brought you into orbit. Her elegance, her confidence, her wealth.

The professor was there to greet us, pipe in mouth. His excitement for this project was palpable as he introduced us to everyone at the party with the pride of a parent whose child just graduated from med school. This project was as much ours as it was his. He wanted this information out in the world, out in society.

Champagne, whiskey, and crab puffs bombarded us from every corner. We went on and on about BVR, boasting about her art, so much so that she started to sound more like the new Frida Kahlo.

Ariana and I found a corner to smoke and gossip. It was decided I'd be staying on this side of the river tonight after everything I'd imbibed.

"Ari, seriously, you have become like my best friend here. I don't care that you're my boss," I slurred, holding up my white wine.

"Awww, darling! I don't say this often, but you're one of my people. I don't know what the gallery—or I—would be without you," she puffed. "I'm so stoked you're here."

We were mid-laugh when Ari's face turned serious, as if seeing a ghost. She dragged one more puff.

"Migu—"

His voice cut off her warning.

"Can I join in on the laughter?"

My heart skipped a beat as I tried to maintain composure at the sound of a familiar voice. I turned towards him.

"Alessandro. What are you doing here?"

"Didn't mean to crash the party." He flashed a coy smile. "Just wanted to say *ciao* to my old pals."

I scoffed, leaving my glass of wine on a coffee table nearby. "Pardon me, Ari." I walked away.

"Miguel!" she called. "Where are you going?"

I turned. "If I don't come back, I'll see you at your place."

I stormed out of the party without grabbing my coat.

¿Qué importa?

The heat from the alcohol combined with the *empingue* I felt was more than enough warmth for an evening. We were on the 34th floor, and although I knew insistently pressing the button to call the elevator wouldn't make it come sooner, I had to release my rage somewhere.

Who the hell does he think he is? Showing up here like that? *Sin previo aviso*, as if nothing happened. As if he'd written every month. When had he even come back? Just as the elevator door opened, he turned the corner behind me, catching up.

Cojones, did he have to be so beautiful? He'd trimmed his beard and his hair, making way for the chiseled features of his face.

"Miguel—*aspetta!*" He slid his hand between the elevator doors as they closed. They opened like curtains on the inaugural night of this shit show.

"Don't come in!" I warned him. "I'm really not trying to deal with this here, Alessandro."

"Let me explain . Come out of the elevator. *Err...*We can talk, and I can tell you everything that happened."

"No. I don't want to know everything that happened. You had an entire year to reach out to me. You had a million ways of contacting me."

All the anger and sadness I suppressed for a year was now effervescent. My eyes pooled with tears I angrily wiped away. "What are you doing here, anyway?"

"Please, come out—" he started.

"*Oye*, I'm not stepping out of the elevator. Answer my question and let me go."

"I—" he hesitated. "I'm here for *you*."

I scoffed, "For *me*?"

"*Sí*, for you." He put his hands in his pockets. "The professor told me about your discovery, the painter. He said you needed an expert in Latin to help with the show. Miguel, I promise that things are more complicated than you can understand. I know that I messed up. *Cazzo*. You don't have to forgive me, but at least let me explain what happened."

"No," I said sternly. "I don't want an explanation. I lived with your ghost for a year in every corner of this fucking city. Whatever we had is buried, and I have no intention of digging it up. The professor was wrong. We *don't* need someone to help with the Latin part of the show. *Así que*, please, go back to wherever you were where you didn't need me. You're not the only one who gets to choose when to walk away."

The elevator doors closed, and I broke down, tears streaming onto the shirt *Mami* spent two days ironing. As I descended from the party that celebrated my new life in this city, this country, my past had returned to haunt me. A sick reminder that my heart still skipped a beat at the sound of his voice.

Alessandro came after me, winded from taking the stairs, closing the door of the building to prevent me from leaving.

"Five minutes," he pleaded. "Then you can go back to hating me."

75

AMORE A LA SICILIANA

Miguel

New York, New York —1985

We sat on the sidewalk in the chill of the night. The only sound between us was our breathing and the cars passing on the road. You knew things were bad when a Sicilian and a Cuban weren't uttering a single word. Typically, people had to shut us up. Called us obnoxious and loud. *Those islanders.* I'd given him thirty minutes to speak and was growing impatient by his hesitation.

"Alessandro, if you don't want to talk or have nothing to say, you can go home. I'm fine. *En verdad,* I would welcome being on my own for a bit," I said, breaking the silence.

He opened his mouth to speak, but couldn't utter a word. His head hung down with what I hoped was shame. "*Dai,* Miguel," he finally said. "I—this is not that easy for me. Please. I just don't know where to start."

"*Mira,* just start from the moment you left New York for three days and instead disappeared for a year. Sounds like a good place. Plus, you've already wasted fifteen minutes figuring it out."

"I went to Italy to take care of my *mamma* as I told you. Things were much worse than what I expected them to be, *eh*. The mafia, the *Cosa Nostra,* they're still everywhere in Sicily. Part of daily life. Constant, quiet terror. When I left, nobody there knew I was gay. But when I returned, somehow many people from our village in *Siracusa* knew. When I would take *mamma* to the clinic for her treatment, they would whisper '*guarda, guarda il frocio e sua mamma.*'"

I could sense his pain as he told me everything, bringing back memories of the fear I endured in my teenage years, and even later, just for being me. When you're gay, even if you don't say anything, even if you try to conceal your identity, a sliver of your truth always remains. If someone knew what you were hiding, and didn't like you, they start rumors that could cost your life—or even worse—bring shame to your family.

Although Alessandro's family was widely respected in Syracuse, the *Cosa Nostra* found out the son of the Romano family hadn't moved to New York to work as a professor—he was a *frocio* looking to get fucked by men. It started with higher rent on his mother's tailoring business, then demands for free suits and pieces for their men. One day, Alessandro's sister refused to design a cashmere suit for Lino Dipinto, a local capo. The next, not a single hospital from Syracuse to Noto would give them oxygen for their mother. Alessandro drove to Catania, outside of Dipinto's reach, where an old friend of his from university sold him three tanks.

"I wanted to reach out to you, Miguel, I wanted to tell you what was happening, but if the letters were intercepted, or even the calls, I could have been killed. They plant bombs in cars, or make it look like you had an accident one morning while fishing." He wrung his hands. "*Ma,* I had to take care of *mia famiglia*. I know you understand that. I know you also would do anything for your *mamma* and your aunts if you had to."

Cabrón, he knew where my soft spots lay. I looked up at him, "Would you have forgiven me if I didn't let you know and returned like nothing happened? *¿Así como si nada*?"

He grabbed my hand. "*No, no, non è* like nothing happened. *Miguel io so* that I hurt you and that I didn't do things the proper way. *Lo so*. I know you also think that this is all un *cazzo, una bugia, ma ti prego, perdonami*. I have buried my mother. My sister is safe. I could have stayed in Roma, but I returned here to be with you."

His last words took me by surprise. I always questioned the sincerity of this charm. I looked up at him, eyes wide. *Dios mío, ¿qué hago?* His tinted blue eyes made me want to dive into the clear waters of his soul and surrender to the current. I could fight with him eternally, stand tall in my pride, or I could forgive him and move forward. There was one more thing I needed to know to make my decision.

"Did you know I was in an accident last year?" I asked.

"No, not at all. I would have surely reached out if I had known, I promise. What happened?"

"I was hit by a car while I was walking home from work," I said. "It took fourteen units of blood, nine shocks to the heart, and several minutes of compressions to bring me back to life. The driver's cassette was stuck, he was trying to fix it, so distracted he didn't see me crossing the road. *Siempre hay algún come mierda.*"

Alessandro stood, running his hands through his head.

"The ambulance came fast, my people slow. No one knew where I was for three days, just gone. I had forgotten my wallet at the gallery. I had three broken ribs, a fractured femur, a concussion, and two head lacerations. All on top of this heartbreak you left behind. I've healed from almost everything, except a slight limp. This cough that won't go away, the legacy of the broken ribs, I suppose."

76

ABANDON ALL HOPE

Miguel

New York, New York — 1985

We rushed to Alessandro's loft on the corner of St. Marks' Place, just above a pizzeria. I retraced the three flights of steps that led to the tiny sign at his door that read, "Abandon all hope, ye who enter here."

The phrase was the most quoted line from Dante's *Inferno*, the first book of *The Divine Comedy*. It was how Alessandro and I initially connected. He had seen me reading while I waited for a snowstorm to pass when I worked at Tito's.

A new thought flashed through my mind.

How long had it been since we slept together? Because for sure that's what was about to happen.

With my body still healing, I was unsure what was left from the fire that once burned through both of us. We stood in the middle of the room, watching each other. His black waves with strands of gray looked like rays of moonlight in an *apagón*. The constellation of freckles descending from the back of his neck to his shoulder, three tiny ones on the corner of his eye, forming a triangle. He walked over to me, leaning in for a kiss.

I pulled his face toward mine, kissing him hard, passionately. My body, on fire, betraying my heart. He released a soft moan, his hand leading me to the bed. I felt my desire for him rise between my legs, his hands reaching down to confirm it. He whispered something in Italian that I didn't understand. I was too lost in the feeling of him to care.

"*Ven, bésame,*" I said. "I want your tongue in my mouth."

"*Non ti preoccupare, caro*. It's about to trace every inch of your body." His touch was a symphony of contradictions, soft, then hard, then soft again, releasing the mixture of suppressed desire with the knowledge of my fragility.

"Don't be gentle with me," I moaned. "I want to feel you, all of you, hard and inside me."

With the slightest hesitation, he reached for a condom in the drawer of his nightstand, and set it aside before lowering his face to my cock. I moaned as his tongue rolled up and down my shaft, stopping to suction the tip.

Ah, pinga. *Qué ricooo.* I dug my fingers into his scalp, pressing myself deeper into his mouth, leaving it there until his eyes watered. "*¿Así?*" I asked. He nodded.

"*Qué rico, papi,*" I continued. "*Dios*, I want you to fuck me so badly. Just do it, don't torture me anymore."

Wiping his face, he stroked his bursting cock, handing me the condom. "*Dai,* help me put it on. You don't expect me to do all the work, do you?"

He lowered himself over me, lifting my knees up to my chest before entering me. It hurt. I was tight after such a long time without sex.

"Am I hurting you?" He leaned in to kiss me without thrusting. "We can stop if it hurts too much. We can do other—"

"—No." I lowered his face back to mine, sticking my tongue in his mouth. "I want you inside me. I *need* you inside me, right now. *Te necesito*."

And we flowed, like two rivers destined to meet at the ocean.

77

THE DIAGNOSIS

Miguel

New York, New York —1985

I couldn't ignore the cough anymore. Or the swollen lymph nodes. Not to mention the constant hammering in my head. I scheduled my appointment with the doctor and went by myself, even though *Mami* had asked if she could come with me.

The fluorescent light of the halls brought chills to my body as the nurse walked me through a corridor and into an examination room. Undress and stay in your underwear, the doctor will be right with you. A rash had formed where my ribs fractured previously, and the constant cough probably wasn't helping.

Ay, virgencita, que no sea nada grave.

The doctor came in with his white coat. He had a thick Brooklyn accent as he greeted me. My file in hand, he's eyeing it, eyes widening. Silently, he sifts and shifts, back and forth. *Hmm. Hmmm.*

Hmm, ¿qué? Compadre. What is it?!

"Alrighty, Miguel. It looks like you've been coming in and out of here for your recovery from your accident." He continued leafing through the file's pages. "With doctor Abernathy."

"Yes, yes. I have returned a few times since, because my leg still hasn't healed...and this cough. It feels like I've had a cold for months that won't go away."

"Well, let's see what's going on with you"

He took the stethoscope out, listening to my lungs. I cough at the cold touch. Then, he takes a look at the rash on my chest, moving his hands toward my lymph nodes.

"Miguel, now, I need to ask you a few questions, if you don't mind. "

"Ok, sure," I say.

"Are you experiencing night sweats or persistent fevers?"

"Yes."

"Have you had any unusual weight loss lately?"

"*Bueno*. I haven't been as active as before. I have probably lost some muscle."

"Are you sexually active?"

"What?"

"Are you sexually active with men...women, or both?" He looks up from the file.

"Eh...yes."

"Yes to what?"

"I am sexually active, sir. I'm 33 years old; who is a virgin at this age?" *Sapingo*.

"With men?" He says judgingly.

I hesitate, looking down at the examination table, guessing what he was implying. "Yes, with men."

"Hmm...." He flips through the pages of the file.

"My symptoms started after I came here for treatment following the accident. I know everyone thinks that all gay men have anonymous sex at bathhouses without condoms, but that's not me."

"Well, I see here you've had several blood transfusions after your accident. Has anyone called you about this?"

"Called me? No, no one has called me." I racked my brain for the possibility of someone reaching out, calling the house and *Mami* answering. No messages were left on the answering machine.

The doctor rolled his chair forward toward an examination counter, drawing a vial and needle. Then rolled over to me.

"Miguel, I need your permission to take your blood for an examination. To test for Human Immunodeficiency Virus."

My heart stopped with fear. "AIDS?"

"Miguel, a few months ago, we called several recipients of blood transfusions who came into the hospital the same week as you. We realized that some of that blood was contaminated with the human immunodeficiency virus. It is known to cause AIDS."

I felt my world crumble before me as the air left my lungs. Blood drained from my face, replaced by pin needles. "Are you telling me I have—" I thought of Alessandro, the night we spent together.

"Do not panic for now. We need to test you first." His words felt further and further away. The room started spinning, my breath shortening. "Miguel" I heard my name in the distance.

"Miguel!?" I felt my body collapse on the examination table. "Help! Nurse."

Then, it all went dark.

78

POSITIVE

Miguel

New York, New York—1985

HIV-positive. That was my death sentence. It came neatly typed on white paper, not a single smudge. Tucked in an envelope for me to take home in secrecy. In 1985, there was still no cure for this, and I chuckled ironically on the subway as I thought of *Mami* always telling me "*Si tu mal no tiene cura...*"

Well, *Mami,* this time, my illness really doesn't have a cure.

It's not just the illness, either; it's everything that comes associated with it. *El chu-chu-chu,* the "he was probably promiscuous." The stigma kills you before the disease. As if many of the same people who criticize you aren't mere mortals, just like me.

Heck. I wish I had contracted it like that—in bed with someone I wanted, someone I chose. At least there would have been warmth, an orgasm, some moment of trust and thrill.

No. Mine was just a case of medical negligence, a system that *still* hadn't figured out a way to effectively screen blood samples. They pushed it straight into my veins, no margin for failure. Maybe when the gays aren't the only ones dying in masses, they'll figure it out. In the meantime, I would die.

I looked down at the pamphlets the nurse handed me for support groups, transfer documents for the new hospital I'd have to go to for palliative treatment, since they didn't take any HIV+ patients there.

We're sorry we fucked up, but here's a place that won't discriminate you.

79

A SOUL VESSEL

Miguel

New York, New York — 1985

It was opening night at the gallery, and I found myself at a hospital on the Upper West Side of town. It was far, even farther with the cane I now relied on. It was also the only one available to people with AIDS. I had four hours to get to the exhibition in SoHo to ensure everything was going smoothly. I had with me a change of clothes for tonight.

The support groups were bullshit. All I did there was meet other people in the same situation. It wasn't exactly how I wanted to spend the rest of my limited days, but they would give us intravenous vitamins, and those made me feel better. Tonight, I needed to feel better. Not like I would die at any moment.

The thoughts sent my body into panic. My hands were damp with sweat in the nearly empty subway car, thick with the smell of old cigarettes and metal. I clutched my cane. My mouth went dry, and I tasted the familiar rust. Then the almost imperceptible tightness in my chest started.

Respira, Miguel. Respira.

My heart ignored the deep breathing crap the psychologist fed me, drumming against my chest in an almost ritualistic beat. The car felt too small, the ceiling too low, my breathing fast and shallow. The fluorescent lights flickered as the car rushed through another tunnel. A surge of heat rose at the back of my neck, followed by a wave of nausea.

I reached for the cold metal pole, but it slid through my sweaty palms. I gripped tighter, pulling myself up, desperate to escape the train at the next stop, which happened to be near Columbia University.

"Excuse me, excuse me," I pushed past the doors onto the platform, breathing the hot heavy air into my already beaten lungs.

A familiar voice found me.

"Miguel Ángel?" It was the professor. "Miguel Ángel, come." He led me to a bench, where I collapsed. "What's happening? Do you want to go to the hospital? Are you all right?"

The world around us started softening, tears finding their way into my eyes. I stared up at his gray face, sobbing.

"I don't want to die, professor. I don't want to die. I don't want to die."

"Slow down, slow down now."

"It's killing me, professor. This disease, it's going to take me."

"Just try to breathe for now. We are all dying, just taking different routes to get there."

I shot him a look that could kill.

He cocked his head. "Just reminding you."

"Have you ever been terminally ill, professor? Right before your grand moment?"

"I can't say I have ever been in your position, and you have every right to be angry, Miguel." He put his hand on mine in a fatherly way. "I am, however, a bit older than you. And if the theories of life are right, at some point soon enough, I will die. I think, give or take, in a decade or two. It seems like a lot of time, but it goes by in a blink. I believe our bodies don't know what dying feels like, but our souls remember."

"I don't follow," I said, still nauseated.

"We have lived many lives before this one, Miguel. This is not your first time here. We have also died many times. Your soul remembers those deaths. Some which may have been violent. Others hopefully less so. Each one is a transition into another life experience where our soul grows like a vessel navigating through time."

I had never heard the professor speak this way before.

"Be gentle with yourself, Miguel. Forgive yourself for the events that may have led you here, which, may I remind you, were *not* your fault. There is no right way to live or die. And you are doing both quite valiantly."

"I don't want to die in pain. Or even be too sick to move."

"Then don't. In any case, what goes unfinished in this incarnation, you will resolve in another."

"Professor, how do you know about all this? You're an academic..."

He snuffed. "Academics also have souls, Miguel. I have an inkling we've had this conversation in another life already."

80

UN PADRE NUESTRO

Miguel

New York, New York — 1985

P*adre nuestro que estás en los cielos, santificado sea tu nombre... La muerte está en la puerta.* I can feel her. She's the promise of life no one wants to believe in, until she comes, and we have no other choice but to surrender to her.

Venga a nosotros tu reino, hágase tu voluntad en la tierra como en el cielo...

I never learned how to pray, at least not to the God I was told hates women and the gays. Is this his punishment? I used to pray to Yoruba gods, and now I'm wondering if they felt the same. Rafael at the clinic is helping me learn the *Padre Nuestro*, so I can place my burdens in God's hands. He says God loves me.

Danos hoy nuestro pan de cada día...

Perdona nuestras ofensas como nosotros perdonamos a los que nos ofenden...

This disease—this incurable thing eating away at me—

requires a certain kind of understanding I can't find anywhere else. No one warns you of the loneliness. The anger. The pain.

No nos dejes caer en la tentación, y líbranos de todo mal...

Death is at the door. I can feel her. And even though the professor says this isn't actually the end, I'm not sure what I'll find on the other side.

Today, I tell death, "Just not before the premiere of my show, *hija de puta*."

Grant me this wish, God. We will see to the rest when we meet.

Amén.

81

RENAISSANCE FLOWERS FROM THE CARIBBEAN

Miguel

New York, New York —1985

B*eatriz, llegó nuestro día. Everyone will know who you were now, Beatriz. Lo prometido es deuda.*

I stepped into the gallery in my seafoam linen suit, light as air; it felt like it was spun from summer itself. I was the first one here.

The fabric breathed easily against my skin, loose enough to conceal my war wounds, and sharp enough to let everybody know I was the person behind putting this all together. I limped through the gallery, the faces of the women BVR turned into flowers, staring back at me. They were their own pantheon of goddesses, each in their respective powers and hues. Ariana had bought me a special cane for the occasion. Black lacquered wood, smooth as piano keys, the base decorated with poppies and sunflowers in red and gold. The silver handle was fitted to my hand, a symbol of security and grandeur.

The door opened behind me, and Ariana walked in, arms wide open, her laughter filling the room.

"¡Miguel Ángel García! You did it, *Papi*!" She crashed into me, her enormous hair sticking to my lapel pin. "There is so much buzz around this opening already. Someone from the *New York Times* is coming to cover it and everything. They want to interview you today."

"Me!?" I was shocked. "You're the owner!"

"HELLOOO you managed to get these paintings out of CUBA, my love. Everyone wants to know who you are and where you've been hiding!"

She caught herself mid-sentence. "You know what I mean, sugar."

The caterers, bartenders, and musicians arrived first. Then, with the light of the sunset, a crowd lined up outside the door of the gallery. To my surprise, dozens of people showed up. And not just the people I knew. Members of New York's elite had made their way down to SoHo to see the work of Beatriz Velázquez de Rossi. They wanted the *chisme* on how this Renaissance woman made it to the Caribbean, and somehow, ended up on the island of Manhattan. Within the first few hours, three of her paintings were sold.

Ariana took the stage, thanking everyone who made it down to our little gallery for their incredible support of our work. The place was so packed, there were people standing outside the door sipping on their small cups of white wine. Alessandro stood in the back of the room, gleaming next to the professor.

"And now, I want to pass on the microphone to someone very special, without whom we wouldn't have even known about the existence of BVR. I have to say, when he first brought the idea over to me, I was concerned about putting up the artwork of a potential colonizer. That is until Miguel proved me wrong. While she did immigrate, like so many of us have from our countries, this woman came forth to the Caribbean not seeking to colonize, but to tell stories through her art...and today we're honored to share her work and legacy. Miguel, *por favor*." She handed the mic over to me.

I could hear the cameras shuttering in the back. It wasn't just the *New York Times*, it was also the *Post*, the *Native*, and *Columbia's Daily Spectator*. The confidence I'd felt all evening washed away as I neared the microphone, which echoed as I held it close.

"*Bueno*...my English is not very good, but I hope you will move past my accent to what truly matters today: Beatriz. I first heard of this incredible painter by chance, wandering the halls of Columbia University one day. I sat in on a lecture about a woman who made my island her home. We don't know if she was rich, poor, or if she chose the place I was born to spend her final days. What I did know was that I needed to know more about her. The paintings you see here today sat in a closet in Trinidad for centuries. It's a miracle no one used them to light a fire on days of scarce electricity." The crowd laughed.

"There are always questions of who owns or doesn't own art. If it belongs in one specific place or if it should be distributed. Maybe we'll never agree. All I know is that for 500 years, no one cared to look at these faces and think they deserved a place in the world. That is why we paint, why we create, why we write and sing. To give things a place, to make things known. As I curated this exhibit while fighting the epidemic of our generation, I felt the same urge as Beatriz to portray things not as people saw them, or thought they did, but to portray their soul. Their essence. These bodies we carry change, fade—often betray us. Our souls are trapped in them for the duration of our stay on this planet. As you look through each of these images tonight, whether you choose to purchase one or admire them here, know you are not simply taking a portrait of a woman, you are taking her whole story. I hope you will help me make the artist's name known. She deserves the same attention as so many of her male contemporaries did, and I'll be happily quoted saying '*no tiene nada que envidiarles*'. Enjoy tonight. *Salud*."

By the end of the evening, the gallery turned into a center for celebration. The wine flowed and laughter roared. I sat near the entrance, observing patrons basking in commentary over the exhibition. In the corner, Alessandro and the professor spoke ardently with their students, his Italian hand gestures speaking louder than his words. *Mami* left an hour before with *Tía* Teresita, Margarita, Tamara and their work friends. She gave me a kiss before leaving, radiating in pride.

"*Estoy muy orgullosa de ti, mijito*. I loved it." She kissed my forehead. "I'll see you at home."

Watching it all unfold, I felt the sudden urge to stand and step into the evening breeze. I crossed the street, looked back at the gallery, and smiled.

82

LOS ARETES DE LA LUNA

Miguel

New York, New York — 1985

At first, I didn't know where I was going, simply strolling down Watts St. toward Canal. The moon was full, gleaming over the buildings like a lantern illuminating the way. I kept walking until I reached the edge of the river. The park was empty for a Thursday, the dark water of the Hudson still. I slid my jacket off, letting it fall first; the weight lifted. I felt the breeze. It caressed my head, held my hand, and led me closer to the edge.. The river was high enough to slip into it, like I did when I went to the coast in *La Habana del Este* with my cousins as a child. Memories.

I didn't bother taking off my pants, just my shoes, as I glided into the water. It felt like velvet against my hot skin. I rolled onto my back, eyes wide open, as I gazed at the moon. I wasn't scared.

Los aretes que le faltan a la luna, los tengo guardados para hacerte un collar...

The water held me like the sound of my *abuela's* voice making me *el almuerzo* after I returned home from school while she sang along to Vicentico Valdés.

Los hallé una mañana en la bruma...cuando caminaba junto al inmenso mar...

Let's walk together, *abuela.* I've missed you so much, *mi vieja.*

Privilegio que agradezco al cielo, porque ningún poeta los pudo encontrar...

My body floated, drifted. My eyes closed slowly as I surrendered to the current.

Yo los guardo en un cofre dorado. Son mi única fortuna, y te los voy a dar.

The letters are on top of the dresser. A goodbye note. *Mi cadenita de oro.*

Ariana will know how to distribute the money from my commissions of the sales.

Todo salió bien. Perdóname, Mami...Ale.

Los aretes que le faltan a la luna, los tengo guardados en el fondo del mar.

And in the arms of the Yoruba river goddess, Oshun, I left.

83

DROWNED IN SORROW

Mar

Florence, Italy – 2024

It all made sense now. My fear of drowning, the dying pain, the failure. I bawled as Almaguer watched from the other side of the screen and I released the memories.

"Perhaps this is what you needed to see Mar, before moving forward," Almaguer said. "Let it out. Release it."

I held my hands up to my face, wiping away the tears.

I sat with my grief for a moment, thinking of how short-lived that life was. Thinking that now I had the opportunity to live what he did not. Dario was also right—he was the reincarnation of his uncle Alessandro, who had been Miguel's lover. He had been Dante and Alessandro and all the other souls that had accompanied me through these lifetimes.

"Tell me, Mar, what have you learned from this experience?"

I couldn't stop the tears long enough to tell her.

84

NEW TERMS

Mar

Florence, Italy – 2024

I was set to return to Madrid. I woke up to the subtle rays of dawn peering through Dario's window. He rested on his side, facing me. I watched his breath rise and fall as I took in every detail of his being. His thick, bushy eyebrows, the tight curve of his jaw, prickly with his dark beard peppered with white hairs. The scar on the side of his cheek from when he fell into his mother's rose bush. I pushed back the desire to touch him, slowly rising from the bed to gather the remains of my things.

I grabbed some clothes, still sitting out, and headed into the shower. Soon enough, his black hair appeared at the door. "May I?" He pointed at the shower.

"*Sí, sí,* sure," I rinsed my hair. "I'm almost done."

He towered over me as water spilled over him. "Have you ever seen the statue of Juno that is at the Galleria Dell'Accademia? The one where she is lying on her side?"

A PowerPoint slide flashed through my memory. The ancient Roman goddess with her firm breasts out, soft belly, chest proud and chin up. Her long waves draped over her, a diadem keeping them in control.

"Yes, it's housed in the hall of models, if I'm not mistaken," I said, spreading soap all over his body.

"I had a dream last night that she was you. *My Junone*," he teased. "She looks just like you when you're naked. Radiating your inner power."

I laughed, pulling his wet face toward mine for a kiss before I stepped out of the shower, feeling like a *diosa*. Drying myself, I felt the inevitable conversation we'd been avoiding for days creep up on us. We decided to have breakfast out in the city, finding a small coffee shop without too many people to hear how we would move forward with our relationship.

"Dario, I want to start off by saying *grazie*," I said. "In a time when ghosting, indifference, and fleeting moments are the norm, I'm sure that our connection can feel a bit...intense. I'm not going to say that we're meant to be together. Because you're right, it should be a choice. But I have to be honest with you, Dario, because over the last year, I've discovered something about me. I'm not the ghosting, fleeting, or acting cool type. I'm the send love letters, leave you the last slice of pizza, love you with the door open type. And it might be too soon to make 'relationship' decisions, and you may not even want to. I just can't go back to Spain without you knowing how I feel."

His eyes smiled back at me, glistening with tears. He reached over for my hand. "Mar. Ever since I saw you get off that tram, all I've wanted to do is sit at the kitchen table with you. Go to the grocery store. Make love to you as if I came back from another life to do just that. Be your lover, friend, and accomplice. Hold your hand and kiss you whenever I want. All of this you're feeling, I feel it too."

He paused, taking a moment to think of his next words. "It's just not the right moment for me. Before you walked into my life, I had projects and plans—I don't even know how long I'd be in Florence. I know that if we do this, I'm going to lose myself."

Despite how much it hurt, I understood. It was the wound he had carried with him throughout his lifetime, of not choosing who he loved, of losing the sense of who he was within the people he loved.

"We have a choice now, though, isn't that something?" I said. "Isn't that worth thinking about? Can you really go on as if none of this happened?"

He stared back at me with a pained expression. "No, of course not. The past few months I will remember for the rest of my life. I just think it's best that we return to our normal lives."

And with those words, we had lost each other again.

The tears came without summoning, flowing on their own. I walked through Florence alone. Feeling the agony of knowing what I lost here, what I lived here. Knowing that our souls hadn't met by chance, but traveled through time until we could be together. Now that we could choose, that we'd found each other in a time when the choice was ours to make, he wasn't sure.

If the trap of our previous lives was that we couldn't be together, the trap of this one was that maybe we didn't want to choose each other at all. Whatever it was, it was time for me to take my desire by the hand and lead it, instead of letting it lead me.

I thought back to my session with Almaguer—Miguel's bravery. He had carried the pain from all our previous lives and transformed it. Doing things on his own terms. Now, it was time for me to do the same.

After picking up my things from Dario's apartment, he walked me to the tram, where we said goodbye quietly, in gratitude. And like turning a page, I was back in Madrid.

85

THIRTY

Mar

Madrid, Spain – 2024

My thirtieth birthday came around that fall, a couple of months after my return from Italy. I had not heard from Dario since. The first weeks I cried desperately, waking up in the middle of the night, dreaming of a life I'd already lived. Sometimes, I'd see him in a dream and send him peace. Eventually, the dreams faded, and I learned to rest.

My friends prepared cake, candles, and a huge party that celebrated my life, but I couldn't enjoy any of it—despite all my attempts at healing, my wounds were still open. I stepped away from the party while everyone was dancing and stared at myself in the mirror.

What did I *actually* want out of life now that my twenties were behind me? Was I ready to embrace it? What was I going to do with everything I knew now about my past lives?

Once again, I had more questions than answers. The only thing I *truly* had all along was myself. Wine poured all around me, as friends showered me with the love I knew I deserved. The love that wasn't afraid to embrace the parts of me that weren't always a *diosa*. And I would have to live with that, for now.

"I'm not calling for a past lives session. I just want to talk," I told Almaguer over the phone, standing outside her office. "Can you come down for a coffee?"

A few minutes later, we had picked up cappuccinos from Alma, finding a spot in Plaza de Olavide to sit.

"How was the big milestone birthday party?" she said. "I'm sorry I couldn't make it. My daughter was graduating that day. How are you feeling now that you've been back for a while?"

"The party was nice, but I don't know, I'm still sad? A part of me is still moving forward. I'm just bummed I didn't break the curse, you know?"

She sighed. "Mar, can I be honest with you?"

"Always."

"There has never been a curse. There is no such thing as curses," she said. "I know that you *believe* in it—it's been looming over you all this time. You thought that by breaking it, you could get Dario to love you, your family would move on from tragedies you couldn't explain, and that you would finally get the fairytale we've all been sold."

"What?" I said in shock.

"We believe in curses because it is easier for us to grasp than to take action in our own lives. Your happiness is in your own hands, Mar. You just have to accept yourself, give yourself the love you want—the love you deserve. *You* are the love you have been looking for."

86

THE LOVE WITHIN

Mar

Madrid, Spain – 2024

Almaguer was right. As much as I had grieved over Guille's actions a year ago, the recent events with Dario, even my belief in the curse—they wounded me so deeply only because I was searching for validation everywhere except within myself.

Now I knew exactly what I had to do. The path I had to walk was one of love and forgiveness. How could I expect love from the outside world if all this time I had been rejecting the love I felt for myself? I had been looking outside for the answers, in the past, in my family, and in others. And the answers were here, in the woman I was today.

I looked at myself in the mirror, recognizing that within me lived a woman of multitudes that can be many things at once, bold *and* shy, talented *and* self-conscious, creative *and* in a rut, happily single *and* a hopeless romantic. I took off the armor I'd built all my life to keep me from accepting myself, ready to leave the past behind.

87

FORGIVENESS

Mar

Madrid, Spain – 2024

I walked into La Vaquería in desperate search for coffee as I ran late for a client meeting. "Mario! Quick. A lactose-free *manchado*, no sugar. To go. Thanks!"

While I waited for my order, I turned to the sound of a familiar voice: Guille. He was sitting at the table where our story started, with Silvi. He stared out into the window while she looked at her phone. He asked her something, but she didn't respond. Neither looked at each other now.

Huh. I thought.

Here we were, all of us. The same bodies, but now different people. Seeing him here, at our spot, with her, didn't hurt anymore. It was as if we were strangers. I realized I had finally forgiven him.

The last time I had seen him in my apartment, I was in so much pain that I didn't even know where the light would come in from ever again. I thought our relationship was everything to me, but if it hadn't been for how he left me, I would have never come to terms with how disconnected I truly was from love.

I knew now that love should feel safe. It should be a place of peace to be oneself. Most of all, the heart should be with whom it chooses to be, not with whom we think we should be with because they fit some idea of love we have in our mind.

"Here's your coffee, Mar," Mario said, breaking me from my spell.

I looked over at Guille once more before leaving. He raised his head, acknowledging me.

I never looked back.

That same day, I wrote Dario a letter. I told him of how I regretted the way things ended between us, even how they started.

Dario,

I hope you live freely and happily with whom you want to be with. Finding a love that fulfills your desires in the way that you wish, not by force, but with ease. For love is freedom. That is what you have taught me.

I gave him an address where we could meet if he wished to. Otherwise, I would let our love go forever and be at peace with what it was.

Finally, I headed home to Miami.

I drove to *Papi's* grave first. His tomb was empty, his tombstone rested next to *Abuela* Cristina's. I brought them both a bouquet filled with the sunflowers they both loved. *Mami* came with me, sitting quietly.

"Thank you, *Mami*," I said. "Thank you for raising me on your own, even through all the pain you must have felt. The grief of losing the love of your life."

She looked at me, her mouth agape. "It was my honor, Mar." She placed her hands on my face. "I wish I would have known how to be more gentle, how to allow you to carve your own path. I didn't want to raise you with fear, but I didn't know another way. I was also scared."

"I know, *Mami*. We're going to do it differently from now on."

That afternoon, I drove to the beach on my own. I put on a bathing suit, walked into the water and let the waves crash into me. I was fearless. I closed my eyes, letting myself take in the feeling of water flowing through my hands, and I knew then in my heart that all this time, the love that moved the sun and all the other stars in my universe was the one I felt for myself.

88

FIELDS OF POPPIES

Mar

Dozza, Italy – 2026

Dozza looked completely different two years after my first visit. Not much had actually changed, except the town was stripped of all the murals previously decorating every corner of it. The town had invited me to participate in the 30th edition of the Biennial of the Painted Wall after I'd dedicated my latest mural in Madrid to Beatriz's work.

I'd opened a space to heal the wounds of my soul by honoring both her talent and the work Miguel Angel initiated over forty years ago. My soul had reached this milestone. His mother, who was still alive, gifted me with his research, two paintings, and a few diaries he'd written before his untimely death.

"*Ay mijita*, I'd rather someone bring light into that dark period of our lives," she said when I visited her at her home in New Jersey. "Go on, do something big with it."

There was something surprisingly healing about being

seen. About working on myself and living in my love. Lucas published an article about the forgotten female contributors of the Renaissance in a prominent art magazine, with Beatriz leading the story. All the other *Fiori*, with the help of Alessandro's research, were mentioned too.

The town, already popular for its murals, became even more prominent as people were moved by Beatriz's story and the love she didn't have the opportunity to live here. They had also added Dante's contributions to the town through his writing, publishing his works during the event. After all, this story was, in part, his too.

Dozza buzzed with anticipation as artists and tourists alike flocked to the week-long event. I passed painters and organizers on my way to the house we had rented for the weekend from a meeting they had for muralists. It coincidentally sat across the field where Beatrice held Dante as he died 500 years ago.

I saw Sol's mural, the replica of the one I'd seen at the Prado all those years ago, was being washed over with egg-yolk colored hues in preparation for my mural. Sol had found me—or I'd found her, I still wasn't sure—and now it was time for her to rest.

I walked into the house, where Lucas and Tania were drinking coffee at the garden table. *Mami* and *Abuela* Mariana would arrive in two days to see the festival. They were visiting Rome and the pope first. Even Almaguer made the trip to see my work take up more blank space.

I took advantage of their distraction to organize my materials. The cans of paint, my sketch of the mural, my notes. Everything was ready and in order, but I felt an itch, a calling, to go to the field where so long ago Dante had perished. I went back into my room, arranging what I'd wear later that night to the welcome event for the muralists, deciding to take a walk before sunset.

My feet led me down a path to what from afar looked like a

wheat field, but as I got closer, I saw them. Thousands and thousands of poppies in bloom, swaying in waves as the wind caressed them. This was the field where their original home was, where the tragedy happened, where now life had taken over. All of it, liberated. I ran my hand through their soft petals, taking in their intoxicating scent. I felt the corners of my mouth form into a smile. If past lives regression therapy had taught me something, it was that the eternal nature of our souls always awarded us opportunities to heal.

The sun was starting to set, painting the sky with hues of oranges, pinks, and violets over the fields. Taking a deep breath in, I continued walking toward a single stone wall with a window that stood in the middle of the field. The surrounding grass was so tall, I barely noticed it, like an optical illusion.

I reached the corner when a tall figure emerged. He didn't startle me. Somehow, something bigger than me knew he would be here, waiting. Standing there, he grinned as if he'd come to the same conclusion.

"Mar." He walked closer to me.

I looked for the right words for this moment. I'd asked him to meet me in Florence last year, and he hadn't shown up.

The only words I could utter were, "Dario, what are you doing here?"

He looked out at the field, then at me. "Lucas told me you'd been selected for the festival. I'd been meaning to reach out to you earlier…it's just I felt like an idiot writing or calling you after so much time apart. I didn't go to our meeting place. I've regretted not taking a chance with you ever since you left Florence. I guess I was more of a coward than I gave myself credit for."

"I guess so." I looked up. "Don't worry, Dario. The situation was murky. Painful. It was difficult to understand. All debts are paid. We're both free to choose as we wish. I'm not resentful. I'm in a great place now."

"What if my wish is for us to get to know each other again?" he asked. "What if I want to find out why my soul chose to come back time and time again to find *you*?"

I stood, quiet, my heart pounding at the softness of his words. The ones I'd longed to hear for so long.

"If your feelings for me are not the same, if they have changed, I understand," he said. "Two years is a long time. A week, a month, all of it was a long time. But I'm here for you, now, Mar. Willing to take that next step, if that's what you want too. I know that this love isn't just fated, or destiny, or a thing of soul mates. I have chosen you every day for the last two years, and I am willing to withstand the trials that it may bring, if it means I get to love and be loved by you."

I stepped forward, finding the groove on his chest where I'd rested my head during our last night together. I pressed him against me, taking in his scent, letting the sunset seal this moment. Then, I stepped back, finding his hand and intertwining it with mine.

"It's getting dark, *andiamo*."

THE END

AUTHOR'S NOTE

To all who read *The Sun and All the Other Stars*,

It is often said that grief is the price we pay for love. But over the course of the two years it took this novel to bloom, I've learned from my own experiences that to sit with grief is to sit with love, and to sit with both means you are alive.

Writing *The Sun and All the Other Stars* was, for me, a way of healing many of life's complex moments. During this time, I fell in love, went through breakups, experienced a miscarriage, and even lost my beloved dog, Lucy. While entirely a work of fiction, this book is a place where I hope readers can ask themselves the same questions I so often found myself asking during my journey to the other side of grief.

In this book, you will find historical figures, locations, and events inspired by real life but reshaped by my imagination to bring this story to life. This includes the personality of Sandro Botticelli and the artistic contributions of BVR. Finally, while the past-life regression experiences depicted here are informed by my personal experience with these therapies, I recognize that such experiences vary deeply from person to person.

All that being said, while it is uncertain how many lives we will live and how many incarnations we go through, take this novel as my token of gratitude for the chance to coincide in *this* life as reader and author.

With love,
-Karla

ACKNOWLEDGMENTS

When I started writing *The Sun and All the Other Stars* on pen and paper, sitting under the shadow of the Santa Maria del Fiore in Florence, I never imagined this story would come to life as it has. Though I've been a writer for as long as I can remember, this, my first novel, has been a transformative labor of love and the truest work of my soul. I would be remiss if I didn't share my deepest gratitude to the people who helped this book flourish.

First, to Jeanell English and Tanya Sam, thank you for believing in *TSATOS* from the very beginning, and to the entire team behind Elizabeth & Minnie—you are all truly the best!

To my incredible editor, Chersti Nieveen, for your unwavering brilliance and guidance. You helped me transform this manuscript into the novel my soul truly wanted to write. I couldn't have done it without your insight.

A special thank you to my dear friend and fellow author, Yamily Habib, who was the very first person to read *TSATOS* and tell me, "You need to write this to the end." Thank you for that vital push.

I now turn to the people in my life who continuously believed in me, loved me, and held me through this process.

To *Mami*, who showed me that with passion and perseverance, any dream is possible. Thank you for the sacrifices you made so I could build the life of my dreams.

To my grandparents, Clara and Eddiwson, for being my

unwavering pillars and my constant inspiration. Your love is a great protagonist in this book.

To my big, loud Cuban family, who have always supported my creative spirit and inspire so much of the familial love in this book.

To my uncle Ariel, for sharing invaluable anecdotes that shaped one of my favorite characters, and inspiring me with your love life.

To Marian, for helping me transform the world of *TSATOS* into Spanish.

To Vane, for showing me that the most important thing one has to be in life is oneself.

To Kris, Erika, Luis David, Emely, Tania, Daniel, Michelle, and Mirtle—thank you for listening to pages upon pages of text at every hour of the day and night. Your friendship is invaluable to me.

To Yudi, for your detailed counsel and support.

To Antonio, for being my Alberto.

To Milo and Lucy, my pups—the long nights would have never been bearable without your unconditional love and furry cuddles.

To Agustina de Belaustegui, the real Adriana Almaguer of my life. Thank you for leading me through every inferno and helping me find the profound love that lives within. Thank you for pushing me to write this book and see it through the end.

To Sheila Flores and the team at SER, for teaching me the intricacies and cycles of the soul. Including their sacred contracts.

To my friend and photographer, Jorge Andrés Alonso, for my author photos, and for reviewing Miguel's chapters and helping me depict his experience as authentically as possible.

To Maria Teresa, a promise is a promise.

The entire team at La Vaquería, Madrid, thank you for

keeping me fed, watered and caffeinated throughout this entire process.

Finally, to every immigrant woman out there who was once a girl dreaming of being an author. KEEP GOING. Your story is important and necessary. Believe in yourself and the force of your ancestors, and build the life you want for yourself.

In gratitude.

ABOUT THE AUTHOR

Karla Montalván is a Cuban-born writer shaped by migration, memory, and longing. Born in Havana in 1994 during a severe economic crisis, she migrated to Ecuador as a child and later settled in Miami. A graduate of Miami Dade College and the University of North Carolina at Chapel Hill, she has spent the past decade telling stories centered on identity, gender, and diaspora. Her work has appeared in *People*, *People en Español*, *Cosmopolitan*, and *mitú*. *The Sun and All the Other Stars* is her debut novel.

ABOUT THE PUBLISHER

Elizabeth & Minnie Publishing is an independent, women-led publishing house devoted to discovering and amplifying the stories that reshape our understanding of the world. Named for the grandmothers of its founders, the press seeks out bold, resonant narratives that honor the complexity of identity, history, and imagination.

Founded by Jeanell English and Tanya Sam, Elizabeth & Minnie believes that books are catalysts for change, beginning with a good story and an engaged community. The press champions emerging authors and underrepresented perspectives, developing works with the power to live beyond the page and reach into film, television, and the broader cultural conversation.

At its heart, Elizabeth & Minnie is committed to lifting voices, lifting stories, and building a more inclusive literary landscape—one book at a time.

Elizabeth
& Minnie